W Hollywood
Beverly Hills
LOS ANGELES
SANTA MONICA F'WAY
101
405
Culver City
Univ of S Calif
HARBOR F'WAY
AT & SF
Huntington Park
Hughes
Inglewood
Lennox
Segundo
Hawthorne
Lynwood
Compton
Gardena
Lawndale
TORRANCE
Clifton
Carson
PE
SP

Night Train To Sugar Hill

A Novel
by Iceberg Slim

Introduction
by Justin Gifford

Contra Mundum Press   New York · London · Melbourne

Night Train to Sugar Hill
© 2019 The Estate of Robert Beck;
introduction © 2019 Justin Gifford.

First Contra Mundum Press
edition 2019.

Library of Congress
Cataloguing-in-Publication Data

Slim, Iceberg, 1918–1992

Night Train to Sugar Hill /
Iceberg Slim; Introduction by
Justin Gifford

—1st Contra Mundum Press
Edition
324 pp., 5 x 8 in.

ISBN 9781940625294

   I. Slim, Iceberg.
   II. Title.
   III. Gifford, Justin.
   IV. Translator & Introduction.

2019936601

Table of Contents

Introduction

In 1990, an aging pimp-turned-novelist named Robert "Iceberg Slim" Beck steadily worked away at one of his last novels, *Night Train to Sugar Hill*. His eyesight was poor from the effects of diabetes, but he was still able to write in longhand. His wife Diane Millman Beck typed up his manuscripts as he wrote them. For twenty-five years, Beck had been a player in the sex trafficking business in industrial Chicago *&* throughout the Midwest. During the 1940s and '50s, he had pimped hundreds of women. He drove custom "hogs" (Cadillacs) and wore tailored "vines" (suits). When he wasn't living this life of "phony glamour," as he later called it in interviews, he was in and out of state and federal penitentiaries or running from the FBI.

In 1967, he published his autobiography, *Pimp: The Story of My Life*, a gritty urban picaresque of his rise and fall as a pimp. It mimicked the confessional storytelling of Malcolm X, but with a more explicit focus on the hidden underworld of pimps and sex workers. It was so infused with slang that at the request of his publisher Beck had to include a glossary at the end of the book so readers not familiar with the milieu could decrypt the street vernacular. It was an instant bestseller, and it became standard reading in prisons *&* inner-city neighborhoods across the country. Beck went on to write essays, short stories, and novels, and he helped establish a new genre of black American literature known as "street fiction." Black writers like Chester Himes had popularized African-American detective fiction a decade earlier, but Beck's experience as a pimp brought a new on-the-ground perspective to the urban literature genre. His work inspired Blaxploitation films like *Superfly* and *The Mack*, as well as gangsta rappers Ice Cube *&* Ice T, who both named themselves after Iceberg.

In the early '90s, toward the end of his life, Beck lived in a small studio on Crenshaw Boulevard in the middle of South Central L.A. His publisher at Holloway House had cheated him out of most of his royalties, so he lived modestly. When he was working on a novel, he spread his books and papers out on his bed so that he could visualize the project as a whole. Diane had given him an exercise bike, but ever since his diabetes had gotten worse, he had stopped riding it. Beck kept framed pictures of his three daughters on the headboard above his bed.

His years as a pimp had hardened him, and he preferred to live alone. Diane came down from her home in Silver Lake to visit three times a week. She helped him prepare his manuscripts and took him to his dialysis treatments. He wore a silk shirt and slacks, and he sported a black leather Kangol cap to cover his bald spot. Sometimes Diane drove him around the neighborhood in his 1948 Lincoln Continental. The majestic car was his last possession from his days as a writer. When Beck was noticed at a stoplight, adoring fans would run up to his car window to pay tribute to the legendary Iceberg Slim. Most days he smoked weed, listened to jazz records, and checked out the action on the streets using a pair of binoculars. He read occasional letters sent by convicts seeking advice on how to create their own best-selling novels. But it was writing that Beck loved most of all, *&* even with his failing health, he worked diligently on two final books, *Shetani's Sister* and *Night Train to Sugar Hill.* Set on L.A.'s mean streets, Beck's last novels feature his familiar cast of characters—pimps, crooked cops, drug dealers, and sex workers—who try to transcend a life of crime only to succumb to its violence.

Night Train to Sugar Hill is Beck's most personal work of political fiction, a fast-paced crime novel about the 1980s L.A. crack crisis. It is an epic tragedy where no one escapes from the deadly orbit of the drug industry. Nearly everyone dies by the book's end. The innocent and the damned alike fall victim to the artificial allure of crack cocaine — a teenager accidentally overdoses, junkies smoke rock laced with cyanide, a gang member is shot down in the streets, a mother is murdered by her alcoholic husband, and a major drug dealer is killed by an ordinary man who is fed up with the drug game.

The central protagonist of the story is Baptiste Landreau O'Leary, an old ex-con who is Beck's alter ego. O'Leary is the moral center of the novel, a character who calls for political action as the crack trade infects all of their lives. He is one of the many characters who serves as Beck's mouthpiece, indicting Reagan and right-wing Republicans for their lack of compassion for the lives of black Americans. "The racist policies of Ronald Reagan, George Bush, and the Republican party must share the blame with the killer of Leroy and all of the others," a minister preaches at the funeral of a young man killed in the streets. "Any nigger in America who votes for the enemy Republican party is stupid, misinformed, or afflicted with the Uncle Tom need to be punished and to kiss the ass of his master. Wake up to the truth."

Night Train is a reflection of Beck's growing alarm over both the crack crisis and police repression in L.A. In the early 1980s, a Colombian cartel rerouted a major supply of cocaine into the United States from Florida to California. This flooded the streets of L.A. with crack, a cheaper and more dangerous drug cut from cocaine. With deindustrialization and suburbanization changing the economic landscape of L.A. and unemployment among black men hovering around 45%, selling crack was one of the few options remaining to working-class African-Americans. Crack houses sprung up all over L.A., and at that time the media created a moral panic over "crack babies" and "welfare queens."

In response, under Chief Daryl Gates, the LAPD implemented Operation Hammer. A new militarized police raided black communities, using massive battering rams to knock down doors. They performed illegal searches of black and Latino youth, often roughing them up or arresting them on baseless charges. At the national level, Ronald Reagan signed into law the Anti-Drug Abuse Act, which created the now infamous 100 to 1 ratio for prosecuting crack possession. This meant that a person holding 5 grams of crack would receive an automatic minimum sentence of 5 years in prison. A suspect had to get caught with 500 grams of cocaine to receive the same sentence. This disproportionately affected black defendants, who flooded America's prisons in the late 1980s.

Night Train to Sugar Hill's urgent message also came out of Beck's personal encounter with the drug. He had snorted *&* injected massive quantities of cocaine while he was a pimp, and it had destroyed his health. Worse yet, his daughter Camille had very nearly died because of her involvement in the drug trade. In September of 1983, she was arrested for transporting over 20 pounds of cocaine in Richmond, Virginia. She was released on 1 million dollars bail. Soon after, she mysteriously fell from a 7th floor balcony, breaking a number of bones on one side of her body. Miraculously, she survived, and after Beck discussed the case with the D.A. in Virginia, she was eventually released with time served. In the novel, O'Leary's daughter Opal operates as a surrogate for Camille. At the conclusion of the book, Opal is one of the few people left alive, though she is forming an addiction to cocaine. "I'm not a dopefiend. I'm not hooked. I can stop using whenever I want to," Opal tells herself at the end of the novel. Given all that we have witnessed throughout the book, it is difficult to be optimistic about her chances.

If there is any optimism in *Night Train*, it is focused on the relationship between fathers and children. Perhaps the most loving relationship in the novel is between O'Leary and his surrogate son Isaiah, a former Golden Gloves fighter. Isaiah was modeled on Mike Tyson, whom Beck met in 1988. Tyson was a devoted reader of Beck's work and was impressed by the elder's sense of style, with his ascots and French cuffs. They shared a love of literature, particularly the classics, and Tyson used to come to Beck's apartment to get advice about relationships and life. Beck used to sit on his bed in his silk pajamas and draw on psychoanalytic theory to show how Tyson's problems with women could be traced back to his mother. Beck tried to mentor Tyson, to show him how to understand and control his emotions. Beck himself had not had a dependable father figure in his life, and in his impressionable days he had looked to well-heeled pimps to guide him. Now he wanted to provide Tyson with the mentorship that he had never had. In *Night Train*, Beck represents this kind of vulnerable alliance between O'Leary and Isaiah as one of the few bright spots in a world of darkness and violence.

Those who are looking for an Iceberg Slim novel with his typically flamboyant prose and bleak vision of the American city will not be disappointed. Like the L.A. novels of Raymond Chandler, Chester Himes, and Walter Mosley, *Night Train* shows that L.A. is anything but a city of angels. With his sharp eye for counterfeit opulence, Beck writes of the Hollywood strip, "A variety of sweaty hicks in cheap clothing moved along the sleazed boulevard, searching for the fantasy hoax called Hollywood. They wandered in confused flabbergast among the moil of five buck cuties, brute-faced men in miniskirts." *Night Train* has all of the features of a Beckian noir: young people destroyed by a life of crime, the psychological torture of prison, women abused by the sex industry, criminals haunted by nightmares about their crimes, and the inevitable fall of the anti-hero.

Beck also experimented with elements new to his fiction, like incorporating Haitian voodoo into the plot of *Night Train*. Like the magical realist novels *Kindred* by Octavia Butler and *Beloved* by Toni Morrison, *Night Train* features realist settings infused with mythical elements. Throughout the novel, O'Leary's cook Helena prays to Loa, the gods of Haitian voodoo, to kill drug dealers and other dangerous characters. The voodoo spirits grant her wish, but they also kill innocent people as a price for their dark magic. *Night Train* is ultimately a hybrid novel, a mix of hardcore crime fiction, mysticism, L.A. noir, literary naturalism, and street literature.

Beck's novels have never been easily digestible, but they have always been true. *Night Train* gives us Beck's end of life vision, with him looking back over his abusive childhood, his career as a criminal, and his later years as a family man. It is set against the backdrop of an America whose so-called dream is more of a nightmare, its underclass one often deliberately preyed upon. *Night Train to Sugar Hill* is Robert Beck's last remaining major work to be published, and it offers an opportunity to read a mature Robert Beck, one who saw America teetering on the edge of apocalypse and felt compelled to protest it in his fashion.

Justin Gifford

Night Train to Sugar Hill

Prologue

Baptiste Landreau O'Leary is the author's alter ego. Certain people cast in this fictionalized social drama are composite characterizations of real people who have been given pseudonyms. The events depicted have been drawn from general public media sources and from the personal experience of the author. Because of story material that includes drug abuse, graphic murder, and bizarre sexual peccadillos, parents are advised that this book should not be made available to minors.

Chapter 1

It was past midnight in Long Island, New York. A violent June rain and thunderstorm bombed the enclave of posh homes. Baptiste Landreau O'Leary, the 10-year-old son of an interracial couple, lie sleepless in his weeping mother's arms on a bed in a guest room of the two-story family mansion.

After a brutal beating, Iris Landreau O'Leary had fled from the master bedroom that she shared with her alcoholic husband Frank. A flash of lightning revealed the awful effect of Frank's fists on Iris's puffed and battered face. Baptiste blurted, "I usta love Daddy when he usta play funny games and stuff with me and make us laugh. Now I hate him! I hate him!"

She caressed his mop of curly black hair. "Bap, don't hate him or anybody, ever... You will love him again after I convince him to get help to stop his drinking."

"But why does Daddy beat you up all the time?" he whispered as he clung to her.

She heaved a sigh. "His whiskey is driving him crazy. And also, because he hates me, blames me for things that happened to him after we got married... Your Uncle Chester warned me not to marry him."

Baptiste raised his head from her bosom to exclaim, "Mom, I wish you had listened to Unc."

She said softly, "Bap, love can make you deaf, dumb, and blind."

Baptiste whispered, "Why does Daddy hate you? And what does he blame you for?"

She reached across him to a bedside table for tissues to blot her tears. "Bap, I was just a dancer in a Broadway musical when your father and I started meeting and falling in love in secret, hidden places. You see, Bap, all of his high society friends and relatives, even his mother and father, cast him out of their lives. His stock brokerage business went broke when his racist customers heard of his marriage to a poor Haitian dancer. His whiskey makes him blame me for everything bad that happened to him." She squeezed herself close. "Bap, don't worry about me... I've got you and that's all I need to make me happy."

Baptiste sat up in the bed. "But Mom, we gonna have to leave here. Let's go live with Unc Chester in Harlem. We can..." The little boy's face froze in terror as he stared at his father's fearsome 6'6" frame standing in the doorway of the bedroom.

Frank switched on a ceiling light as he moved to the bedside. His bloodshot pale blue eyes glared down at her for a long moment. "Iris, get your ass back in my bed. Now!" he shouted as his fists banged his thighs.

Mother and son scrambled away to the far side of the bed. Iris said coldly, "Frank, I'm not sleeping with you again until you keep your promise and go to A.A. for your drinking problem. Get out and leave me alone."

Frank hollered, "No black bitch orders Frank Phineas O'Leary the Third to do a goddamn thing!" He lunged across the bed to seize her right wrist. He jerked her across Baptiste to the floor and kicked her buttocks with a house-slippered foot.

Baptiste screamed, "Stop! Leave her alone!"

Frank grabbed her arms and pulled her to her feet. She clawed at his face and missed his crotch with a knee smash. He punched her in the belly. She vomited and crashed against the bedside table, shattering a porcelain lamp on the table against the wall.

Baptiste leaped from the bed to hook his hands around his father's neck. He rode his father's back. He bit his father's neck and shoulders with the ferocity of a rabid wolf.

Frank howled in pain as he tore Baptiste's arms away and hurled him against the wall. Frank stooped to hammer his fists against the head of the boy.

Baptiste rolled away and got to his feet. He ran to his room down the hall to get his baseball bat.

Iris snatched up a dagger-like shard of the broken lamp. She gouged a spring of scarlet from Frank's neck. He backhanded her to the carpet. He rubbed his hands on his wounded neck and stared slack-jawed at his bloody palm.

"I'll kill you!" he yelled as he vised his hands around her throat.

She fell to the carpet as he straddled her and tightened his stranglehold. She was dead when Baptiste rushed back into the bedroom with the bat. He held it high above his head to strike the back of his father's head. Frank caught a flicker of motion in the corner of his eye. He tilted his torso and took the crunching blow to the top of his shoulder.

Baptiste dropped the bat and ran for the doorway. Frank scooped up the bat and pursued Baptiste into the hallway. He caught him and swung the bat against the side of the boy's head as he was about to enter his bedroom. Baptiste fell into a bottomless chasm of nothingness.

Chapter 2

Now 75 years old, Baptiste Landreau O'Leary was awakened from the nightmare that had recurred to stomp his sleep for decades. He closed his eyes against the dazzling lasers of the Beverly Hills, California sun firing through a bedroom window.

He lay motionless, depressed in his great white oak bed as he started his daily visualization therapy for his several life-threatening medical problems. As if watching a video tape playing inside his head, he saw the lump of cancer in his prostate dying in a freezing blizzard, cracking, dissolving into tiny fragments that would leave his body when he urinated. For his defective heart, he visualized a gargantuan clock glowing in the heavens, regulated by the master of the Universe to tick thunderously, with celestial precision compelling his ailing heart to beat in sync with the same strong perfection. He visualized his kidneys, on the brink of dialysis, awash in a blessed healing waterfall that burst rainbow colors.

As always, he felt physically better, energized after the visualization ritual. But he was still depressed. He swung his long lean frame from the satin-quilted nest onto the white carpet. He mounted an exercycle across the room. Pajama clad, his long legs were a gold silk blur as he furiously pedaled for 10 minutes.

He was still depressed after showering and dressing in a black mohair suit. He shoved a compact disc of Ellington into a player. But not even the "A" Train could haul away his pain. He was going to the funeral of a friend today.

He closed his eyes, his knees quivered. He remembered the funeral of his mother Iris after his father had strangled her to death and fractured Baptiste's skull. He remembered how sweet and funny and lovable Frank had been before whiskey changed him into a monster. Shadowy black wings of guilt flapped inside his head. Perhaps if he, in his childish rage and panic, had not brought his bat into the bedroom... A ghost of remorse for his father's murder haunted him for an instant.

He looked at his impeccably dressed image in a floor to ceiling mirror. He studied his face, which always reminded him of his father. It was almost a perfect replica of his square-jawed handsome Irish father's face, except for the coffee tint of his mother's face and her dreamy sable eyes.

He felt painful remorse when he remembered how, at 16, had ambushed his father in Long Island and shot him to death with one of Uncle Chester's hand guns. He had been sorry an instant after he pulled the trigger.

Frank's money & political clout had gotten him off with a year in prison for involuntary manslaughter for the murder of Iris. After all, Iris had been just a nothing black dancer to the judge and prosecutor. But Frank had stolen the life of the most precious person on earth from Baptiste.

Yes, he had served 5 years in prison, until he was 21, for killing Frank, and it had been worth it. At that time in his youthful rage & pain he would have been happy with a life sentence to make Frank dead.

As he turned away from the mirror, he shivered. He remembered that he had asked his daughter Opal to bury him in the suit he was wearing. He pressed a button on a console to alert his live-in maid and cook, Helene, to start breakfast. He left the bedroom and went down a winding staircase to the sunken living room. He walked through the beige and gold living room onto a red tile patio. Pale blue fiberglass roofing tinted his silver hair as he sat down at a marble-topped table for breakfast.

Zephyrs of fragrances wafted from a flower garden ablaze with colors in the sunshine.

"Good morning, Mr. Landreau," Helene, his Haitian housekeeper said as she placed his breakfast from a silver tray before him.

He smiled. "Good morning Helene... Please look out for Isaiah's car and buzz him through the gate."

The statuesque young beauty's radiant dark eyes sparkled. "Oh! That will be a pleasure, Mr. Landreau. He's so tall and strong and handsome." She fingered a lacquered, dried walnut-sized Haitian seduction root dangling from a gold chain around her neck.

Baptiste said, "Watch yourself, Helene. That root around your neck can't catch Isaiah. He's married and in love."

The lavender silk of her uniform shimmered in an elaborate shrug. "So, I catch another man that I want who is not married and in love." She smiled mischievously and pranced away.

He made a mental note to watch for any voodoo paraphernalia in the house and especially in his personal effects. The necklace was not conclusive evidence that Helene was a voodoo fanatic, he thought as he ate the Wheaties with mocha mix and salt-free rye toast.

Voodoo fanatics made him uncomfortable. He'd gotten a bellyful of them when he lived with his Uncle Chester in Harlem. Chester had lived in an apartment above his voodoo accessories shop. Unlike Chester, he had never believed in any of the store's products to empower customers to win love or to achieve the insanity or death of one's enemies.

Ironically, Chester had dropped dead behind the store's counter while packaging for a customer a powder guaranteed to ward off death.

Baptiste stared at his face reflected in a silver water pitcher. "Jesus!" He looked so old and worn. His once bright and vibrant eyes looked dull and fearful of sudden visitation of the grim reaper. Despite the fact that his face had no major wrinkles, he shuddered. He remembered how fresh looking his face had been at 20 when Chester died.

Isaiah Jones came onto the patio. "Hiya, Pops," the 6'5"-giant said as he sat down at the table. He placed a large manila envelope fat with checks and cash from the scores of tenants in the dozen apartment buildings and homes he managed.

"Oh, I'm still kickin', but not that high."

Isaiah finger-stroked a lapel of his midnight blue silk suit. "Like my new suit?" Isaiah asked with mock anxiety in his voice.

Baptiste played the game. "Hell no! You look like a Harlem pimp."

They laughed. Baptiste looked at his watch. "Even though you were 20 minutes late, you have time for a cup of your black poison before we leave for the funeral."

A bell on the tabletop brought Helene to the patio.

"Baby doll, please bring Isaiah a cup of black coffee," Baptiste said sweetly. She smiled. "Be back in a flash. I just made some."

Baptiste leaned toward Isaiah and lowered his voice. "Helene has the hots for you."

Isaiah chuckled, "She's gorgeous all right but Haitian women are too intense for this Georgia boy... but I'll put her on my list..." Isaiah paused when Helene brought his coffee. When she left, his handsomely boyish face hardened. "I'm seriously thinkin' about cuttin' Sabina loose."

Baptiste tried to remember how many times he had heard him say he would during the two years of their marriage.

Baptiste said irritably, "Nigger, you can't dump your alcoholic goddess. She's kicked your emotional ass a thousand times and you're still rooting your nose in her pussy like a hog in a bucket of slop. Don't tell me any more you're gonna kick her out. Nigger, do it and then tell me."

Isaiah flinched under the verbal barrage. "Damn, Pops, lighten up. I'm not the only sucker to fall in love with a tramp."

Baptiste studied him with slitted eyes for a long moment. He knew and loved Isaiah like a son. Isaiah's weakness and mistaken notion that lust was love infuriated Baptiste. "Love, Nigger? What is there to love about a lyin', dog-ass alcoholic blue-eyed blond piece of garbage? Love, Nigger? Unless you get strong and learn the difference between lust and love, you're gonna have the alabaster blues till you die." He placed his hand on Isaiah's wrist. "Son, you know I love you, but…"

Helene appeared in the doorway to interrupt him. "Opal is on the living room phone," she said.

Baptiste affectionately patted Isaiah's back as he got to his feet. He said, "Come on, pal, I'll only be a minute on the phone with Opal."

Isaiah picked up the manila folder and followed him into the living room. He was so relieved that the old man's anger had vanished quickly as always.

Isaiah dropped the manila folder on the living room sofa beside Baptiste. Isaiah went out the front door and sat on a lawn chair in the late June sunshine.

Shortly, Baptiste finished his conversation with Opal, calling from Sugar Hill in an upscale section of Harlem. He placed the manila envelope in his bedroom safe before he joined Isaiah.

Baptiste nodded toward a monstrous 1938 black Rolls, sparkling in an open garage. Because of eye problems, Baptiste drove it infrequently.

"How about you drivin' ol' Betsy to South Central?" Baptiste said.

Isaiah opened a door of his Thunderbird in the driveway. He shook his head. "Not me, Pops. I might get sideswiped and give you a heart attack."

Helene stood at the open front door of the house watching them as Baptiste got in Isaiah's car. Isaiah drove down the long driveway to the steel gate. Baptiste buzzed it open with a genie device from his coat pocket.

They drove through an affluent colony of spectacular homes and perfectly manicured jade lawns into Hollywood.

"Say, man, why are you taking the long way to South Central?" Baptiste asked.

Isaiah chuckled. "You keep me so busy, Pops. I haven't seen Hollywood in a long time... Don't worry, we'll make the funeral on time.

They cruised down Hollywood Boulevard. Panhandlers with gimmicks and pitches galore played on tourist suckers. A tall black man in jeans scored repeatedly after he pitched his tale of woe. He pointed out his female accomplice, teetering nearby on prop crutches.

He begged for bus fare to take his ailing, crippled wife to County Hospital.

A variety of sweaty hicks in cheap clothing moved along the sleazy boulevard, searching for the fantasy hoax called Hollywood. They wandered in confused flabbergast among the moil of five buck cuties, brute-faced men in mini-skirts.

Some of the tourists snailed along the sidewalk gazing down at the implant of stars honoring their past and present movie idols. Some of them, like bumpkin cattle, crowded into tour buses. They would gape at the homes of stars in Beverly Hills and Bel Air. Perhaps they would get lucky and spot a star to get an orgasm of the eye. But their idols would be hiding from murderous fanatics in their luxurious prisons.

Baptiste said, "Turn off this nightmare alley at the next corner."

They headed to South Central. Driving down Crenshaw Boulevard, the racket from high decibel car radios pummeled their eardrums. Fast food joints, gas stations, bars and liquor stores marred the scenery.

They parked beside Angelus Funeral Horne. They entered the quiet ambience of the elegantly furnished foyer. They were directed by a flashy high yellow woman behind an ornate desk to the chapel where the services would be held for the slain young gang member. Baptiste had known Leroy Wilson from babyhood when his mother had been a tenant in one of his apartment buildings.

The chapel was packed with mourners and spectators, drawn to see and hear preacher Eli Brown. Baptiste and Isaiah sat in the last two vacant seats in the rear of the chapel. An obese black woman, wearing a polka-dot dress, sat at an organ playing "Amazing Grace."

The open coffin of Leroy Wilson sat in front of the empty pulpit. Leroy's grief-ravaged mother sat with seven staircase brothers and sisters of Leroy's only a few feet from the casket.

The room was graveyard quiet when the organist concluded the piece. The outrageously candid and fearless black activist minister would soon make his appearance.

Baptiste said, "Reverend Eli is gonna be hotter than hellfire today. Leroy was his nephew."

The flamboyant old soldier of God suddenly materialized through a curtained door behind the pulpit. As usual, for the funerals of young gang murder victims, he wore a blood red ankle length red smock over his street clothes.

He stood motionless in the pulpit for a full half-minute to achieve his favorite effects: drama and divine mystique. His long-shaved skull was tilted skyward like a blueblack missile ready to fire. The whites of his large, light brown eyes flashed like white flame as he gazed at the image of his master painted on the chapel ceiling.

His leathery, savage face would be perfect casting as a Zulu warrior in a Hollywood film.

He lowered his head and swept the crowd with his compelling amber eyes. His *basso profundo* voice amplified by the pulpit microphone exploded like a cannon shot in the hushed chapel. "My nephew, Leroy Wilson, died a gangster. He and his kind are hated and feared by many across America. But I baptized him when he was an innocent baby in his mother's arms. I loved him then and I love him now, lying there in his coffin. Today, God has directed me to fill your hearts and minds with the truth about Leroy and all of our black youth like him, dead and condemned to die on the streets of America. Perhaps with God's truth and wisdom delivered through me, you can learn how the generation of Leroys in this country were psychologically brutalized and satanized by the indifference and cruel neglect of the symbolic political father of our country, Ronald Reagan. He cut and sabotaged many of the government programs necessary for the stability of Black underclass families and other minorities. He created a climate, a cult of greed and corruption in America."

"The coroner's report was that Leroy Wilson died from multiple gunshot wounds from an automatic weapon. Police have the triggerman in custody."

He paused to vigorously shake his bullet head. His voice quavered a bit as he went on.

"The racist policies of Ronald Reagan, George Bush, and the Republican party must share the blame with the killer of Leroy and all of the others. It pains my soul that some of us are so politically naive. Some of us helped to vote George Bush into the White House. Yes, voted for the enemy of black people, even though he had publicly vowed during his campaign for the Presidency, to continue the policies of Ronald Reagan. I'm aware that all Americans have the right to vote for any candidate or party of their choice."

He leaned and thrust his ancient face across the pulpit. "But any nigger in America who votes for the enemy Republican party is stupid, misinformed, or afflicted with the Uncle Tom need to be punished and to kiss the ass of his master. Wake up to the truth!" The crowd gasped. Eli boomed on.

"Needless to say, the clique of social climbing nigger money junkies who seek and grovel for so-called important positions in the present Bush administration are beneath contempt."

"Do you really believe that a president who vowed to perpetuate Ronald Reagan's racist policies would appoint blacks he couldn't control that would oppose or challenge such policies? I ask you, what has the present black Secretary of Health done to improve the health care of blacks and other minorities? Bush's black Army Chief of Staff did not dare to strongly oppose the decision to ship thousands of our young men to that potential death trap in Saudi Arabia. Instead, he timidly suggested that our boys would suffer in the oven heat of the desert. Believe, friends, that a black man of Jesse Jackson's principle and courage would have resigned the so-called lofty position. Black men like Jesse would not have put their principles and righteous conviction on hold to please a boss. But then, a black man of Jesse's stature could not have been Chief of Staff anyway, and certainly not a fall guy."

"My friends, high level black lackeys rationalize that if they join the enemy, they can change things for the better. But they never do. I know from personal experience that the Democratic Party is also tainted with racism and the need to recruit black men that they can control. But at least many of its white members have compassion and concern for our plight. Racism, as even a fool should know, exists on every corner in America. Thirty years ago, I was offered a chance by a group of powerful white Democrats to prepare for a run for State Assemblyman. My present white wife, Ida and I, were engaged to be married the week following the offer."

He paused to smile down at silver-haired Ida seated in the front row. Time had ruined her dollish face.

He went on. "Many of you here today know Ida and love her as I do. The political bosses gave me a choice. Postpone the wedding until after the election or I would be unacceptable as a candidate for the office."

His eyes were on fire as he smashed his fist down on the pulpit. He roared, "I told them that only God controls this nigger! So, barricade your souls from the Satan that controls Bush and his black lackeys. Learn to love Leroy, the political victim lying there. Don't hate the enemy. Pray for Bush, and especially for old insensitive Reagan and his wife Nancy."

He leaned and gazed down at the corpse of his nephew. Tears spilled down his wrinkled cheeks. "Goodbye, Lil Leroy. God told me we'll meet again in Heaven."

The string-bean dynamo turned away to disappear into the curtained area behind the pulpit. The crowd sat in utter silence when the fat lady finished playing "What a Friend We Have in Jesus" on the organ.

Baptiste and Isaiah left the chapel to wait in the parking lot for Laura Wilson, Leroy's mother. On the lot, a funeral director and his female assistant were lining up cars and placing funeral stickers on windshields for the trip to the cemetery.

Laura staggered into the sunshine like a sleepwalker, followed by her children. Baptiste embraced her for a long moment. He said softly, "Laura dear, my heart is almost bursting with pain and sympathy for your loss."

She tiptoed to kiss his face as they disengaged. She walked away to a black limousine. Baptiste and Isaiah watched the procession of cars move from the lot, led by tan uniformed men on motorcycles. Baptiste and Isaiah went to the Thunderbird.

As Isaiah started the car, he asked, "Pops, is there anybody you want to visit over here before I take you home?"

Baptiste loosened his tie. "Yeah, since this is Sunday, a lot of my kid pals will be at the Center."

Isaiah turned into heavy Crenshaw Boulevard traffic and drove south for a mile or so. On the way Isaiah said, "What did you think about Reverend Eli's rap?"

Baptiste hesitated. Finally, he replied, "Eli's rap was pretty much on the money... except that he should have excluded Mayor Dinkins in New York and Assembly Leader Willie Brown here in California, along with Jesse from that category of so-called black political lackeys."

Isaiah said, "How about Tom Bradley here in LA?"

Baptiste shook his head. "No comment to that, pal."

Isaiah reached an imposing five-story apartment building. He opened the garage gate beneath it with a genie device. A large red lettered sign on the gate read "Garage for Tenants Only." Isaiah pulled into a vacant space marked "Manager" in white paint. The spacious garage, as usual, on a balmy Sunday, had only several of its spaces filled. As they walked toward an exit at the rear of the gloomy expanse of concrete, a melon-red Excalibur caught Baptiste's eye. "Hey, son, you didn't mention to me that I had a tenant who could afford a 150 G crate like that red convertible."

Isaiah jerked open the door of the security building. "Pops, Sabina drives it... She, uh, said a girlfriend in Malibu loaned it to her until she gets back from France."

Baptiste grunted as they went down a hallway to a walled section behind the apartment building.

"I didn't believe that lie either, Pops... I'll talk to you later about other Sabina bullshit that's got me uptight." He violently jerked open a heavy oak door.

They stepped into a pleasant oasis. In the middle of an expansive green lawn ringed with flowerbeds was a swimming pool. A half dozen black pre-teeners frolicking in the pool chorused, "Hi, Pops!"

Baptiste smiled broadly and waved as he followed Isaiah into a large gymnasium. Twelve to fifteen aspiring young boxers were busy on punching bags and in a ring.

Isaiah, a former heavyweight California Golden Gloves champion, was their trainer. In 1985, Baptiste had financed the entire installation. He had done it without the help of the Reagan or Deukmejian administrations. He had known they had no interest in such inner-city projects at all.

Baptiste and Isaiah sat at ringside. The scent of sweat was heavy in the air. Two ten-year-old interracial sluggers in boxing trunks flailed huge leather gloves in the ring.

Eric, the elfin-faced white opponent, was beating the black boy to the punch with a lightning left hook every time the black boy telegraphed a right cross. Isaiah bragged, "My stepson has sure got a sweet left hook. He's the only white kid in the program, but everybody respects and likes him... I don't know how Sabina gave birth to such a fine boy... Maybe I haven't beaten her rotten ass or thrown her out because I don't want to lose his love or worse, have her disappear with him."

Alvin, Isaiah's salaried assistant and former gang member, called time. Alvin stooped to tie Eric's shoelace. Eric looked down at his stepfather and Baptiste. "Hi, Daddy! Hi, Pops!" he exclaimed a second before Alvin rang a bell to send him back into combat.

Baptiste glanced toward a far corner of the domed structure. A tall black Amazon in the kitchen waved a hand holding a spatula. He waved back at Liz, the cook that he paid to prepare non-fancy but nutritious meals from noon to 6 P.M. for hungry kids. Adults down on their luck were never turned away.

Isaiah said, "Let's go upstairs."

Baptiste nodded and followed him into an elevator inside the apartment building. They rode to the 5th floor. Isaiah keyed into his apartment entrance hall. They heard Sabina's syrupy Texas drawl. She sounded intoxicated. The strong odor of incense filled the hallway. They stepped into the living room. Blue velvet drapes were drawn across the windows. Sabina glowed, like a lewd ghost in the blue dimness. They were shocked to see her buck-naked cooing on the phone.

The Swedish sexpot was sprawled out on the blue silk sofa with her legs wide open. She was oblivious to their presence as she stroked her jutting breasts and inner thighs. She giggled as she inserted a finger into her sex nest. She stage-whispered to the person on the line, "I'm doing it now. Ooo-wee it's good."

Isaiah scooped Eric's binoculars off the carpet. He threw the heavy plastic missile as hard as he could at her head. It thudded against the wall inches from the back of her blond head. Startled, she spun around to a sitting position. Her blue eyes widened, then slitted. "Goddamn you, Isaiah," she yelled as she slammed down the receiver. She covered her crotch with a sofa pillow. Isaiah galloped toward her.

Baptiste said, "Be cool, son. Easy!"

She scrambled from the sofa before Isaiah could grab her. She dashed into her bedroom and shut the door. She bolted it from the inside an instant before furious Isaiah turned the doorknob.

Isaiah gritted his teeth. "Pops, I'm gonna waste that stinkin' bitch."

Baptiste put an arm across his shoulders and said, "Come on and sit down."

Isaiah shouted through the door. "You're a low life mother, bitch! What if Eric had come in on you?"

She shouted back through the door. "Eric forgot his key. I thought I had the chain on the door Saint Isaiah bastard!"

Baptiste guided trembling Isaiah to the sofa to sit beside him. He said softly, "Now son, let's get this situation into nitty-gritty perspective." Baptiste's eyes scanned the coffee table before them. He didn't see a half-empty glass of booze or even a reefer roach in an ashtray to explain Sabina's horny scenario. He removed

24

his straw hat and started to place it on the coffee table when he spotted the glass crack pipe. It had been almost invisible against the glass tabletop. The strong incense had deodorized the acrid stench of crack smoke.

Baptiste dropped his hat over the pipe before Isaiah could spot it. Isaiah would be uncontrollable if he knew she was on crack. He'd kick in the door to get at her. He hated crack for the ruined lives, the bloody gang wars, and murders it had caused.

Isaiah half-whispered as he glanced toward Sabina's locked door, "Come on, let's go to the dining room."

Baptist left his hat on the coffee table and followed Isaiah to sit at the dining room table. Baptiste said, "Since it's obvious that you can't cut her loose..." He paused to glare Isaiah into silence when he saw him open his mouth to protest the remark. Baptiste said sternly, "Shut up white pussy freak & listen. Stop lyin' to yourself. You love the kid and you're hooked on his mama's cunt. You have two options. If, by some miracle, you can bear to blow to kid, you can cut her loose. Or you can keep her and let her drive you to murder. Let me remind you that I doubt that any nigger has ever killed a white woman in California that wasn't executed or sent to the joint forever. Look son, you just turned 30 a month ago. You can get all kinds of women. You've got the worst jones for anglo pussy that I've ever seen. So, dump this bad one and with patience you can find another good white woman. Start planning Sabina's non-

25

violent exit from your life. I know your choices are a bitch, but the secret of survival and happy living can sometimes force us to drop even people we think we love from our lives. Can I count on you to be sensible, to understand what I just told you? I need you to manage for me. I trust you, son."

Isaiah said, "Pops, thanks. I'm cool now and I won't let you down... I would like a favor that could relieve some of the pressure she's puttin' on me."

Baptiste smiled. "Sure, anything."

Isaiah leaned across the table and said in a half whisper, "Stokes and Lee, a pair of retired LAPD black vice cops, have opened an office up the street to handle private investigations. I want to hire them for about a week to find out just what shit Sabina is into... If I can find out everything, I can stop imagining and draining myself. Maybe I can even get custody of Eric. Loan me a coupla grand and you can deduct whatever you say from my salary every month until you get it back."

Baptiste stood up. "I'll give you a check when you take me home... but your chances as a black stepfather to get custody of Eric are lotto slim."

They went to the living room. Baptiste went to the coffee table to pick up his hat and the crack pipe. He positioned his body to block Isaiah's view. He lifted his hat off the table. Sabina had vanished the pipe... He put on the straw and followed Isaiah to the elevator.

26

———

Isaiah drove from the garage down busy Crenshaw Boulevard past the office of Stokes and Lee. Isaiah noticed a sign in a front window that read, "Open Seven Days a Week."

As they stopped at a red light next to The Liquor Bank they watched a crowd begin to gather around two young black men who were having a bloody fistfight.

Isaiah proceeded down Crenshaw. At Martin Luther King Boulevard, a young white hooker leapt from an older black man's car and dashed into a chicken joint.

Isaiah broke a long silence. "Pops, I, uh, really feel bad, embarrassed about that skunk's lousy show that you saw... I've gotta get her out of my life, and somehow out of Eric's life. She screams at him, punishes him when he forgets to speak white American English in her presence and slips into ghetto lingo..." He paused to sigh, "Pops, maybe you know and understand, why would a beautiful young Southern white woman leave the white world to hook up with a struggling nigger in the ghetto that she hates."

Baptiste started to reply when a bedraggled old black crone in a fright wig suddenly stepped into the path of the Thunderbird. Isaiah slammed on the brakes to miss her by inches. "Damn," Isaiah said, "somebody's mama is in bad shape."

Baptiste cynically said, "Somebody's mama is full of bad booze!"

They resumed driving as Baptiste responded to Isaiah's question. "About your woman's horny display of her, uh, abundant physical assets, comfort yourself by the fact that I've suffered in affairs with anglo and black women who were synthetic ladies with the manners of princesses and the sneaky morality of wild tomcats. Other anglo and black women that I'm happy to forget were pure to the bone skunks. They all had pretty faces and eyebombing curves like your skunk in residence."

Isaiah said, "What can a guy do to find a real woman?"

Baptiste said, "In these times, great patience is needed to find a stable and good woman of any color. My advice to any black man who prefers white women is to search in the social bin marked Jewish for a loyal, lovable woman like my Deanna. Now, about understanding why Sabina hooked up with you in the ghetto. Shit, I ain't psychic, but I think there are as many reasons as there are white women who flee into the ghetto. Some of them have secret embarrassing reasons. After all, a bad minority of white men in America are the undisputed champs of the sexual abuse of their daughters and other female members of their family. These females are forced by rock bottom self-esteem to seek emotional comfort, acceptance, and even worship, in the arms of black men. It's sad, but true, Isaiah, that some black men will take tons of long-term shit from a finely stacked blonde and kick a black woman's ass for cussing him. Sabina, like many of the others, has secret reasons for running into the ghetto."

Baptiste chewed his bottom lip. "I'd hazard a guess that when Sabina rented that bachelor apartment on the first floor from you two-and-a-half-years ago, she got the impression that you owned the building. After all, I'm almost an absentee landlord, except when I visit the kids in the back. I'm sure that after she laid a sample of that pussy on you, you didn't tell her that you were just a manager. You waited until after she married you, right?"

Isaiah nodded. Baptiste went on. "Perhaps the truth might have soured her fantasies of ripping you off for a chunk of dough. Then she could re-enter the white world with a bankroll for a front to catch a handsome big shot white man. Whatever the case son, you're in quicksand."

Isaiah drove the Thunderbird into Beverly Hills. He gritted his teeth. "I hate white people! I want revenge! Sometimes I feel like taking a machine gun to a mall in Beverly Hills or Bel Air and just kill, kill until they kill me."

Baptiste said gently, "I'm sure the racism in America has driven other young blacks to similar foolish thoughts, but hear me clearly friend, it's stupid to think that way, and worse, to do the act. Killing for revenge is wrong ex…"

Isaiah cut him off. "You wouldn't kill someone who killed your mama and all your brothers and sisters?"

Baptiste said, "I was about to say that revenge is a fool's trap, except when you kill someone who kills a person that you love and the killer slips through a legal loophole to freedom, or just receives a slap on the wrist. But for the hell of it let's assume that you went on a murder rampage like that. What if you killed many good white men and women along with some of the racists that mingle in every mall. Machine gun fire would kill innocent children, babies. Why, shit, nigger, I might be at the mall shopping and get caught in your crossfire."

They laughed together as Isaiah drove through the gate to park in the driveway in front of the house. Baptiste said, "Want to come in for a moment for the check and a cup of coffee?" as he got out of the car.

Isaiah hesitated, "No thanks, Pop, I'm in a hurry to get back to South Central."

Baptiste said, "You all right?"

Isaiah laughed. "Pops, your rap could make Manson cool. I want to get back and sic those private investigators on Sabina."

Baptiste smiled and turned away. He said over his shoulder, "I'll send Helene out in a moment with the check."

Shortly, Helene pranced to the car. She came to the driver's side and gazed at Isaiah's face with smoky eyes for a long moment before she gave him the check.

"Hope you visit again soon," the Haitian temptress purred before she moved away into the house to buzz him through the gate.

Twenty-five minutes later, he walked into the office of Stokes and Lee, just a block from his apartment. A faded brown-skin glamour girl wearing purple eye shadow and a matching micro-mini sat behind a battered reception desk.

"I'd like to speak with Mr. Stokes or Mr. Lee."

She said, "You are ... ?"

He said, "Jones, Isaiah Jones."

She fluttered her fake eyelashes. "Please make yourself comfortable for a moment."

He sat down and stared at the worn maroon carpet. Five minutes later he seated himself in the office of Billy Stokes, Lee's gargantuan shoe-black partner draped in a pin-striped suit.

"Mr. Jones, is your, uh, problem, domestic or industrial?"

Isaiah said, "I guess domestic, an industrial strength domestic problem."

Stokes laughed at the pun. "We also handle investigations of dishonest employees in stores and other businesses."

Isaiah said seriously, "I want a complete report on every move that my wife makes out of the house, night and day for at least a week..." He paused to remove from his wallet a close-up Polaroid shot of Sabina seated on their living room couch.

Stokes studied the picture. "Our fee is two hundred dollars a day plus expenses... You want us to take the case?"

Isaiah said, "Start tomorrow."

Stokes nodded and picked up a pen.

Isaiah thought of his modest life savings in the bank. He'd go broke to know the full truth about Sabina's life in Texas.

"Mr. Stokes, I also want you to investigate my wife's past life in Austin, Texas. Her maiden name is Nillson. Can you also do that?"

Stokes said, "Of course, but it will cost you at least an additional 1500 to 1800 dollars to send an investigator down there. I'll personally call and check the Austin police Hall of Records and the FBI for a criminal history."

Isaiah said, "I want that."

Stokes opened a notebook. "Okay, give me your address, a description and plate numbers of any vehicles that she drives, and other important information about her."

———

Isaiah's inner pressure was much relieved when he left the office. He hurried home to let Eric into the apartment just in case Sabina had hit the streets as she often did of late, without a thought of Eric's meals or care. He took a letter from the mailbox. It was from his father's sister Melba in Macon, Georgia. She was the only person in the state that knew he wasn't dead.

Sabina was in her bedroom completing a paint job on her face when Isaiah got home. He sat on the sofa and watched her through the open door. She came into the living room decked out in a new champagne-colored silk micro-mini, coco sling pumps with matching clutch bag.

"Bye, bye, King Kong," she said as she walked past him to the front door.

He laughed. "Bye, bye, Slick Fox."

At that moment the doorbell chimed. She opened the door for Eric, who was clutching a small bouquet of flowers behind his back from the back yard. His enormous blue eyes were bright with intent to surprise her.

"Yo, Mom! I copped some blossoms for you," he said joyfully as he gave her the bouquet.

She glared down at him, with her face distorted in sudden rage. She threw the flowers to the floor & seized his shoulders. She shook him violently as she shouted, "I'm sick of hearing you speak that nigger slang."

"Daddy, Daddy," the boy wailed.

She shouted, "I've told you how it upsets me for you to speak like that. Don't ever do it again! Understand? Under..."

Isaiah rushed off the sofa to jerk her away from the mauled little boy. Eric cried as Isaiah hugged him.

She screeched, "Eric, that nigger isn't your father. You're white!" She left and slammed the door shut.

He took Eric to sit on the sofa. He held Eric close and said, "Your mama is just nervous and uptight...

she loves you... and you know I do and always will...
I'm the only father that claimed you... so I'm your father,
black, green, or otherwise. Right?"

Eric looked up into his face. "Yes Daddy, you are...
and I love you too."

After preparing an early supper of spaghetti and
brussels sprouts for Eric and himself, he went into his
bedroom next to Sabina's to relax. Eric was engrossed
playing Nintendo in his bedroom.

In the quiet beige and brown sanctuary of the bedroom, Isaiah lay with eyes closed. He saw inside his head
a vivid video of himself at 18. Then, his real name had
been Hershel Johnson. He was lean and strong enough at
harvest time to help his mother and father and his seven
younger brothers and sisters on the Johnson farm. He'd
worked with them from 6 A.M. to late afternoon. After
that he would usually go across the road to help his
Uncle Henry in his business. He'd shoe horses, sharpen
tools, and wait on the ailing old man — sometimes until
midnight. He often stayed overnight.

He remembered how and why his total being had
been infected, contaminated with his insensate hatred
for white men. He visualized as clearly as the starry
skies of country Georgia that day when he, his father
Philip, and Suzie Mae drove into Macon for groceries.
16-year-old Suzie Mae was so abundantly endowed
physically that most men, black and white, would gape
lecherously at her.

They got out of the battered family truck in front of the store. Four white men played cards at a table in a small alcove adjoining the store's entrance. A fifth of gin and glasses sat on the tabletop. Three of the card players were decrepit old men in their late seventies. The youngest one with them was 50ish, powerfully built Jimmie Joe Franklin, Grand Dragon of the local Klansmen.

As the Johnsons approached the store, Jimmie Joe whistled in a familiar key. He leaned and darted his hand under Suzie Mae's dress to finger-poke her pussy as she followed her brother and father into the store. She screamed, "You dirty dog! Daddy, Hershel-Jimmie Joe put his hand on my private part!"

The Klansman laughed and turned back to his game. Hershel's 6'7" father almost bowled over Hershel to grab the molester. Hershel tried unsuccessfully to restrain his father. His father beat and kicked Jimmie Joe into a bloody heap on the sidewalk. Fortunately, the street was almost deserted because of a big softball game with a team from Rome, Georgia. The Johnsons shopped at another store before they went back home.

Elroy, a visiting cousin about Isaiah's age and size, helped bring in the sacks of groceries. Mama Tillie Johnson was terrified when she heard the bad news. "Oh, lawdy!... what we goin' do when them night ridin' devils come for us?"

Papa Johnson took an automatic shotgun off a wall rack. "We gonna kill every peckerwood in a white robe...

you, Jimmie, Marshall, Joe, and Lester, load your shotguns and rifles and keep them near your beds. Hershel, you and me will stay up tonight to watch out. Go across the road and tell Henry what happened."

At midnight, 77-year-old Henry stumbled into the Johnson home with chest pains that doubled him up. Hershel drove him to the emergency room of the Macon County Hospital. He stayed until 3 A.M. with Henry until he was told the old man had died.

As he drove down the country road toward home, he saw a geyser of flame and smoke shooting into the night sky. He reached the raging inferno that had been his home. His father's body lay riddled with bullet wounds in front of the farmhouse. He smelled the strong odor of gasoline and saw empty gasoline cans scattered about. He rushed toward the mass of flames to enter and save anybody still alive. But a blast of heat drove him back. He felt his father's wrist for a pulse beat. He dragged his father's body across the road into Uncle Henry's house. He locked the door and in a trance of shock stared at his father's body on Uncle Henry's bed.

Soon he heard sirens and the clamor of fire trucks. Someone banged on the door.

He didn't answer.

At 9 A.M. he heard on Henry's radio that all members of the Johnson family, with the exception of father Philip, had perished in a fire of unknown origin.

The news gave birth to Hershel's plot to get his revenge on Jimmie Joe. Since the authorities thought the body of his visiting cousin Elroy was his, he could kill Jimmie Joe and leave Georgia forever. But what about his father's body? He'd leave the front door ajar when he left to stalk Jimmie Joe. One of Uncle Henry's customers would discover his father's body. He knew his father carried burial insurance policies on himself and all the others. It would be assumed that his father had been shot. Naturally not by the Klansmen, but by a person or persons unknown.

Hershel loaded Henry's 30-30 rifle. Since he was presumed dead, he'd have to walk through deep woods for 5 miles to reach Jimmie Joe's house. He lived with his mother in an isolated section outside Macon.

He left Henry's at 9 P.M. He had to be waiting when Jimmie Joe came home from his nightly tour of the town bars. Bone-tired and drained, he lurked in a clump of shrubbery 20 yards from the driveway of the Franklin home.

Midnight passed, then at 10 after 2, he saw Jimmie Joe's red pickup pull into the driveway. When he got out, Hershel aimed and pulled the trigger of the 30-30.

The high velocity bullet blew the Klansman's brains out over the driveway. Lights flashed on in several of the isolated homes as Hershel fled into the darkness. He swung onto a moving freight train a half-mile from the rail yard. He didn't know where it was headed. He didn't care.

A week later in South Central L.A. he met Baptiste while grocery shopping. Baptiste saw him slip a package of lunchmeat into his shirt. Baptiste had come up behind him and whispered, "Son, put that back and take this five spot. I'll talk to you outside about a job."

He had started out mopping and cleaning out vacated apartments for Baptiste. Six months later, he told Baptiste about the Georgia murder and why. Baptiste had said, "I understand better than you'll ever know. I hereby rename you Isaiah Jones. My mother's father was named Isaiah."

Isaiah was startled out of his reverie by Eric in his doorway, carrying a ghetto blaster booming out Kool Mo Dee's latest hit.

"Good night, Daddy," Eric shouted above the din.

"Yeah, goodnight," Isaiah shouted back.

Chapter 3

A week later Isaiah walked the block down Crenshaw to the office of Stokes and Lee. As he went in, Sabina gasped as she spotted him. She was riding beside Big Freddy in his silver Rolls.

"Hey girl, what did you pin to put you up tight?" he asked as he pulled around the corner from her apartment building to let her out.

She opened the car door and started to step out. "It's really nothing for you to know... it's personal."

The flabby mountain of black fat grabbed her wrist and yanked her into his lap. He twisted her wrist until she winced in pain. She lay trapped on her stomach. He fiercely whispered in his sinister hoarse voice, "Look at me bitch and get hip to what I'm rappin'!"

She turned to look up into his brutish face. "There ain't a motherfuckin' thing I ain't 'spose to know about you. Bitch, you ain't got no personal business that Big Freddy shouldn't be hip to. When you take a shit bitch, remember it concerns Big Freddy. Hey, I ain't no trick. I copped you that ride and mashed the bread on you to cop that pile of new threads from Rodeo Drive. I treat you righteous 'cause you my lady... ya jus' livin' temporary with super square until I make arrangements to move you and your crumb cruncher out. I send suckers to the cemetery that fuck me over. You my woman."

Despite her fear and anger, a bit of hysterical laughter slipped out. She couldn't remember the musical drama in which a black singer sang the line, "Bess, you is my woman now."

He growled, "Bitch, you crazy?"

She said, "No, I always laugh when I'm getting my fuckin' wrist broken."

"Girl, you hip to what I been sayin?"

She nodded her head vigorously. He released her. She sat up. He took a wad of C-notes from a blood-red silk shirt pocket. He shoved the wad down her bosom. "Buy your crumb cruncher some new threads and a trip to Disneyland. Now give Daddy some sugar."

She leaned toward him and endured, without flinching, his long slobbery kiss. She left the car. She walked away, then turned back. "You got any special candy left?" He gave her a vial of crack laced with China White heroin. She rushed into her apartment. She spent five minutes gargling and spitting out Listerine. The wad of C-notes counted out to 3500 dollars.

"What a vicious, uncouth, despicable trick Big Freddy is," she thought. But he was the most generous she'd known. And also the most dangerous, she reminded herself. But she was sure she could handle him until the time was right to flee from the ghetto into the sanctuary of the white world.

She remembered seeing Isaiah go into the investigator's office. She vowed to be careful and make sure that she was not followed.

Sabina undressed and stepped into the shower to cleanse herself of Big Freddy's afternoon lovemaking in a Hollywood motel.

Isaiah was admitted into Stokes' inner office at the instant that Sabina entered the shower. He passed a sad-faced older man exiting Stokes' office. "Good afternoon, Mr. Jones. I'm sorry you had to wait. Sit down and take a deep breath."

Isaiah sat down. "The unpaid amount you owe is 1,900 dollars with the 2,000 dollar check you gave us. The total for everything is 3,900."

Isaiah took a checkbook and pen from his pocket. He quickly filled out the check and gave it to Stokes who gave him a receipt. Stokes said, "I'll give you a brief summary of what our investigation of your wife revealed..." He paused to glance over his shoulder at a bony black woman in a yellow dress seated before a computer printer.

"Miss Morris is printing out a complete report for you... Young man, I'm afraid you married a very promiscuous king-sized headache."

Isaiah felt faint. "How, uh, bad is she?"

Stokes blew a gust of air through his gold-plated uppers. "She's freaking off with Big Freddy for openers. She is also..."

Isaiah, shocked at the mention of the notorious drug dealer, interrupted. "You can't mean Big Freddy Evans, the dope dealer."

Stokes said, "One and the same. He's rumored to be not just a garden variety dope dealer. He could be the main distributor, the godfather of crack cocaine — not only in California, but to franchises across the country. As I was about to say, your wife also has been observed in the company of affluent young & middle-aged white men. She picks them up in upscale restaurants and bars in Beverly Hills and West Hollywood. Several of these gentlemen have taken her to motels for brief periods of time. She almost hit the jackpot when she was 18. She got pregnant with a young rich man's kid, a boy. They were about to be married when the young man's parents ran a check on her background and killed the romance. I'm..."

Stokes's thin, high yellow assistant dropped the sheaf of printout information on his desk. Stokes continued, "I'm old enough to be your father. I hope good advice won't offend you. Your wife is poison, Jones. Let her go... Her police record down in Texas started at 13, everything from theft, dope usage, and prostitution. In fact, an investigator saw her in the company of one of her early girlhood hooker pals from Texas right here in L.A. The pal is Lisa Lundgren. She deals cocaine to upscale white men and women from her West Hollywood apartment. Here's the report, and please take extra care, Mr. Jones."

Isaiah stepped out into the late afternoon sunshine in a fog of shock and turmoil. He was stricken beyond anger or sorrow. He was totally numb as he entered the apartment.

Sabina was seated on the sofa in a filmy lavender negligee, buffing her gold nails. She looked up and smiled. "Hi, pretty boy."

He muttered, "Hey." He went past her like a robot with glazed eyes.

She said to his back, "Daddy darling, I'll be waiting for you after Eric goes to sleep around 11."

He went into his bedroom and locked the door. He sat on the side of the bed and read the 20-page report. He collapsed on the bed and stared at the ceiling. He had to rid himself and Eric of her. But how? The monster, murder, invaded his mind. She would be waiting for her pussy slave at 11. He'd go in and strangle her, then he'd wrap her corpse in a bundle of sheets. He'd wheel the body in the large clothes hamper onto the elevator. If a tenant saw him, it would be assumed that he was going to do a big gymnasium wash for the athletes in the first-floor laundry room. But he would go to the garage. He'd stuff her body into the trunk of his Thunderbird. Then he'd go to the tool shed where Alonzo, his all-around assistant, kept rakes, a mower, and a shovel. He'd drive to the desert and bury her deep... then he remembered Baptiste's remarks about the gas chamber or life forever in the big joint and the monster inside his head was rousted from his mind.

The solution to his problem was inside himself as Baptiste had told him a hundred times. He'd have to commune with the truth and stop lying to himself.

He'd have to handcuff every man's mortal enemy. His ego. He'd have to face the stark, painful truth about himself, no matter what. "You hate her," he told himself and knew that to be true. "Am I stupid enough to be her pussy slave?"

With uncommon bravery of will he recognized that truth. He got a vision of her lying naked in her gold and lavender lair as she waited for him tonight. He asked himself what the hidden reason was for why he was hooked on her flesh when he hated her so much. Then suddenly he realized that Sabina was the accessible embodiment of every blue-eyed blond that had ached his balls and stiffened his dick with forbidden desire since his boyhood in Georgia. Sabina was Marilyn Monroe, Christy Brinkley, and every other ball blaster that had tantalized and inflamed him from TV and movie screens.

He felt his shackles loosen. All right, she was poison as Stokes had told him. Maybe he was taking killer doses of her poison. He'd slack off and fuck her fast only every 10 days instead of three times a week. Maybe taking her pussy in small doses would make him immune over time. Yes, he'd develop the emotional numbness of a pimp. He'd shame her until he could break away. But he'd need a fill-in pussy to take off the fierce pressure in his balls.

He made a mental note to call Helene, the Haitian sexpot, and set up a date. He undressed and went into the shower that adjoined his bedroom. After the shower, he relaxed nude on the bed. He fell asleep.

At 11:15, he was awakened by a knock on the door. "Yeah," he growled.

"Daddy darling, did you forget our date?" Sabina cooed through the door.

"No, I'll be there," he replied.

Five minutes later he left his bedroom. Her door was wide open. He paused in the doorway. She lay in the lavender glow, 5 and a half feet of naked, curvaceous alabaster poison. The heavy odor of incense hung in the air to cover the crack she had just smoked.

His 12" weapon erected beyond reason, beyond hate. As he went to lie beside her, he wished that his dick was a scalpel so he could slash and butcher her insides.

He caressed her from head to toe with gentle fingertips. He barely resisted the impulse to rip her flesh open with his teeth as he toured her body with tender kisses.

She moaned when he trapped her knees against her chest with his shoulders. "Oh, please don't hurt me," she whined as he eased in his vengeance pole to her belly. He fantasized that he was a murderous slave, who had slipped in to kill ol' massa's precious daughter with his dick. He rode her hard and long. She was barely conscious after the crack and brutal ride. He spewed enough hate seed into her battered cave to spawn a million sex slaves. She was oozing sweat and gulping air.

He put his ear against her chest to hear the riot of her heart.

"You're going to kill me baby," she said raggedly. He abruptly, contemptuously got to his feet without the usual cuddling and tender baby talk he had lavished on her in the past. He left the room.

He stumbled into his bedroom, exhausted. He hadn't been the victor in Sabina's bed. He was depressed, regretted that his dick had ruled him once again. But at least he thought, I get a draw for fucking her into a semi-coma. He fell asleep five minutes after his head hit the pillow.

The next morning, he called Baptiste. "Good morning, Pops. I'd like to come over in a coupla hours to show you the report I got on my wonderful wife. Okay?"

Baptiste laughed. "No. You're barred until you dump her... Get here before I have to leave for a bone scan at 2:00 P.M."

Isaiah said, "I'll be there... Would you mind putting Helene on?" Baptiste shouted, "Mind? Hallelujah!"

Helene came on with her throaty voice vibing hot Haitian passion. She had implored the loas, her voodoo gods, to reel him into her bed. "Isaiah, you are very wonderful to thrill me so with this chance to speak with you. Thank you," she excited him.

"It's my pleasure, Helene... Think your boss would let you take off this evening for fun and sweet games with me?"

She giggled. "Maybe if I ask him, certainly if you did. Will you?" Isaiah said, "Sure, put him on."

Baptiste picked up the phone. "I heard everything. You young handsome son of a bitch. I hate you... she can take off. I'll see you later pal."

47

Isaiah hung up feeling great for a change. He showered and dressed in a blue silk leisure suit with blue and dove grey shoes and a grey banded blue straw hat. Sabina had hit the streets and Eric was in the gymnasium when he left at 11:30 for Beverly Hills.

Helene buzzed his car through the gate and let him into the house. He embraced her and feather-stroked his lips across her mouth before he went through the house to the patio.

He saw Baptiste swimming in his kidney shaped pool. Baptiste said, "Get your trunks from the cabana and get some big time exercise."

Isaiah entered the igloo shaped building to undress. Shortly, he emerged and dived into the pool. Helene gazed at his heart-thumping body from her bedroom window. She thanked the loas for sending her such a body on which to lavish several years of starved passion.

Chapter 4

In a Beverly Hills restaurant Sabina enjoyed lunch with Lisa Lundgren. They had chosen a smoking section in the balcony overlooking the crowded main floor. They sat at a table near a wide window with a view of the street.

Fashionably dressed men in sports clothes and three-piece suits paraded past with impeccably attired women. The older women wore designer hats and gloves.

Lisa spooned chocolate mousse into her wide but sensual mouth. She was a pretty brunette who looked a lot like a young Hedy Lamarr, except that her large brown eyes had a piercing coldness.

Sabina said, "Look at those pampered lucky bitches... I wonder how many of them live in mansions? I'd kill to be respected and live like them."

Lisa took a cigarette from a gold case. "Not all of them are lucky or happy. Some of them are married to rich pricks... maybe half of them live in mansions or six-figure condos. The other half live in high rent apartments. By the way, when are you going to dump your crazy Japanese sucker in Orange County?"

Sabina had lied because hooking up with a nigger, even a rich one was, in Lisa's opinion, the absolute pits for any white woman. Sabina said, "Old slant eyes will receive that big inheritance soon. I've got the sick old bastard's power of attorney. I'll take the hunk of bread and stick him in a rest home. Then la de da, Sabina will be on the prowl to catch a handsome, rich husband and live like a big time lady."

An elderly man smoking a cigar took a table a few feet away with his young female companion. Lisa blew a gust of smoke against the window.

"How's the kid?"

Sabina frowned. "He's well but... he... is attached to old slant eyes. He infuriates me when he speaks Jap shit."

Lisa leaned across the table. "We've come a long way Sabina, since we hooked tricks together in Austin when we were kids. You've got a dream to hook a rich guy. I've got the dream to expand from a lousy retail dealer of cocaine into a big wholesaler dealing kilos."

Sabina was instantly energized by the kilo remark. There was a big buck angle somewhere in the triangle of Big Freddy, herself, and Lisa. She'd have to think it out. She raised her glass of champagne toward Lisa and toasted. "Here's to the early realization of both our dreams."

Across town, in Inglewood, an adjoining section of South Central L.A., Big Freddy sat down to lunch. His elderly mother, Esther Evans, brought him and seven-year-old Freddy Jr., the thin image of his father, a plate of freshly baked biscuits to go with the smoked pork chops, hash browns and gravy. Esther's doe face was heavily wrinkled. Her snowy hair was in a tight bun on her neck. A gold chain around her throat dangled a gold crucifix.

"Mama, ain't nobody can burn like you," he mumbled with his mouth loaded with food. Junior agreed, "You ain't lyin', Daddy."

She gently slapped his barn door shoulder. "Hush that jive & eat slow." She stood beside him and studied him for a long moment. She had lost two much younger sons in gang wars. She walked away into the kitchen. She prayed silently that God would let her keep Freddy. She reassured herself with the thought that he was now 40. He owned a thriving Fried Chicken Shack and didn't have to lead a crooked & dangerous life. Junior's mother was dead. She wished Freddy would get married.

The phone rang on the table beside Freddy. He was startled by the call. He picked up on the first ring. He heard the voice of Ernesto Portillo. "Yes, it's Freddy."

Ernesto said, "Hello, my friend."

"Come to see me in the next half hour." The slightly accented voice of the Colombian cocaine cartel member commanded.

"Daddy, can we go see the Dodgers home game next week? Can we?"

Freddy said, "Yeah, sure buddy," and gulped down the last of his meal, grabbed his hat, kissed Mama Evans and left the palatial house.

Fifteen minutes later he drove into the walled estate of his boss in Baldwin Hills, an area that overlooked South Central. A pack of six huge killer Rottweilers descended to surround Freddy's Rolls. A squat, dark complexioned Colombian in shirtsleeves shouted out a command in Spanish. They sprinted away to patrol the grounds of the estate.

Freddy got out of his car and was escorted by two Portillo henchmen into the two-story white stone castle-like home. He was taken through the opulently furnished home into the white and gold den on the ground floor.

58-year-old Portillo, a tall, darkly handsome man, was seated on a white leather sofa. He was flashing even whiter, nearly perfect teeth as Freddy entered the room. Bianca, Portillo's statuesque wife, placed a tray of cookies and lemonade on the coffee table. "Hello, Freddy," she said in her husky voice.

"How you doin', Mrs. Portillo?"

Her haughty face shaped a little smile as she left the room wearing a red satin ribbon in her waist-length silver riddled jet-black hair.

Portillo looked at his watch. His palm patted the sofa. Freddy sat down beside him.

"My friend, it's very good to see you arrive five minutes early. In our business, proper timing and planning can give us an edge on local and Federal cocksuckers with badges. Right, Freddy?"

Freddy grinned, "Mr. Portillo, you ain't lyin'... you sounded a little upset on the phone. Is everything cool?'

Portillo threw his head back and laughed mirthlessly. Freddy stared at the widow's peak of black shiny hair that gave Portillo's face a satanic cast. Freddy laughed with him at the thought that he'd ask a dude that looked like hell's landlord if everything was cool.

Portillo's fiery black eyes sparkled with irritation. "Cool, my friend? We're like red hot foxes hiding and running from hounds that chase and trap us with technology of every kind. One mistake and everything that gives life joy can be lost, even life itself." He took a folded map of the USA from a pocket of his gold satin robe. He unfolded it, spread it out on the sofa between them. Arrows in red ink had been drawn from circled Chicago to Detroit, New York, and Philly. Portillo put a perfectly manicured index finger on Chicago. "Three thousand kilos of my merchandise have been stored in a safe house in Chicago." His finger moved across the target cities. "I have delivery commitments that must be completed within a week."

Freddy looked puzzled. "I thought Juan left for Chicago yesterday to deliver the kilos to those cities."

Portillo sighed. "Juan was unfortunately arrested on an old murder warrant. Fortunately, he was arrested in his hotel room before Tony had arrived with the kilos for Detroit. My friend, you share the responsibility with me, your business associate and friend, to help me in this matter."

The thought that Portillo was suggesting that he, Freddy, go to Chicago to replace Juan popped sweat out on his flat nose. "Mr. Portillo, I don't look right for slippin' past the DEA and a bunch of other heat lollygaggin' in airports in Chicago and them delivery cities."

Portillo smiled slyly. "My friend, I've decided that men and women with dark skin have become high risk mules whether black or Latino... I heard that you have been fucking an all-American young blond. Is this true?"

Freddy fidgeted. "Yeah, for a month or so, but she's... uh... married."

Portillo banged the heel of a hand against Freddy's arm. "You've been screwing her for six weeks my friend. Married? Tell me more."

Freddy said, "Well, she's beautiful with a knockout body... she's 27, 28 years old, but looks 20. She's got a kid, a boy 9, 10 years old."

Portillo stroked his heavy black mustache. "It's good she has a child... tell me about her husband."

Freddy snickered. "He's straight & stupid. I call him Super Square. He lets her go and come as she pleases."

Portillo said, "She sounds perfect for the job, she..."

Freddy cut him off. "But Mr. Portillo, she ain't the type to stand no pressure if she gets nailed dirty in one of them air terminals... she'll flip and finger me."

Portillo said, "That's nonsense. Her kid is insurance against that possibility. Give her a good fuck and tell her she'll get 10 grand to make the deliveries. I'll see you tomorrow and give you detailed instructions to pass on to her... Oh, yes, we won't have to worry about her honesty or the cash she'll handle. I'll send a pair of shadows with her on all her flights & transactions. Have her on a plane to Chicago within 72 hours my friend. This is more than an emergency. Understand?"

Portillo was addicted to his heroin-laced crack. Freddy loved it and planned to request a key of China White when he put in his next order from Portillo. Freddy said, "I understand, Mr. Portillo... do you have any of that special rock you can spare?"

Portillo smiled and took a large vial from his robe pocket. "Here, my friend, is enough for a few days. This is pure joy without a wrecking of the nerves and a black hole of depression when you come down."

"I know... thank you, Mr. Portillo."

They got to their feet and shook hands. The two guards stepped into the room to escort Freddy to his car. While driving to South Central, he decided that he would proposition Sabina to take the gig for 10 grand. But with his ass in Portillo's vise, he'd double the payoff.

In Beverly Hills, Baptiste and Isaiah sat at the patio table after the swim and breakfast. Isaiah picked up a thick manuscript from the table top. "Damn, this is gonna be a humongous book... have you finally finished it?"

Baptiste took a sip of iced tea. "Yeah, the first draft... I need to change and rearrange a few minor things." He finished reading the investigator's report on Sabina. "Whew! Son, you hooked up with Satan's pet."

Isaiah ruefully shook his head. "Yeah, I know; if I stay with her I'm afraid I'm gonna get stupid and hurt her real bad."

Baptiste placed his hand on Isaiah's arm. "There's something I kept from you... It would hurt my heart if I told you something about her that you couldn't handle... Oh shit, I shouldn't have cracked anything."

Isaiah frowned. "Why the fuck are you torturing me? I ain't gonna kill that slut bimbo... lay it on me."

Baptiste sighed. "I covered her crack pipe on the coffee table with my hat at your place so you wouldn't see it... when we came back from the living room. It was gone when I picked up my hat... Can I trust you to stay under control?"

"Yeah, I'm in touch with the truth about her & myself."

Baptiste looked at his watch, "Guess I'll see you later. I have an appointment for a bone scan... Old age is the worst curse."

Isaiah started to rise from his chair. "I'll drive you, Pops."

Baptiste put a restraining hand on his shoulder. "I'll drive old Betsy. You can stay and keep your new sweetie company."

Forty minutes later, Baptiste lied on a table in a starkly white, quiet room in his shorts. He had been injected with a trace substance. He had been instructed to lay motionless on his back. The automated scanner started to move its hood-like x-ray component which was attached to a long flexible tube. It inched at a snail's pace from his toes to the top of his skull. He ached from boredom as he lied there listening to the dulcet whir of the robot scanner.

Finally, it was over and he dressed. He went to sit and read a dog-eared magazine in a lonely little room. He waited for his urologist and the results of the scan.

Within an hour, his doctor came to sit down on the couch beside him with his usual inscrutable expression on his pale, worn face. He looked at Baptiste through horn-rimmed glasses for a long moment. "Mr. Landreau, I'm deeply sorry that I have bad news…"

Baptiste grabbed his arm. "Tell me doctor… how long… Don't con me."

The doctor looked at the ceiling and bit his bottom lip. Baptiste had a morbid thought as he stared at his glasses. The doctor's glasses reflected the ceiling light that looked to Baptiste like the silicone chips sparkling in granite tombstones. "Well, Mr. Landreau, you have, uh, maybe a year as an extremely optimistic prognosis… perhaps 90 days… perhaps not that long. You refused testicular surgery, chemotherapy, and radiation therapy treatments for your prostate cancer… It has metastasized, spread throughout your body. It's regrettable that you…"

Baptiste cut him off. "I don't regret any of the decisions I made. I'm going to the grave a whole man with my balls intact. Chemotherapy and radiation would have debilitated me at my age. I don't want to die in bed."

They stood. Baptiste shook his hand. "Good luck, Mr. Landreau. If you need help to face your situation, call me. I'm also a clinical psychologist."

Baptiste squared his shoulders. "Thanks doc, but Baptiste Landreau knows how to live and die on his own."

He left the hospital for his car. He drove home in a mental whirlpool. Would he live long enough to finish the polishing of his book? How, where, when would he die? Did he have time to get his business affairs in order and get himself to his daughter Opal in Sugar Hill?

He got home and went to Deanna's shrine in a guest bedroom. He sat on the silk pink chaise lounge that she cherished. He gazed at a life-size painting of Deanna. The artist had captured the real life glow in Deanna's strong, sweetly sensual face. "Well, pretty brown eyes, looks like reunion time for us. I don't feel no pain baby. I'll be so glad to join you." He sat for an hour in the pink ambience. He went into his bedroom to call Opal just to chit-chat. He had concealed the whole truth about his health from her. "Hi, sugar pie."

"Hello Daddy, what a wonderful surprise," she joyfully exclaimed. "How are you feeling?"

He cleared his throat. "Fine, baby. Just fine."

"Daddy, you wouldn't tell a fib to your one and only child... your voice sounds — well, tired and a bit strange. Come on now, you know how well we know each other."

He felt tears on the brink. "Hey, I've felt better... but you've got nothing to worry about. Oh shoot, the phone is ringing downstairs and Helene is off."

"Daddy, I'm coming out there to see you next month. Bye."

He hung up and picked up his manuscript to read for changes.

———————

At that moment Sabina lay nude and exhausted in bed with Freddy at a Hollywood motel. She smoked crack and watched his white teeth flash like neon in his ebonic face, reflected in the ceiling mirror. "You want me to rundown anything again baby?"

She moved out of his arms. "I don't need another rundown... I need a hike in pay for your risky gig... how about 25 thou? After all, I've got a kid and I could be middle-aged when I got out of the joint if I take a fall. No hike, no dice. Well?"

He nipped her nipple with his teeth. "You're a stuck up bitch. But you got it. Again. Just pack a couple of changes and necessities in a small bag. Get to Pan Am at 10 in the morning. Your ticket is paid up front. Deal?"

She slipped out of bed to her feet "I want half now and the other half when I get back. Deal?"

He grinned. "Shit, you think I ain't got chicken feed like that in my pocket." He pulled his trousers off a nearby chair. He took a roll of c-notes and thousand-dollar bills from a pocket. He counted out 13,000 into her palm. They left the motel separately at her request. She didn't want to be seen with him after seeing Isaiah go into Stokes' office.

She went to her convertible. He drove into a South Central grocery lot to use a public telephone to call Portillo. "Hey, Mr. Portillo, I just installed that new transmission and she's ready to go."

"That pleases me very much my friend." Portillo hung up. Freddy called his mother. "Mama, I'm at the grocery. You want me to bring you anything?" She replied. "You, just you Freddy."

In Baldwin Hills, Portillo summoned Emilio Sanchez and Frank Carillo, his trusted bodyguards of 20 years. Frank was his wife Bianca's nephew. "You guys leave tonight for Chicago. Any questions?"

Emilio shrugged. "No. You explained everything perfectly. We'll be there when the all-American girl checks in." They left the living room.

Portillo made a brief call to Lisette Fontaine, an 18-year-old platinum blonde with whom he was totally infatuated. Then he left the house to feed his killer pack of Rottweilers. They were trained to take food only from his hands.

Chapter 5

Sabina was apprehensive on the flight to Chicago. Maybe she shouldn't be risking her freedom for the less than fabulous money. After all, she couldn't buy a mansion or a private jet with it.

She arrived in Chicago at twilight time. She took a cab to a modest hotel in the downtown section. She checked into her room. A wardrobe trunk sat in a corner of the room. She went into the bathroom. She had pulled down her panties to sit on the john when the door to the connecting room opened. She pulled up her panties. "Who the hell are you?"

Wiry Emilio's dark face wore a pleasant smile. Fat, short Frank leered at her over Emilio's shoulder. "Don't be alarmed. I'm Emilio, and the guy behind me is Frank... Sabina, we're your friends and protectors. Lock the door when you come in here... we'll talk to you after you get settled in." He shut the door. She locked it and relieved herself.

An hour later she tired of TV. She examined the padlocked trunk and tilted it. It was fairly heavy. She wondered what it contained. A knock came on the bathroom door. She unlocked it. Emilio & Frank entered the room.

"What's in the trunk?"

Frank said, "Sixty pounds of lead bars and lots of shredded paper... don't sweat about anything. The boss has figured out everything to the smallest detail."

She moved to sit on the side of the bed. "Who's the boss?"

Emilio said softly, "You don't really want to know. That could be dangerous... relax, while you can. We leave at midnight."

"What, uh, where are we going?"

Frank laughed, amused by the virgin mule's trepidation. "A guy checked in downstairs is gonna bring us 30 kilos for Detroit delivery."

Her hand shook as she lit her cigarette. "How will I get 30 kilos past the DEA agents and the cop dogs in the airport?"

Emilio said, "You don't. At midnight we drive a rental car to Rockford, Illinois. We separately board a 2:30 A.M. pre-paid flight to Flint, Michigan. Then we drive a rental car into Detroit. We use the same method to deliver to Philly and New York. Feel better?"

She sat down on the bed. "Yeah, a lot better."

As they left her room, Emilio said, "Be dressed and ready to leave at midnight sharp for the drive to Rockford."

She couldn't sleep, not even catnap. The tension inside her was horrific and she had no crack to medicate her nerves. She thought, "If I could get to the South Side I could cop. But how do I get away from these goddamn bloodhounds? I feel worse than I felt since Texas when I was 8 years old. Fuckin' stepfather's four sons tore my nerves apart coming into my bedroom to lay me in relay..."

At five minutes to midnight they separately left the hotel to get into a black, rented Chevrolet parked a block away. Emilio took the wheel for the two-hour drive to Rockford. Along the way Emilio went into a Kentucky Fried Chicken restaurant to bring back three dinners. Even though Sabina's stress had been lowered by Emilio's rundown of the delivery method, her mind was magnetized by the king-sized bag in the trunk that contained the 30 kilos.

Twenty miles from Rockford, Emilio pulled to a stop on the shoulder of the highway. "Your turn Frank," he said as he slid out from behind the wheel.

Frank got out and went around the car to take the wheel. Sabina sat on the back seat with her eyes closed. They went into the airport separately. Emilio and Frank had small, clean carry-on bags for show.

A skycap put Sabina's big dirty bag of kilos on a cart to ride beneath the flight in the storage hold. She made only two over-the-hill plainclothes cops as she went to pick up her pre-paid ticket. They seemed hypnotized by her blond radiance and gorgeous gams revealed by a short black linen skirt. Her frilly white lace blouse lent a delicate purity to her image. The flight was on time and uneventful except when a drunken older woman puked in the aisle before she reached the john. Sabina sat two rows behind Emilio and Frank who sat on opposite sides of the aisle.

They disembarked at Flint. Sabina stood watching and waiting for the big bag to show on the carousel. Finally, it came bouncing into view. A skycap carted it out to the sidewalk and loaded it into the trunk of a cab.

A half mile away Emilio and Frank were in a parked rented Ford. They carried two automatic pistols and a portable counting machine that had been left in the car. The trio drove to Detroit. At a drive-in theater they parked behind a black Mercedes with a designated license plate. Two young black men in sports clothes with hard faces came to get in the Ford. They brought a large valise stuffed with 450,000 dollars for the 30 kilos at 15 thousand a kilo.

Sabina sat behind the wheel. Frank got out to get the machine and kilos from the trunk. He put the bag on the lap of the younger man. Frank got back in the car. Emilio counted the C-notes and thousand-dollar bills on the rear seat with his gun beside him. Frank, a black belt in karate, sat beside Emilio. He leaned and watched one of them prick a plastic wrapped kilo from the middle of the bag. He dipped from the kilo with the tip of a penknife and dropped a bit of the crystal coke into a vial containing a pale tan liquid. It turned deep purple when the coke fragments dissolved.

The younger man said to the older, "It's pure enough to stomp on and get 60 kilos." The pair counted the kilos. They smoked cigarettes while Emilio finished counting the bundles of bills. Finally, he said, "See you next month." The pair got out and entered their car. They drove off the lot.

A moment later Frank drove the Ford from the lot. Sabina sat alone on the back seat. The valise was on the front seat. A thought gnawed at her. "Emilio, somebody is going to have a tough time changing all those thousand dollar bills into smaller ones without a lot of heat."

Emilio laughed. "You think we're fuckin' amateurs? The boss owns or controls two banks and a Savings and Loan. Beautiful, you're in fast company."

They drove to Flint, Michigan to take a flight back to Waukegan, Illinois. Waukegan was a short distance from Chicago. They drove a rented Toyota to their Chicago hotel. Tony Baca, the delivery man, came to their room a half-hour after they arrived. Tony, Frank, and Emilio knocked and entered her room. Tony unlocked the padlock on the trunk. He opened it and removed two 30-pound lead bars & a mound of shredded paper that was used to keep the bars from thumping and bumping while the trunk was handled.

He stuffed the bars and paper into two large plastic garbage bags. He placed the big buck valise into the empty trunk and locked it. Before he left to dispose of the bags he said, "See ya in the morning about 10 with the merchandise for New York." He went to the street. He entered a gray Cadillac driven by his beauteous black long-term wife, Delphine. She drove away for their apartment on Chicago's South Side. They smoked crack on the way.

Emilio and Frank went to their room. After they left, Sabina lay staring at the trunk. Her mind searched frantically for an angle to rip off the small fortune. But she realized it couldn't be done. "Eric pisses me off a lot," she thought, "but I love him in my own ambivalent way. If I didn't have a kid thousands of miles away that could be kidnapped & killed, I could slip out and buy a hacksaw from a hardware store to cut the padlock. I could buy a duffle bag from the Rexall Drugstore across the street, and I could split when I was sure the pair on the other side of the bathroom were asleep. Why oh why did I ever have a kid?" she asked herself as she drifted into fitful sleep. The next morning Emilio ordered breakfast from room service.

They drove a rental Pontiac to Milwaukee, Wisconsin, 90 miles from the concentrated police heat in Chicago airports. At noon in Milwaukee they separately boarded a flight to Trenton, New Jersey, a stone's throw from the Big Apple. They left the plane. Emilio and Frank went to a rental car five blocks from the terminal. They checked the trunk to find a counting machine and pistols inside.

Sabina, as usual, waited impatiently for the kilo bag to be unloaded with a mountain of other bags from the belly of the plane. Finally, the bag came tumbling down onto the carousel.

A skycap loaded the bag into a cab that took her to the Pontiac. Sabina got in the back seat with the bag. "Well, Big Apple, here we come."

Emilio and Frank burst out laughing. Emilio said, "Only a lunatic would deliver 30 kilos into New York City."

Frank said, "There's more heat and busts here than anywhere in the world... bulk cocaine is in short supply in the Apple."

Emilio said, "Yeah, I know. That's why we're gonna get 20,000 a kilo from the Puerto Rican..." He paused to glance at his watch. He continued, "When he gets here from Spanish Harlem."

Frank drove to park in a lot behind a pool hall on the fringe of the black ghetto. They got out of the car, took the kilos and counting machine from the trunk. They knocked on a sheet metal back door. Joshua Johnson, a small black man who was the pool hall owner, opened the door with a dazzling gold-toothed smile. He was also the younger spitting image of the late Sammy Davis Jr. "Come in and relax... My, my, what a pretty lady."

Emilio said, "How you doin', Josh? This is Joyce."

Sabina said, "I'm pleased to meet you and thanks for the compliment."

They sat down on a long-battered sofa in a large room that contained a brass bed, stove, refrigerator, and a clutter of throwaway furniture. There was the sound of raucous voices and the sharp impact sound of pool balls coming from the adjoining pool hall. Frank looked around the room. "Where's your German Shepherd, Josh?"

The middle-aged bantam sat in a faded green leather chair and gritted his goldcapped teeth. "Some lowdown motherfucker... excuse my French, lady... must have put some poisoned meat in the alley and Big Stuff gobbled it and died. A dirty bitch I throwed out must have did it."

Emilio said, "I think I heard a car pulling into the lot."

Joshua went to pull back heavy dusty yellow drapes from a grimy window. He opened the back door. Shortly, a stout, high yellow woman and a handsome Puerto Rican man in a 500-dollar pale blue suit and a pearl grey straw hat entered the room. "Hi folks, this is Connie, my old lady and business partner."

Frank said, "Congratulations, Connie, when you caught Leo you got a winner." He nodded toward Sabina. "That lady is Joyce."

The Harlem pair sat down on the long sofa. Frank shoved the kilo to Leo who gave the money to Emilio. He and Sabina started to feed the 600,000 dollars in large bills into the denominational slots of the machine. As the various denominations of bills passed through the machine, Sabina repacked them into the bag. A tiny screen flashed 600,000 when they finished.

The Harlem pair had selected a kilo from the bottom of the bag and were very pleased with the high quality of the goods. "It's been a pleasure to do business with you," Leo said as he and his woman stood. He shook everyone's hand before he led his woman out the door into the backyard parking lot.

Emilio stood up, followed by Sabina and Frank. Emilio gave Joshua 3,000 dollars in C-notes before they left to get into the Pontiac. The follow car, this time a blue Toyota, was behind them as Frank drove to within a mile of the Mercer County airport near Trenton. He parked. They got out and put the counting machine and pistols into the trunk.

Emilio got into a cab for the airport. Frank and Sabina took another cab; the tailing Toyota parked beside the Pontiac. A tall Colombian got out. He removed the money machine and pistols from the Pontiac and placed them in the trunk of the Toyota before he drove the Pontiac away to be returned to a rental agency. The blue Toyota followed him.

Sabina, Emilio, and Frank separately boarded a flight for Chicago 45 minutes later. When they went into their hotel rooms Sabina went into the bathroom and knocked on the men's door. Emilio opened it. "Have you got any loose cocaine? Or even a stick of grass?"

He shook his head. "Sorry, the boss says no drugs, not even grass, which I miss... until business is finished."

She pouted her lips. "Would the boss care if I went directly to the bar downstairs and had one Margarita?"

He shook his head resolutely. "Alcohol is a drug. Go to bed. I'll spank your ass if you call room service or go to the bar for booze."

She pulled the door shut in his face with a bang. "Bastard," she exclaimed as she went back into her room.

She picked up the phone to call room service for the booze to defy Emilio. She replaced the receiver. She thought, "The cunning bastard probably has called the bell captain and promised him a bribe if he will report any request for service from my room."

She watched TV and chewed her fingernails until she fell asleep on the bed fully dressed. At 3 A.M. she was awakened by Tony the delivery man. He was putting the 600,000 dollars into the trunk with the cash from the Detroit deal. "Do you think it's smart, Tony, to leave all that cash in this room when I leave? A maid, or..."

He cut her off. "It's safe. I move in when you move out."

Next day they drove with 30 kilos in a Buick to the Racine, Wisconsin airport, not far from Chicago. They, as usual, separately boarded a flight to Allentown, Pennsylvania. A car containing a counting machine and pistols was parked a short distance from the airport. Emilio drove the Plymouth into Philly.

They parked in a corner of a huge chain grocery parking lot. Ten minutes later a large blue van parked beside them. They got out and carried the machine & the kilo bag into the van. It was furnished like a living room, with a couch, thick carpeting, and leather chairs.

Two older, punchy Colombians tested the goods before they passed a duffle bag to Emilio for counting out 450,000 dollars.

Within an hour, Frank drove the Plymouth off the lot into traffic. He drove to within a mile of Lancaster,

Pennsylvania. A brown Mercedes followed them. They parked the car and took cabs to the airport. The Mercedes stopped behind the Plymouth.

The same tall Colombian who had taken the guns and counting machine from the trunk of the Pontiac in New Jersey repeated the ritual. He got in the Plymouth and drove away. His accomplice in the Mercedes followed him.

An hour later the trio again separately boarded a flight for Waukegan, Illinois. Sabina was so drained and exhausted that she fell asleep as soon as the flight took off. They disembarked hours later.

A Lincoln was parked a short distance from the airport. They took cabs to it. Sabina protested but drove the Lincoln to within a half-mile of their hotel. She parked the Lincoln in a designated drug store parking lot. They took cabs to the hotel.

Tony was in her bed watching TV when she went in. Emilio came through the bathroom with the 450,000 dollars. Tony stuffed it into the trunk. He left.

An hour later Sabina was awakened by a phone call from Tony. "It's okay to let a black bellboy named Leander take the trunk." He hung up.

Ten minutes later she opened the door to a bellboy's knock. He was a huge young black man with a pleasant moon face. He looked ridiculous in his too-tight red and black uniform.

"Your name is…"

He smiled, "Leander, baby... the sweetest stud in town." He put the trunk on a dolly and wheeled it out of the room.

Next day at noon they checked out. They took separate flights into LAX. Sabina took a cab home. Isaiah was seated on the living room sofa when she walked in. He gave her a dirty look and said to her back as she passed him. "Damn, Slick Fox, you look wasted, like you've been humpin' in a two buck whore house."

She turned and stopped in the doorway of her bedroom. "Fuck yourself, flunkey."

He rose from the sofa menacingly. She quickly stepped into the bedroom. She shut the door and locked it. Isaiah went into the kitchen to prepare an early dinner for Eric and himself.

In the afternoon of the next day Sabina visited her long-term girl pal Lisa. They sat in the sunken living room on a white satin sofa in Lisa's ritzy penthouse condo in West Hollywood. They silently smoked crack in the sunless room. Heavy sable colored drapes were drawn across panoramic windows through which, at nightfall, fabulous neon fireworks of the City of Angels could be viewed.

In the swank gloom they were like pretty, animated manikins in a store window on Rodeo Drive. Lisa broke the silence. "Kiddo, tell me more about the hunk that took you out of circulation for days... I missed your daily phone calls. I was worried about you."

Sabina took a sip of Harveys Bristol Cream from a crystal goblet. "This blond guy was so beautiful, Tom Cruise would feel like an ugly ducking in his presence. When we got to Vegas, he checked us into a gorgeous suite at Bally's. Girl, I swear, I was lubricating with my clothes on for this six-four lump of wipeout sugar. When I looked into his magnetic blue-green eyes I could have eaten him with a spoon. He..."

Lisa burst out laughing and playfully slapped Sabina's arm. "Stop dangling me and get to the meat of what happened in bed."

Sabina lit a cigarette. "Bed? The gorgeous bastard pulled me out to the casinos five minutes after I freshened up... as we played at various craps and roulette tables, several men and a woman slipped notes and money into his coat pocket. At midnight we went to our suite. We had toured most of the casinos. But how could I be too tired for a water bed transport to heaven with the hunk? After a shower I got all sexy in some shit from Frederick's of Hollywood. When he came out of the shower and sat down nude on the edge of the bed, I was salivating. I got down on my knees and started licking the feet of this golden god. I had traveled to my delicious destination when the lousy phone rang. He went to one of his bags and took out a medium sized package, gift-wrapped. "Darling, put on some clothes and deliver this to a friend at the Aladdin. His name is Lonny Smith, Suite 400." I started to protest, to let the friend wait for the package, but the hunk's eyes had rattled my brain and my cunt was sizzling. I rationalized that if little doggie-me ran the errand, he'd be extra sweet when I got back. I rushed back and..."

Lisa exploded laughter. "I've got bad news Sabina, your hunk is a drug dealer..."

Sabina said, "Tell me what I didn't find out. I must be brain-damaged because I made four other deliveries to hotels before I fell into bed with him. I picked up where I left off when the first phone call came in. He loved it when I got him off. I rolled away and closed my eyes for my deserved ride to heaven. I waited like forever. He had fallen asleep. I shook him. He opened his eyes. I said, 'Billy, I want you, need you inside me. Please!' He hugged me and whispered, 'Sabina, you're a sweet and lovely girl but we can only be friends. You see, I'm gay and in love with someone in L.A.'"

Lisa hooted, "What a kindly payoff for risking your ass in the penitentiary."

Sabina hit the crack pipe. "I got a payoff."

Lisa took the pipe. "What?"

Sabina kept her in suspense for a long moment. "The hunk is the connection to cop kilos of high-quality cocaine at 25,000 a key. It could be cut to make two keys... if you're interested, Billy will give me a nice commission."

Lisa turned her head away toward an entrance hall and exclaimed, "Donald!" A moment later, a smallish young man with a soft, most girlish face entered the living room wearing black silk lounging pajamas. He Said, "Hi, Sabina," and sat down on the sofa between the women. Sabina said, "Hello, Donald... nice seeing you again."

He lit a cigarette. Lisa said, "Sabina has a connection to cop keys of coke at 25,000. The stuff is so pure it can be cut to make two. This is our chance to go really big time. How much bankroll do we have?"

He hesitated, "30, 40 grand." Lisa gasped, "I can't believe this... we had at least 75,000 dollars in the bank just 10 days ago. I feel a headache coming on." He sighed, "Baby, believe me, I know how you feel. I made a vow that I wouldn't bet on another racehorse in this lifetime... I'm sorry."

Lisa gulped down a half goblet of Bristol Cream. "Well, what the hell, we'll start modestly with one key."

Sabina shook her head. "Billy won't deal under five keys. Save your bread and I'll help you make a deal with Billy when you're ready."

Donald eased sheepishly from the room. They smoked crack in a long silence before Lisa said, "I've been dealing grams to a handsome British multimillionaire land developer and aspiring movie producer. He's shy, a gentleman to the bone. But he loves a fast buck. He's ready to buy five to ten keys of quality coke. Tell you what, you can meet Stanford William Leeds III here at my place next week in the last part of July. I'll let you know the precise time later."

Sabina left the penthouse in a glorious crack euphoria. Her mood soured as she drove her Excalibur into South Central. She went into her apartment. She saw Isaiah stretched out in street clothes on his bed. She heard a dish strike the floor in the kitchen. Eric was scooping crab salad from the floor into a paper sack. She stood in the dining room and watched him stuff the bag into his shirt. He threw the broken platter into the garbage can. He mopped up the mess on the floor with paper towels before he hurried from the kitchen. He nearly collided with Sabina.

She grabbed his arm. "Hey, let go, Mom. I'm late for a sparring session." She twisted his arm. "What the hell are you doing with that crab salad in your shirt?"

His forehead popped perspiration as she twisted his arm harder. She slapped his face repeatedly with her other hand. Finally, Eric said, "It's for the starvin' cats in the alley behind the gym... a mother cat just had kittens... Let me go, Mom!" She held her grip.

Isaiah rushed into the dining room. He grabbed one of Sabina's arms & flung her violently against the wall. The impact stunned her. She sat on the carpet staring up at him with glazed eyes. Finally, she pulled herself to her feet. "You goddamn idiot. He was taking expensive food to mangy alley cats. Stop interfering and spoiling my child.

Stop roughing me up or I'll kill you in your fuckin' sleep! Remember *Burning Bed*, stupid?"

Eric ran from the apartment. Isaiah stood, shaken by her reference to the Farrah Fawcett movie based on a real case in which Farrah's character murdered her husband by torching his bed while he slept.

Sabina stomped away into her bedroom. She locked the door and stood quivering with rage before her dresser mirror. She excoriated her reflected image. "You beautiful dumb Texas moron. Are you retarded or what? You wind up in a fuckin' black ghetto getting room and board, married to a dead-end nigger who bosses you and bounces you off fuckin' walls... so Eric will be torn apart when you split from the only father he's ever known. So split, idiot! Eric will heal fast with a new rich white daddy." She lit a stick of incense. She opened the dresser drawer. She took lingerie to stuff under the slight gap between the bottom of the door and the carpet so King Kong wouldn't smell even a wisp of her crack smoke.

She drew the heavy gold drapes across the windows to blot out the sunlight. She lay in bed in black panties and bra. She smoked a special mixture that Freddy had given her. It was smokable China White heroin blended into the crack. Her mind explored the history of the cause and effect downslide into her present hated existence. Her life had been sweet and happy when she was six years old. Her big, affable father, Herman Nillson, and mother Ella were in love. They lived a modest but happy life in a mortgaged small house in Austin. A week before her 7th birthday, Herman, who was an oil field worker, was killed accidentally at work. Ella fell apart. She drank heavily at home and in rough saloons. She lost the house. She and little Sabina lived in the family's battered old Ford. Ella met a mean-spirited alcoholic oil worker and married him. She and Sabina moved into the stepfather's house, occupied by four teenage sons. Soon, father and sons were molesting Sabina in relay fashion while Ella lay in drunken stupors.

Sabina's bitter reverie was interrupted by a torrent of tears. She recovered and remembered how she suffered in the house until she was 12. She ran away to live in the streets. She slept in abandoned cars and houses. She panhandled and scavenged throwaway food from chain grocery dumpsters. One day, 15-year-old hooker Lisa Lundgren came out of a grocery store and went to her pimp's Cadillac. He was about to drive away when he saw Sabina bring her blond head out of the dumpster.

"Lisa, get out and get that pretty young bitch," he commanded. Lisa always did as Felix commanded because he got his jollies kicking ass.

"Hi kiddo, I'm Lisa. Let's go get some nice food and some new jazzy clothes." It had been that easy for Felix, the half-Mexican, half-Irish mongrel pimp to get the fifth young girl for his stable working the streets of Austin.

Sabina learned the skills of prostitution and stealing from people and from stores. She was busted a dozen times for theft and prostitution. When she was 15 she was kicked and beaten by Felix because she bought a package of cigarettes without getting his permission. The week before, he'd taken his five girls to an abandoned barn. At five bucks a pop, three hundred Mexican migrant workers had lined up and punched their tools into the girls who were lying on piles of straw. Sabina was sore and raw for a week.

She split to Houston, Texas. She set up her sex service in a big hotel with the cooperation of the bell captain. He would send businessmen tricks to her room for a 20 % payoff from her fees, which ranged from 50 dollars to a C-note for brief sessions.

One day in a fancy bar in downtown Houston, she was approached by a young, handsome man. She liked him instantly, so she played innocent little square to hook him. What a prize she had caught. He was the only child of a tremendously rich oil family. After a long romantic holiday in Acapulco, Link Rosenthal told his mother and father he planned to marry Sabina. They had met her and agreed that she was indeed beautiful. But privately they were deeply concerned about her background. They hired an investigator who ferreted out a rap sheet in Austin. Link's parents were horrified by the close call. Link was devastated, turned off by the revelations. Sabina fled to Hollywood.

Six months later, Eric was born, the image of his father Link. She went on welfare and turned a few tricks until he was 5. She paid a baby sitter and took a job as a doctor's receptionist until Eric was 8. One day, Nick Papodapoulous, a fast-talking Greek promoter/gigolo came into the office for a minor medical problem. She gave him her phone number when he convinced her with the cliché line about "you're so beautiful you deserve to be a star, and I'm the guy that can make it happen."

She quit her job and moved with Eric into Nick's spacious apartment. Nick paid for dance and vocal lessons. He invested in an expensive array of Western apparel. He arranged a number of bookings for her as a singer of country and western songs. He also told her that in her spare time she could perform in porn movies.

Isaiah knocked hard on the door to startle her back to the present. "What the fuck do you want, Isaiah?" He laughed, "I was just checkin', Slick Fox, to see if you had killed your crazy self." She shouted, "Leave me alone, nigger. Unfortunately, I'm still alive." He said, "That's wonderful... I think," before he left the apartment.

Then she remembered that last day in Nick's apartment. The following day she was to begin her first booking on the showbiz treadmill in San Francisco with a shabby little musical troupe. She couldn't do it. But Nick's reaction to her refusal to go after his big investment might be violent. She also believed he was mob connected. She snatched up a few clothes for herself and 8-year-old Eric and caught a cab. She fled to South Central, the last place Nick would search for her.

She rented a bachelor apartment on the first floor below her present apartment. Isaiah, who she thought owned the impressive building, came on strong and she married him for security, only to discover that he merely managed the building for Baptiste.

For two years she had been trapped in the black ghetto. Three months before she had gotten the news on TV that Nick had been killed in a gunfight in Hollywood. She was free to make excursions into Hollywood. One day she met Lisa there in the Rainbow Bar.

The phone rang on the nightstand. She picked up. It was Lisa calling to tell her she was frantically putting together the affair for Stanford Leeds.

———

Across the alley from the gym, several boys 10 to 15 years of age sat on a railing and passed a crack pipe around. One of the boys Eric's age saw Eric leave an abandoned garage where he had left the food for the cats.

"Hey, Eric, come on and take a hit." Eric shook his head, "Thanks, not today." He had crossed the alley on his way to the gym when he stopped in his tracks. One of the older boys hollered, "You know that sissy ain't hip enough to take a hit." Then derisive laughter erupted from the group.

Enraged, Eric went back to face them with his fists doubled. "Who called me a sissy? Stand up and I'll knock you on your ass." Eric's fearsome left hook and stout heart in the ring were well known. They all just looked at him. Finally, an older boy said, "I was jus' jivin'… Ain't no reason to go to fist city about bullshit… Take a hit and be cool." He extended the pipe. Eric accepted the veiled apology. Almost involuntarily he took the pipe as he thought about the time he had peeked through the cracked door of Sabina's bedroom when she was hitting her pipe.

He inhaled and quickly passed it back. "How you feel dude?" the older boy asked. Eric felt like he would fly out of his shoes. He felt his heart sprint wildly. He felt a frightening but oddly seductive sensation of excitement that thundered blood in his head. "I feel funny… but kinda good." He reeled away to a chorus of laughter.

He went into his apartment. He slipped into his bedroom and fell across the bed to straighten out his head.

In Seattle, Washington, George Nelson, DEA agent, was mowing the lawn and trimming the hedges around his rather modest but comfortable four-bedroom home. He was assisted by his twin pre-teen sons, Damon and Peter. When they finished their work, they went into the house to wash up and sit down for lunch.

Ilka Nelson hummed in the kitchen as she prepared shrimp salad and split pea soup for them. She was a beautiful, fine-featured woman with long, lank golden hair. She was always joyful when George would slip away from L.A. for a day or so, or even for just a few hours as he had done once since his undercover assignment to L.A. as Stanford William Leeds III.

The buxom blonde served the food and kissed her husband and twins. "Dear, I'm off to get a light perm… I'm so thrilled you'll be home for a few days."

He smacked her fanny as she turned away. The twins giggled. Five minutes later the phone rang. George got to his feet. "You guys make sure you clean your plates," he said as he went to answer the phone in the living room.

The twins shouted to his back, "We always do, Daddy!"

It was the soft voice of Joe Wiggins, DEA Regional Chief calling from L.A. "George, Central just faxed me a complete report on Lisa Lundgren, your gram girl. What's interesting about it is that she's running with a pal from Austin named Sabina Nillson Jones. Sabina has a son, Eric, 10. Sabina is married to a black man who is clean. But she's been screwing a notorious black bad guy called Big Freddy. He's been under LAPD investigation for several months for possible collusion with Ernesto Portillo to distribute cocaine in South Central L.A. and possibly to gang members throughout the country. I'll brief you in detail when you get back to L.A."

George said, "Thanks for the info." He hung up and sat looking out a living room window at the peaceful and serene suburban street. He knew he was lucky to have Ilka, the twins, and the house. He was also grateful to get this respite from the snake-pit world of gunmen, drug dealers, and pretty painted human maggots in high heels that would do any filthy, unscrupulous thing for a fast buck or to capture Stanford Leeds and his mythical fortune. He sincerely believed that pretty criminal women were among the most cunning, dangerous, and greedy creatures in the underworld. Why had he, a San Diego Assistant District Attorney, left such a well paying relatively safe career niche to risk his life with the DEA?

His uncle Albert, a DEA agent since its inception in the 70's, had begged him to join the elite drug busters. Albert was slain in Bogota, Colombia by a drug cartel hit team. George was in the DEA service a month after Albert's murder in 1980. Nelson hated with a fanatical passion drugs and the vicious, greedy people from the top to the bottom of the poisonous scale. Like all members of the DEA, he was obsessed with the drive to ultimately take down the producers and importers of drugs. They were the Colombian cartel members and certain Mexican nationals who were their confederates.

Nelson felt excitement when he thought of Joe Wiggins' call indicating that Sabina Nillson Jones could possibly become a link to take down Ernesto Portillo, a known cartel member.

Two days later Opal Landreau Ross arrived at LAX. She called Helene in her quarters to let her know she was on her way to surprise Baptiste and to buzz in the limousine she would hire to take her to Beverly Hills. The 5'10" beauty turned many heads as she walked from the terminal to the sidewalk to enter a limousine. Her short champagne chiffon dress matched her exotic satiny smooth face. She looked no more than 30 despite the fact that she was past 40.

In Beverly Hills, Baptiste lay in bed desperately visualizing that his cancer was leaving his body. For several days, he had felt an odd numbness on his left side from ankle to hip. Wrenching, unbearable jolts of pain in his right leg occasionally forced him to take prescription morphine. He was about to force himself out of bed to start the day when Opal burst into the bedroom.

"Surprise, Daddy!" she said as she flung herself into his arms.

"You imp, you almost surprised the pee out of me."

She kissed his face repeatedly.

"Oh, stop that... I haven't showered or brushed my teeth." She moved to sit on the side of the bed. He noticed stress shadows around her eyes.

"Where's Carl?"

She averted her eyes and stared at the morphine vial on the nightstand. "He's got the flu... He sent his love."

Baptiste sat up in bed. "Baby girl, are you telling me the truth?"

She evaded the question. "Daddy, do you have pain so bad that you need morphine?"

He pulled her into his arms. "Yeah, damn arthritis in my joints... Baby girl, are you and Carl still getting along sweet and lovely?"

She started to cry. She blubbered, "Oh, daddy, Carl ran away with a 21-year-old white barmaid... They're living in Paris... It's getting easier now, but it really hurt a lot, Daddy. Well, I've got the house on Sugar Hill and close to 200,000 in the bank. It could have been worse. Carl could have been a nine to five joker instead of the heir to a fortune and left me broke in some rat hole apartment. Daddy, I really don't need anyone except you to help me mend and be happy. Come live with me on Sugar Hill. Please!"

He got out of bed. "I'll be there as soon as I can wind up business affairs here," he said as he went into an adjoining bathroom.

An hour later he and Opal sat with Isaiah eating lunch on the patio. "Pops, how soon do you plan to split?"

Baptiste took a sip of grape juice. "Oh, in a couple of months. Don't get antsy to become the boss when I go."

Opal opened her purse to get a cigarette. Instead, she closed it. She knew Baptiste hated cigarette smoke and she didn't want him to know that she couldn't keep her promise to him that she would quit smoking. "Isaiah, how are Sabina and Eric?"

Isaiah's face hardened. "She's around every now and then... Eric is well and my stone pal... "Pops, Helene can help me run things when you leave."

Baptiste smiled. "You have my approval."

Isaiah said, "It's a real pleasure to see you again Opal. Hope you stay and go back with Pops." She sighed. "I'd like that, but I'll have to go back tomorrow to host a big charity affair in Harlem for crack mothers and babies."

That evening Opal retired for the night in a guest bedroom next to Deanna's shrine. Opal slept soundly for the first time since Carl had deserted her several weeks before. She was so happy that Baptiste would be joining her on Sugar Hill soon. She would catch a flight at noon back to New York. Baptiste went to his bedroom. He went and stood before Opal's mother's picture on the dresser. His eyes moistened as he stared at the lovely face of 18-year-old Hattie Rambeau, so much like Opal's face. He'd married Hattie a month after Chester's death. Together they operated the Harlem store.

Hattie miscarried three times in her desperation to have his child. He smiled, remembering how happy they were at the birth of Opal, a doll replica of her fiery Haitian mother.

He was suddenly saddened, remembering how he had failed to convince Hattie to make her feel secure, to know the truth — that he truly loved her and was immune to any other woman. But a fiendish demon resided inside Hattie's mind. She became savagely jealous and violently accusative when he smiled and spoke pleasantly to the young attractive female customers. He remembered that fatal day in Spanish Harlem when the demon puppeteer inside Hattie's head sent her to her death. They had closed the store, taken one-year-old Opal to babysitter Grandmother Rambeau. They had gone to the gala opening of a bar and grill owned by a close friend. After glutting themselves with spicy Haitian delicacies and champagne, they left the party at midnight. The sidewalks of Spanish Harlem were infested with night people. The walked toward their new Buick, parked down the street. An outrageously voluptuous Puerto Rican ball blaster encased in a skintight red satin dress walked toward them. She beamed her enormous dark eyes up at Baptiste and bumped her hip against him in passing.

Hattie's hand, which he was holding, burst perspiration. She tore away shouting, "You slut bitch, I'm going to stomp a mudhole in your rotten ass!"

Baptiste remembered how he had stood paralyzed with shock as he witnessed the murder of his wife, in a weird kind of slow motion. The Puerto Rican woman spun around. Her face was distorted by surprise and alarm. Her hand darted into her bosom as Hattie reached her and punched her face.

In the neon glow of the street, a steel switchblade flashed like a striking silver cobra into Hattie's heart.

Tortured and tormented by his loss, he went on a sexual binge in a vain attempt to alleviate his misery. He had brief affairs with a variety of black women, Puerto Rican, and white women from Greenwich Village to Park Avenue.

Opal lived with Grandma Rambeau for most of the time during the 9 years of madness. Finally, without Hattie, he decided to escape the punishing New York winters and the voodoo freaks that he had endured for 30 years. He sold the store, the land on which the building sat with several other adjacent properties inherited from Chester, to a development company.

It had been so wonderful in 1965 when he and young Opal stepped off the train in L.A. in balmy December weather. He had deposited $850,000 in cashier's checks in a South Central bank. He and Opal liked living in South Central until 1975 when the gangsters declared war on themselves and anyone who got in the way.

His real estate investments in South Central and Baldwin Hills had paid off handsomely. He took Opal from the battlefield and purchased his home in Beverly Hills.

He sighed in long term loneliness. Opal had fallen in love with Carl Ross, a young white student at UCLA and eloped with him to honeymoon in the Bahamas.

"I was born to lose people I care about," he thought. His mind followed the bitter path of loss as he looked at a gold ring on his right hand. Deanna Stein, the most important person since Hattie, had given him the ring on the 10th anniversary of their marriage in '86. A month later loyal lovable Deanna was snatched away by viral pneumonia. He thought of the shrine he had created in a guest room in memory of Deanna. He never retired for the night without going to relax for a moment in the room where somehow he sensed Deanna's beautiful spirit was present.

On a morning in the last week of July, Lisa called Sabina. She invited her to come to a birthday party for Stanford Leeds that evening in Lisa's penthouse.

At 8 P.M., Sabina dressed in a silk micro-mini orchid dress that clung to every voluptuous curve of her body. She flung a sable boa around her shoulders and, under Isaiah's icy stare, she went to the garage. She drove her red attention grabber into Crenshaw traffic. Within 30 minutes she stepped off a private elevator into the entrance hall of Lisa's apartment. A caterer's assistant dressed as a butler greeted her. "Good evening, ma'am." He led her into the living room. She heard the dulcet hum of polite conversation between two dozen men and women ranging in age from early 20s to mid-60s. They all looked remarkably attractive and resplendent in the low-beamed softness of a crystal chandelier that showered the room with flattering amber light.

"Darling, I'm so glad you came," Lisa said as she took Sabina's hand and led her to sit on a sable chaise near a panoramic window. The taped, muted piano artistry of Errol Garner's "Misty" hung in the perfumed air like a hymn to these laughing, beautiful mortal gods of movies and finance.

The bright blue uniformed caterer's staff served champagne and hors d'oeuvres from silver trays. A buffet table in the corner was laden with bountiful delicacies. Gold satin ribbons suction cupped to the ceiling dangled dayglo cardboard cutouts of the British Royal family. Other cutouts depicted the London Bridge and other famous Brit landmarks.

Sabina leaned to whisper, "Lisa, no way would our old gang back in Austin believe this."

Lisa caught her breath, "Uh oh, the reason you came is on the way over."

Sabina looked up at the most handsome man she'd ever seen, including in her fantasies. George Nelson, aka Stanford Leeds, stood before the women with his electric grey-green eyes twinkling down on them. "Lisa, please forgive me for the intrusion..." He paused to wave a perfectly manicured hand toward the center of the room. "I must thank you again for this magnificently created party in my honor." He leaned to kiss Lisa's forehead. Sabina was palpitating with excitement.

"Stanford, it was a thrill to do this for you... This is Sabina Nillson, my best friend," Lisa said as the chandelier lights suddenly went out.

"I'm very pleased to meet you, Miss Nillson. Excuse me… I'll be back."

A pair of waiters costumed as palace guards wheeled in a table covered by a rainbow-hued phosphorescent cloth. A mammoth four-tiered cake replica of the Tower of London sat on it. A thicket of flaming candles ringed it. Sabina and Lisa watched Nelson cut the cake before waiters started to serve the guests. The flickering candles against the backdrop of cutouts had the effect of a visual trans-oceanic visit to the land of monarchs.

Nelson returned. He said, "Again, Miss Nillson, it's a pleasure to meet the other most beautiful woman in my memory." His deep rich baritone Brit-inflected voice fluttered Sabina's heart. "I'll leave you two to get acquainted," Lisa said as she got to her feet. She turned and walked away.

Nelson sat down on the chaise beside Sabina. "You are so lovely… you must be a model or an actress, perhaps?"

Caught off guard she hesitated, stared out the open window at the neon light show before she replied. "Breathtaking sight, isn't it?" He said, "It is indeed," as he took glasses of champagne from the tray of a waiter. He gave her a glass. "I did a bit of modeling in Texas and a few TV commercials… I received a rather substantial inheritance several years ago… It freed me as a single parent to care properly for my son Eric, a preteener… Do you have children?"

He took a sip of champagne. "No, unfortunately... My one and only wife died before she could bless our marriage with a child."

Sabina was too personal, too soon, too eager out of refined control. "Are you in love with anyone now?"

He was about to answer when the waiter offered them slices of cake on china plates. They munched on cake for a few moments. He was accustomed to these crudely direct questions from female game players. He was delighted to answer such questions. It gave him the opportunity to play the role of shy, vulnerable Stanford Leeds to the hilt. This role always made the streetwise, arrogant sluts feel superior. He also knew that the main element of charm was to be able to control his ego and deprecate himself, make the other person feel wiser, more sophisticated than himself in certain vital areas of living, like sex, love, and marriage. He portrayed Stanford Leeds as a blue blood wizard of finance and lover of a fast buck.

They put their cake plates on the tray of a passing waiter. "May I call you Sabina?" She smiled. "You may, if I may call you Stanford."

"You may. Sabina, as to your question — I fell in love once... after Hedda died... It was a total disaster."

She leaned toward him, big blue eyes soft with fake empathy. "But why? How a disaster?"

His handsome face became somber, pained. "Suzette was very beautiful, sophisticated, and a very rich French woman. She was also in love with me, enchanted she told me... until she fell more madly in love with a Parisian gentleman about town who was less inhibited in the, uh... bedroom than I... She left me afraid to love again."

She cupped one of his hands in her palm. "You must fall in love again... there are many good, loyal women in the world who would adore you... What is your impression of me?"

He gazed with apparent awe into her finely sculptured face. "I have known many beautiful women but with you I feel really afraid... You see, you bear a remarkable resemblance to Suzette."

Annoyance wrinkled her brow for an instant. She laughed nervously. "Stanford, don't be afraid of me because I resemble Suzette. Why be afraid at all?"

He squeezed her hand. "Sabina, it isn't an unpleasant fear... As a matter of fact, I like being emotionally intimidated by your beauty... Sabina, I'm fearful of you because I don't want to be maimed again... because I have so much to give emotionally, my soul really, to the woman that I love. You see, I have much to lose if I play blackjack love again and bust out... Tell me you understand."

She said, "Stanford, I understand and appreciate your candor with me."

Lisa approached them. "Stanford, London is calling."

He got to his feet and took a calling card from his tuxedo pocket. He gave it to Sabina. "I think I know who is calling me. I'm almost certain I'll have to leave the party to straighten out a business matter. Call me at your convenience." He kissed the back of Sabina's hand and walked away. Lisa sat down beside her. "How did you do with him?"

Sabina lit a cigarette. "He's so fuckin' charming, but so square and naive in the sex and romance departments, you wouldn't believe it."

Lisa laughed, "I believe, but with a guy that handsome and rich, you could get off just lying beside him in bed. You didn't mention keys or anything?"

Sabina drained her champagne glass. "Hell no. You mention that I might have a key connection. Let him ask me after I call him and we date."

Lisa stood up. "Stone self-confidence is what I like about you, kiddo. Here's one of the most desirable hunks in town and you are certain he wants to date you." Lisa went away. Sabina took a fresh goblet of champagne from a waiter's tray. She was going to get smashed on bubbly for a change.

In Baldwin Hills, Portillo hung up the phone in the den of his home. He smoked his special rock mixture. He was very disturbed and aggravated by a mix of anger, shock, and an odd twinge of sadness. The bad news had come from one of his trusted men in Chicago, Julio

Vasquez. Julio was the custodian of the goods in the Chicago stash house. He had left Tony Baca, the delivery man for Sabina, Emilio, and Frank, to guard 2,000 keys of coke while he, Vasquez, went to Mexico for two days to his mother's funeral. The mountain of keys were to be distributed by mules to Kansas City, St. Louis, Pittsburgh, and Buffalo, New York. Julio, a master inventory specialist, discovered when he returned to the stash that six keys were missing. He had been absolutely puzzled and concerned about the matter. The cartel bosses in Colombia and their fellow member in the United States, Ernesto Portillo, would hold him responsible for the missing goods.

Julio could not bring himself to think the unthinkable. Tony Baca, his best friend and trusted Portillo aide, was too smart, and loved to go on living too much, to steal the six keys. But they were missing.

A phone call from a South Side drug dealer informant solved the riddle for Julio. Delphine Thomas, Tony's black common law wife, was putting out feelers on the South Side to unload keys of coke at the bargain basement price of 10,000 dollars. Reluctantly, Julio put in the coded call to Portillo to cover his own ass.

Now Portillo paced the den carpet as he waited for Emilio and Frank, summoned by intercom from the swimming pool in a corner of the huge estate. Portillo felt sadness about Tony's betrayal of trust because he was the son of one of his wife's sisters.

Emilio and Frank entered the den in terrycloth robes, hair still shiny damp.

"Let's sit down. I have sad news," Portillo said. He went on, "Really sad news. Tony Baca, our friend and your cousin, Frank, has betrayed us. That black cunt of his is trying to sell six keys of our goods on the South Side, stolen by Tony from the stash when Julio went to Mexico to bury his mother. I want you both to leave tonight for Chicago. Tony and his cunt must be punished severely. It must be done in a manner that will leave no trail to us."

Frank's voice shook a little. "How should we, uh, punish them, Mr. Portillo?" Portillo closed his eyes in deep thought. Emilio said, "How about yanking out all their teeth with pliers before we..."

Portillo cut him off. "That's no good. Their bodies must not reveal any signs of murder. We must commit the perfect double murder. If their daughter is there when you visit, that would be sad. But she too would have to go. Take her body and drop it into Lake Michigan... What does Tony fear most?"

Emilio said, "The gas chamber. Remember how he was a basket case before he was released and cleared of that bum rap for the killing of a Compton cop six, seven years ago?"

Portillo banged his thigh with his fist. "I've got it! Both of them are crack freaks. Force one of them to write a simple suicide note. Have them both sign it. Threaten to pull out their fingernails and toenails with pliers if they don't smoke the cyanide-laced rock. If the kid is home, tell them you will kill her... Do it after they die from smoking the poisoned dope. Do not, uh, eliminate them until you make every effort to recover the stolen goods. You have my deepest sympathy, Frank, in this matter." Portillo gave Emilio a vial of the deadly crack. He then left the room to return 15 minutes later. He gave Frank two glass pipes.

Frank said, "I got no problems, Mr. Portillo. Tony was stupid and deserves what he gets." The men left. Portillo went into the shower. He came out and dressed for his early Saturday night date with Lisette Fontaine.

At 6:30 he had dressed in a rust silk suit and touched up a sprouting of white hair on his sideburns with a popular instant drug store coloring kit. He was in a state of euphoria after smoking his special rock.

Bianca stood watching him in the bedroom doorway. "You look very handsome, Ernesto... Will you leave again this Saturday night without Emilio and Frank to guard you?"

He frowned, then smiled. "Sweet flower, you must not worry. I need freedom from their presence... besides, they have gone on an errand." He kissed her forehead and left the house. He drove his black '90 Continental to Bellflower, an area outside L.A. proper.

In their bungalow at the rear of the big house, Emilio and Frank finished packing small suitcases for the trip to Chicago. Frank paused on the way through the living room. He stared at the 8 × 10 photographs of his and Emilio's attractive blond live-in girlfriends on the stereo. Frank said, "I miss Grace a lot." He stroked his crotch for an instant. Emilio said, "I miss Pam, but you're the asshole that let Grace con us into letting her and Pam take a long vacation in Europe."

As they went out the front door Frank said, "It cost me a lot of money, too. We couldn't go with them because Mr. Portillo wouldn't let us... Maybe we can find a coupla clean Chicago hookers."

Emilio said, "Have you ever heard about AIDS? The girls will be back after they visit their relatives in Kansas and Wisconsin. Now, forget your prick and concentrate on our job in the big Windy."

An hour later, Portillo went into Lisette's tiny rented bungalow that sat in the rear of a large white house. She had dressed and prepared everything to please and drain him sexually. The drapes were drawn and Lisette was seated nude except for thigh-high black leather boots in a throne-like black leather chair. Her 39 C-size breasts gleamed & thrusted like miniature towers.

He stood transfixed, gazing at the beautiful young sadist. "Hey motherfucker, put the admission bread on the dresser!"

He put a wad of bills on the dresser top. Her world class gams were crossed and a cat-o-nines lay across her fat blond mound of Venus. "You fuckin' slave, cunt lapper, take off your clothes and kneel before me." She cracked the whip like a pistol shot.

"Please, most high mistress, don't be too cruel to me," he begged with piteous eyes as he hurriedly undressed. He started to walk toward her nude.

"On your knees slave… crawl to me," she commanded harshly.

His penis was fully erect as he crawled across the carpet to her feet. "Beautiful Madonna, cruel saint of my dreams, may I kiss your feet?"

She lashed his back with the whip. He whimpered as he kissed her booted feet. "Please, Mistress Lisette, may the slave lick your lovely thighs?"

She lashed his buttocks as he moved to lick her inner thighs. Her green eyes were glittering with excitement. She lashed him as he buried his head between her legs.

In less than 10 minutes he had climaxed under the whip and his frenzied hand on his penis. He collapsed on the carpet before her feet. "Thank you, most delicious, most beautiful mistress. May I visit next week?" he said breathlessly.

She got to her feet. She nudged him with a boot to lay on his stomach. She gently applied coconut oil to his wounds so the welts would fade away in a day or so.

"Thank you, Mistress Lisette. This slave will think of no one but you until next week. I'll bring you a gift on my next visit. I also want to buy you a house near my home. Think about it…" He dressed and went to his car.

On the way home he was thankful that he & Bianca slept in separate bedrooms. There was a very slight risk that his wife would see the welts before they faded. He and his wife never made a move except in the dark.

At that moment Lisette's teacher of her savage craft and pimp arrived in his custom jazzed up Jag. He went into Lisette's apartment and scooped Ernesto's thousand dollars off the dresser top.

———

Next day on Chicago's South Side Emilio and Frank entered Tony and Delphine's rear apartment through an unlocked kitchen window. They were dressed in dark shirts & trousers. They wore black kidskin gloves. They stood rigidly still. They listened to Delphine speaking to her 12-year-old daughter Lucie. "Lucie, I don't want you to visit Leanna. It's too dangerous for you to go into those projects. The gangs…" Lucie cut her off. "Mama, Leanna moved. She lives at 4626 Cottage Grove just around the corner. See ya in a couple of hours, Mom."

Emilio and Frank heard the front door shut. They eased into the living room. Delphine was in her bedroom singing and applying blood red polish to her nails. She wore only white lace panties on her long voluptuous cocoa body. A Sarah Vaughn recording of "Body and Soul" played softly in the living room. Emilio turned up the volume on the record player to a shrieking decibel.

They quickly moved into the bedroom with guns drawn. She stared at them with her mouth open before she said shakily, "Hey you guys, what's goin' down?"

Frank giggled, "You, jive ass, if you don't give up those keys your old man stole. Where are they?"

She waved her hands helplessly in the air. "Keys? Emilio, Frank, please believe me, I don't know what you're talkin'…"

Frank put the muzzle of his huge Magnum pistol against the side of her head. "Where are the keys?" She ashened. "Believe me, I don't know!"

Emilio handcuffed her hands behind her back. Frank said, "One of us will go to 4626 Cottage Grove and kidnap Lucie if you…" Delphine fainted.

Frank went to the kitchen. He brought back a tray of ice cubes. He slipped off her panties and stuffed ice cubes into her vagina to revive her. Within a minute she groaned and opened her eyes. "Please don't kill me or my baby!" she screamed.

Frank said, "If you scream again, I'll blow your fuckin' head off… Where's Tony and the keys?" She blubbered through a flood of tears, "I swear I don't know anything about keys… Tony went to the grocery… somebody told you a big lie about us."

Emilio waved a pair of wicked looking stainless-steel pliers before her face. Frank sat on her back to pin her down. "Tell me where the coke is or I'll yank out every one of those pretty nails."

She hollered, "Please don't! I ain't lyin'."

Emilio stooped and seized the nail on her right little finger with the pliers. He jerked it just enough to cause excruciating pain. She fainted once again. Frank forced ice cubes into her rectum to bring her around. She slowly opened her eyes. Emilio waved the pliers before her face. "How about a thumb nail? Where is the fuckin' coke?"

She gasped. "In the closet in a big leather hat box on the top shelf in the corner." Frank opened the closet door. He reached and got the hatbox. The screech of Sarah's last lyric on the album ended.

He came & dumped the six keys on the bed. "Now, are you going to let me go... I didn't steal the keys. Joe did."

Frank gagged her and bound her feet together with a length of rope. Emilio laughed. "Delphine baby, we want you to write a note for us. Tony is..."

They heard someone coming in the front door. They stepped back from the bedroom doorway. An El train rattled by in the rear of the building.

Tony entered the living room with an armful of groceries. He was whistling a fast-little ditty that Frank remembered singing with him when they were hard core young gangsters in the streets of Bogota. "Hey brown sugar, Daddy's home," Tony said as he went past the bedroom into the kitchen.

Emilio restarted the screeching album. Sarah started singing "Perdido." They barely heard Tony shout, "Del, that's too loud!" They followed Tony with drawn guns.

They stood inside the kitchen and watched him put items into the freezer compartment of the fridge. Emilio shouted above the record din, "Hey, cocksucker! You got company."

Tony spun around, black eyes wild and wide with terror. His knees quivered and knocked together as he staggered to collapse into a dinette booth. "For Christ's sake, you guys gone crazy?"

Emilio said harshly, "No, cunt lapper, you and your slick nigger bitch went crazy. Let's change an old saying to 'don't do crime to friends unless you got the heart to die at any time.' Today is your time to go."

Tony fell to his knees and clutched Frank's legs. "Please don't kill me! I'm your blood cousin. Gimme a break... The coke is in the closet."

Emilio handcuffed Tony's hands behind has back. He said, "Yeah, we found the keys." Frank gagged him and bound his feet together. Emilio dragged Delphine into the kitchen. Emilio took a small pad and pen from his pocket. He decided to force Tony to write and sign the suicide note. He uncuffed Tony and dropped the pen and notebook on the floor beside him. "Write 'Me and Delphine can't go on any longer. Please take care of Lucie, Mama.'"

Tony hesitated.

Emilio continued, "I'm going to 4626 Cottage Grove and kidnap Lucie and kill her unless you do as I say. Now write!"

Tony looked at Delphine. "Is she there?" Delphine nodded. Tony wrote the note. "Sign it," Emilio said. Frank then uncuffed Delphine.

"Sign it." She stalled. Emilio said, "Frank, go and bring Lucie back here."

With tears running down her face, Delphine signed. Emilio lit the fatal crack pipes. "Smoke deep and we won't hurt Lucie." The couple sucked hard on the pipes. In seconds, the cyanide made them jerk, gasp for air, and choke like they were in a gas chamber. They turned blue and twitched before they went into cardiac arrest.

Emilio and Frank untied the feet of the couple. They carried them into their bedroom. They undressed them and neatly placed their clothing on a chair. They then placed them side by side in the bed. They placed the suicide note on a bedside table. They quickly repacked the kilos into the leather hatbox. They placed the pipes and vial on the bed and left the house.

Two hours later they drove into the garage of the stash house in Skokie, Illinois. Custodian Julio Vasquez was overjoyed, to say the least, that the coke had been recovered.

Chapter 6

The Enchanted Lady slashed a frothy path through the sky-blue Pacific Ocean. A tape of Ellington's sensual piano instrumental "My Solitude" lilted dulcetly in the romantic aura. California sunshine bathed Sabina and Nelson in golden light as they danced sensuously, closely, and slowly on the deck of the DEA rented luxury yacht.

"You are so adorable... I'm becoming less afraid of you and of love," Nelson whispered into her ear. She was so thrilled by the declaration that her knees wobbled. He, the consummate real-life dreamboat man of her fantasies, was falling in love with her. Could this all be real? Or was she dreaming? "I am," she thought, "I don't ever want to wake up. I don't want to ever leave this heaven I've found."

They stopped dancing to take a break in deck chairs. They wore colorful shorts and tank tops. They sported visored blue and white hats at a jaunty angle on their heads. A small Asian crew member in a crisp white uniform served them cocktails in crystal goblets. Sabina said softly, "I'm very happy in your company, Stanford. I enjoyed the cruise to Catalina so much. It will always be one of my most treasured memories. Thank you." He leaned to brush his lips across her mouth. "You have been a most welcome and enjoyable distraction from the boredom and grind of business affairs, which reminds me — Lisa told me that you had a friend who has nose candy for sale."

"I do have such a friend... How many ounces do you want to buy for yourself?"

He laughed and tapped his straight Barrymore perfect nose. "I indulge only occasionally. My septum rebelled and threatened to separate. I'm interested in making an investment in say, five, seven kilos, if the product is excellent, and the price is right for me to realize adequate profit in resale. I would be delighted to meet your friend and work out the details with him or her. Can you give me a ballpark estimate of probable unit cost?"

As the boat eased into its harbor dock she said, "I'm sure my, rather, uh, eccentric friend would prefer not to meet you or anyone else. He trusts me to make important deals, for a modest commission of course... I'll guess he'd want 30,000 a key. I will call you in a few days to let you know if a deal is possible."

He smiled. "Whether I do or don't make a deal with him is really relatively unimportant to me. I shall be expecting a call from you soon in any case. I'm becoming addicted to the sound of your contralto voice."

They left the boat. He walked her to her car in a Marina parking lot. She drove directly to a motel in Hollywood. He went back to the boat and dressed in a business suit for his afternoon meeting with Joe Wiggins in his downtown L.A. office. She called Freddy and rented a room.

She lay in bed smoking crack until Freddy arrived an hour later. "Freddy, are you going to cop any more of that mellow rock? This shit jars my nerves."

Freddy picked up his straw hat. "Maybe, if I can cop a key of China White to make my own rock." He spotted the visored nautical hat on the dresser. He picked it up. "Where the fuck did you get this... It looks like a cop's lid." He sailed it into a corner of the room.

"I've been yachting with a group of lousy, rich squares. One of them, who is gay, mentioned to one of my girl-friends that he is interested in buying bulk. He then asked me if..."

Freddy jumped into bed still wearing his street clothes. He rammed his contorted face close to hers. "Did you crack my name to that peckerwood? I'll bet he's bi and you plan to fuck him 'cause he's rich and white. Speak the truth, bitch!"

She scooted away from his high-octane alcohol and crack breath. "Look darlin', you're my main man and you're rich. I don't even fuck my husband any more. Now calm down. I didn't mention your name, or even tell him I was sure I could help him make a deal. Take off your clothes and let's be sweet to each other."

He undressed and plopped his 300 pounds of blubber into the bed beside her. "What's the dude's tag, business, and how much does he wanna cop?"

She moved to place her head on his chest. She tongue-flicked a nipple. Her perfumed blond hair quickened his scrotum. "His name is Stanford William Leeds III. He's a big land developer and aspiring theatrical producer. He's real and he wants five to seven keys of quality coke. You want the deal?"

He squeezed her buttocks hard. "Don't fuck me over with no bullshit about that peckerwood and you. Stay on the real with Freddy and he will stay on the real with you. If Leeds checks out kosher, you can lug him the stuff at 20 thou a key."

She raised her head and gave him a quick annoyed look. "Hey, I figured you would let your woman have it at 15,000 a key so I could sell it to him for 20."

He grunted. "Well, you figured wrong. I'm gonna give you 10 grand, if we make the deal. Now gimme some of that sweet tongue.

At that moment George Nelson sat down in a chair in Joe Wiggins' office. Wiggins talked almost inaudibly on the phone with his whispery voice. Nelson looked out a large skyscraper window. The tops of high-rise downtown buildings seemed to float, submerged in a sea of smog. Wiggins hung up. "How's the family?"

Nelson smiled, "Fine, Chief."

"How did you do with the little Texas tramp?"

Nelson tented his fingertips beneath his chin. "She's romantically interested and gave me tentative promise of a key deal."

111

Wiggins chuckled. "If I had your looks, I'd wear my whang off to a nub screwing show girls and starlets in Hollywood."

Nelson laughed. "Yeah, and you'd probably come up with a horror for which nobody has found a cure."

Wiggins coughed. "I was just kidding. I'm as moral as they come… when my wife is around." They laughed together. "George, Freddy Evans is a very bad guy. He committed his first murder when he was 14. He was out to get revenge on a rival gang member and his family for the drive-by shooting death of one of his pals. Freddy threw a firebomb into the wrong house and killed a mother & her five children. He was incarcerated until he was 21. The psychiatric report at that time indicated that he was a schizoid paranoiac. He's walk-around crazy. He's also a crack freak. While he was doing his bit in a Youth Authority facility, his two younger brothers were killed in gang shootouts. But according to LAPD sources, our boy Freddy gave the killers of his brother's quick justice with automatic rifle fire. He was arrested, but "released for lack of evidence.""

Nelson leaned forward. "Do we have concrete proof that Freddy is linked to cartel member Ernesto Portillo?"

Wiggins shifted his considerable poundage in his massive, high-backed brown leather chair. "Uh, definitely, they are linked. We at present don't know the precise structure of their relationship. You're certain to be checked out. Our manager friend at Channel 2 TV

News has promised that a reporter will mention your name and possibly take a camera and show your house a couple of times in the next week."

Wiggins paused to extend a 6 × 4 photo. Nelson left his chair to take it. He studied the picture of the real Stanford Leeds. "Why Chief, he's my double except for those dark circles under his eyes." Wiggins took the picture. "You look enough like him to go on TV in those Channel 2 spots. Also, the editor of *The Wall Street Journal* will run a series of articles on the financial acumen of Stanford Leeds. Editors of Fortune 500 have agreed to list Leeds' name. I've spoken recently to the real Leeds' parents in London. He is presently confined in a wing of the family mansion under 24-hour guard and care. He suffers from a nervous condition and acute drug addiction."

Nelson said, "That's very good chief. They will check me out."

Wiggins leaned back in his chair. "You know, George, Freddy and Ernesto have a lot in common. Ernesto committed his first of many murders in Bogota when he was 12. He killed his closest friend who led Ernesto's kid gang so Ernesto could become the leader. Under Ernesto the kid gang expanded from theft and extortion of small business people into murder for prices ranging from 50 to 100 dollars. He and others of his stripe grew up to form the present drug cartel that threatens to destroy the civilized world as we know it today. There is substantial reason to believe that Ernesto is the cartel distribution specialist. I'm reluctant to dream that somehow, through Freddy and the Texas tomato, that we could take down Ernesto."

Nelson said, "Dream it, Chief, I already have. What is the surveillance situation at this point on them?"

Wiggins shuffled papers on his big polished mahogany desk. He found the pertinent report. He studied it before he said, "Sabina is under 24-hour watch, as is Freddy. Portillo's estate is watched around the clock. For a year, agents followed Portillo to his Saturday night flings with Lisette Fontaine. But at present, because of a shortage of personnel, we only follow him when he travels with his bodyguards. Lisa Lundgren is small fry that we can reel in later. Any questions, George?"

Nelson stood. "No, I'm very optimistic about our chances to take down Portillo... we bust Sabina when she delivers the keys. We offer her a big downward reduction in charges and possible sentence... she flips, and we nail Freddy. I don't believe he's stable at all. He wouldn't be strong enough or motivated enough to refuse a downward reduction deal to save Portillo and go to the joint for the rest of his life under the new law. I'll fax you all new developments. By the way, thanks for that fake London call that you placed to Lisa's party. I'd had my fill of that Texas slut and her perfume."

Wiggins rose from his chair and waddled to the door with Nelson. He had a big wide smile on his round cratered face. "It's best that your visits here be infrequent. The bad guys may put a tail on you. I'll fax you, in code, anything new that turns up." They laughed and shook hands before Nelson stepped out of the office into the corridor.

———

Next day just before noon, Freddy, decked out in a gray silk suit, drove toward an appointment with Portillo. As always, he was without bodyguards. He was the baddest homeboy in the ghetto, king of the O.G.'s, original gangsters in South Central. He was convinced that he was untouchable. He felt he was too feared, idolized, and especially needed by the ruling homeboys of the gangs to supply them with Portillo's cocaine to be processed into crack. Nobody, he told himself, had the balls to fuck over Big Freddy Evans.

Portillo was watching *The Young and The Restless* when Freddy was escorted into the den by Emilio. "Hello, Freddy. Sit down and watch the tricky cunts play their games."

Freddy sat down beside Portillo on the sofa. "How are you *&* your all-American girl making out?" Freddy loosened his tie, "Jus' fine… I want a favor, Mr. Portillo."

Portillo tore his eyes from the TV screen where an actress playing a married woman was about to get into bed with her lover. "What, my friend?"

The blond hair of the actress, so much like Sabina's, distracted Freddy. "Oh, uh, I'd appreciate you checkin' out Stanford William Leeds III... he, uh, might be a bulk buyer."

Portillo frowned. "His name sounds like he's an Anglo socialite. Where did you meet him at the Beverly Hills Country Club?"

Freddy laughed. "Hey, that's funny... my lady met him on his yacht the other day. She didn't tell him nothin' or promise him nothin'. If he checks out kosher..."

Portillo's eyes narrowed. "Freddy, Freddy, does your lady have suction feelers in her cunt to infatuate you beyond caution?"

Sweat popped out on Freddy's top lip. "Scuse me, Mr. Portillo, I like her, but I ain't in love."

Portillo shaped a Mona Lisa smile. "My friend, I didn't say love. Infatuation is wilder, more dangerous than love."

Freddy crossed and uncrossed his elephantine legs. "But Mr. Portillo, sir, I ain't gonna freak out over no bitch."

Portillo placed a gentle hand on Freddy's sleeve in the careful calm manner of a kindergarten teacher and said, "My friend, the hounds of the DEA are relentless and very clever. A homeboy like yourself becomes vulnerable, an easy rabbit for the hounds when he overvalues beautiful white pussy. I'm..."

Freddy waved his arms to cut him off. "Scuse me one more time, but the lady likes me much as I like her.

Jus' the other day she swore I'm her main man. Don't think that she's shuckin' and jivin' Big Freddy."

Portillo shook his head. "I must demand that you not interrupt me again. I was about to say that I am not technically your business partner. I merely sell you goods at the low sale price of ten thou a key. You are your own boss because you run your own business. You understand the complexities of dealing with your homeboys in L.A. and across the country. I understand the complexities of international business affairs all the way down to the problems of the *campesinos* who grow the coca leaves. I know how to give us all a reasonable chance to avoid the penitentiary. I can, under certain circumstances, suffer with you if you make mistakes in your business. If you make a grave mistake of the heart in your affair with Sabina, you and she could lead the hounds to me."

Freddy bounced his flab on the sofa. "Mr. Portillo, why you insult me like that? Ain't no way I'd flip on you if I caught life in the joint. I ain't no fink."

Portillo leaned close to Freddy's face. He explored the depths of Freddy's maroon eyes with his own black eyes, bright and deadly with suppressed anger and aggravation. "My advice for you is to break off with her before her sex rots your brain. Forget a deal with the Leeds guy. However, my friend, if you want to make the deal against my unfailing intuition, you will deserve what you get. If the hounds trap you or her, Ernesto Portillo will do whatever is necessary to avoid handcuffs and life in prison. Well?"

Freddy shrugged. "I can dig why you're leery of my lady and the gay guy. I ain't. Check him…" Freddy stared at the TV screen with his mouth open. The Channel Two noon news telecast was in progress… A brunette female reporter mentioned Leeds' full name as she was being shown his home in the Hollywood Hills by Leeds himself, aka George Nelson. Both men were transfixed on the sofa, staring at the back of Leeds, the subject of their conversation, as he led the reporter through the splendor of his home. Nelson's face was not shown.

Portillo, needling, cut his eyes at Freddy and said, "He's tall, well built, probably handsome."

Freddy laughed nervously. "Yeah, but he ain't nothin' but a bitch."

They listened as the reporter related how Nelson made his phenomenal rise in the business world in the five years since he left Britain after licking a drug problem and recovering from a nervous breakdown.

The news program shifted to the sports segment. "Freddy, I'm still leery. I'll let you know in a few days whether I'll do the favor for you."

Freddy stood. "I'd appreciate it if you decided to do me the favor… my store is almost empty."

Portillo stood & shook Freddy's hand. "You will have 200 keys at the end of the week, delivered to your homeboy Wade. Will those goods fill your immediate needs?"

Freddy said, "Fine, uh, include a key of China White."

Portillo said, "Bring the money for the goods on the day of delivery to Emilio at the usual place. I can't promise the China White."

Freddy looked very disappointed. "I'll take care of that business, Mr. Portillo."

Portillo patted his shoulder. "I know you will... take extra care my friend."

Freddy left the house. He drove toward home for lunch. On the way, a disturbing thought gnawed at his peace of mind. What if Leeds wasn't gay and Sabina was fucking him. Maybe she was even falling for him. If she was lying... he gritted his teeth and stomped the accelerator of the Rolls. Paranoid jealousy claimed him. He wasn't worried any more about Leeds being legit after the TV spot. He decided he wasn't hungry. He wasn't going home to lunch. He was going to the office of Stokes and Lee, the two corrupt ex-vice LAPD detectives whom Isaiah had hired. Freddy was going to hire them to find out if Stanford Leeds was really gay.

He parked in front of their office on Crenshaw Boulevard. Stokes and his partner Lee were in the inner office. Lee sat in a chair beside Stokes' desk. Husky Stokes, ex-UCLA football star, took a puff of cigar. "Otis, we've got a little money crunch. But I'm sure that those series of ads that Miss Morris has placed in the *L.A. Sentinel* will bring in clients to relieve the situation."

Rangy Otis Lee tapped fingertips on Stokes' desktop. "Reggie, I agree... I don't mind a temporary money problem after chasing hookers & dope dealers for 25 years. I actually get eight hours sleep and my ulcers are gone."

Freddy came in and stood at the desk of the faded glamor girl receptionist. "I want to see Reggie or Otis right away."

She elevated her chin. "You mean Mr. Stokes or Mr. Lee? You are?"

He snickered & slapped his thigh. "Baby, you ain't hip. I'm Big Freddy. How long you been from Mississippi?"

She picked up the phone to ring Stokes.

"Big Freddy is here."

Stokes said, "Send him in." He looked at Lee. "Big Freddy is here."

Lee said, "Ain't this a bitch? Looks like some sweet green is on the turn," as he left the side of Stokes' desk to sit at his desk across the room.

"Sit down Freddy and let's talk," Stokes said pleasantly when uptight Freddy rushed into the inner office. Freddy squeezed himself into a chair facing Stokes behind his desk. "Reggie, I got a job for you. I want a rich white dude investigated."

Stokes relit his cigar. "All right, what's the reason for your interest in the guy and what's his name and everything else you know about him?" Stokes picked up a pen. Freddy's fat lips flapped rapidly. "He's Stanford

William Leeds the second or somethin'. I think he's a faggot, but I ain't sure. I gotta know for sure. He was on the noon news on Channel Two. He's got a pad in the Hollywood Hills. He had a white Jag in his driveway. Oh yeah, he's a big businessman. Can you get on him right away?"

Stokes stalled to pressure him. Finally, he said, "Freddy, finding out the sexual persuasion of such a rich white celebrity will require both external surveillance and a white investigator to rent a suite in say, a place like the Beverly Hills Hotel. Then he will have to infiltrate Leeds' social circle at some level to find out if he is straight or gay. Such an investigation will be very expensive. Are you sure?"

Freddy snatched a wad of bills from his pants pocket. "I gotta know the truth about him. How much?"

Stokes said, "1,000 a day, plus expenses. You still want it?"

Freddy counted out 5,000 on Stokes' desk. "Start now! How long will it take?" Stokes scooped up the money. As he wrote out a retainer receipt he said, "We're the fastest firm in town... maybe eight to ten days."

Freddy took the receipt. "Call me at home when you finish. Freddy Evans is in the book." He stood and leaned across the desk. "Don't shuck me, Reggie."

Stokes said, "Did I ever shuck you when I was a vice cop? Did I ever hassle you when you were a street dealer on Avalon?"

Freddy grunted, "I'm hip you didn't, 'cause I always laid some green on you and Otis." Shoe black Stokes showing his brown teeth, stood up and shook his hand before Freddy left the office. Lee came to sit on Freddy's vacated chair immediately. "Reggie, what did big and ugly, the king of the ghetto, want?" Stokes chewed his bottom lip. "He wants to find out if a rich white guy named Stanford William Leeds is straight or gay... I think Freddy is uptight about more than that concern. Whatever, he's paying a thou a day plus expenses to find out."

Lee's long yellow face was ecstatic. "How many days can we do him for?"

Bone thin Miss Morris, the firm's secretary, sat a cup of coffee on Stokes' desk. "Do you also want coffee, Mr. Lee?"

Lee shook his head. Stokes waited for the secretary to go back to her desk. "Otis, this guy is really upset about Leeds. Freddy is dangerous and will have to be handled carefully. We can find out Leeds' sexual preference in a day or so... maybe we can string Freddy out for a week, maybe even 10 days. Otis, perhaps you had better handle this one personally. Here's the information on Leeds."

Lee took the sheet of paper. "I'll start now." He left the office for his car.

Freddy sat with Freddy Jr., eating a lunch of neck bones and pinto beans at the dining room table at home. He picked up the phone and called Sabina's apartment for the third time without an answer.

In the gym Isaiah sparred with Alonzo in the ring. In a quick hard exchange of punches, Alonzo fell to the canvas from a right cross. Groggy, he got up slowly to his feet. "I'll try you again tomorrow Isaiah." They left the ring to shower and put on street clothes.

Isaiah entered his apartment and heard Sabina's phone ringing in her bedroom. He picked up. "Hello?" Freddy hesitated. "Hello, who is it?" Freddy said, "I want to speak to Sabina." Isaiah said, "I'm her husband. Want to leave a message?" Freddy hesitated again. Isaiah said sharply, "Hey nigger, you must be Freddy. Respect me. Don't call here any more." Freddy laughed. "Keep her out of my bed super square." Freddy hung up.

A moment later Sabina came in. Isaiah said icily, "Your tub of lard boyfriend just called. He told me to keep you out of his bed." Sabina rolled her eyes. "Oh please! He's jiving you. I've never been in bed with him. A few days ago, I was out front on the sidewalk. He drove by and saw me talking to Lettie who did some house cleaning for us. He probably got my number from her."

Sabina went into her bedroom. She locked the door and called Freddy. "Hey midget brain. Hang up when my husband answers my phone. What's happening?" Freddy said brusquely, "The man gets his seven shirts a week from today. I'll hip you to the exact time of day later." He hung up.

Sabina was elated. She called Nelson at home and accepted an invitation to visit his home for cocktails &

to relate her good news at 4 P.M. She smoked crack and relaxed on the bed until 2:30. She showered & dressed in a short pink creation from Sachs and pink and grey sling pumps.

She drove into the Hollywood Hills and was admitted into the stately brown stone mansion by a tall butler, crisply dressed in a blue linen suit. "Ma'am, Mr. Leeds will receive you in the drawing room."

She followed him through the largest, most splendidly furnished house she had ever seen. She entered the spacious room. Many expensive Persian throw rugs lay on the highly polished redwood floor. Excellent copies of master works of Rubens, Picasso, and Van Gogh graced the muted fuchsia walls. Nelson, dressed in a red satin lounging robe over blue silk pajamas, rose from a black silk chaise to greet her. A huge crystal chandelier caught rays of sunlight firing through a stained-glass window and made the chandelier sparkle like a cache of diamonds.

She felt breathless, thrilled again as he embraced her. "You seem more beautiful each time we meet," he whispered in her ear. He almost recoiled from the crack stench in her hair. He took her hand and led her to sit beside him on the chaise.

Theodore, the butler, entered with margaritas on a gold tray. They sipped from golden goblets. A hidden speaker oozed soft classical violin music.

"The good news I've brought is that my friend will make a deal for seven keys of high-grade coke at 30 thou a key."

He crossed his legs. "At that price, what is its purity?"

She stood up. "85, 90 percent... let's dance." They danced and took booze breaks until 6 P.M. He successfully dumped most of his into a redwood bucket beside the chaise that held a fake cactus plant.

She was sitting beside him on the chaise half-smashed when she dropped her head into his lap. She rubbed her cheek against his penis. He reached to push a device on the phone beside him that rang it. He picked up. "Hello... Hi, Harry... gosh, I've been so distracted this afternoon that I forgot our appointment. Forgive me. I'll see you within the next half hour." He stood and held out his arms. She got up and fell into them.

"Are you sure you can drive safely," he said as he held her at arms length and studied her face.

"Sure, I'm all right. I've had an enjoyable afternoon. I'll give you a jingle as to the exact when and where we can make our deal." He kissed her goodbye and Theodore escorted her to her car. He opened its door for her. She got in and drove away, reinforced with the fantasy that Nelson was falling in love with her.

Otis Lee, the investigator, followed her back to her apartment in South Central.

Chapter 7

At that moment in Beverly Hills, Helene prepared for blissful communion with and counseling from the loas, her powerful and adored voodoo gods. Such contact at this time was especially important. Isaiah was coming to spend the night with her. Her otherwise glorious sexual rapport with him was increasingly threatened, marred by the spiritual essence of the white witch Sabina.

Helene was very angry and aggravated. Isaiah was the second lover whom she had ever loved with such fanatical involvement of her total being. The other had been a handsome stud in Haiti. He had deserted her when he fell in love with the near-white Haitian daughter of a wealthy merchant.

In her rage and pain, she had begged the loas to kill the couple. They had assured her that her request would be granted. Ninety days later, her ex-lover and his half-white goddess were drowned when he tried to save her when she fell into the ocean from a motorboat.

Isaiah was forcing her to accept crumbs from the sexual cake that Sabina still possessed in his mind. She felt it, knew it during their lovemaking. The loas had whispered the hidden secrets of his heart to her, even as his giant, wonderful manhood exploded to detonate her orgasms of unprecedented pleasure. He had, on every such occasion, been thinking of Sabina. She had been merely like the sheep that sex starved young Haitian boys fucked dispassionately, mechanically, while they dreamed of beautiful, real young girls.

She had begged the loas to cast out Sabina from his head and scrotum, to kill her so that she could be happy. She would find and kill Sabina herself if the loas did not remove the bitch from the world and her bed.

Helene unlocked a padlock on a large walk-in closet in the bedroom of her quarters in an isolated wing of the mansion. A constant, large bulb spewed scarlet light from the ceiling. A row of black male and female shrunken human heads lay on a shelf like the heads of decapitated, wrinkled old Lilliputians. They had been enemies of her mother, Zeeda. They had died after Zeeda, one of Haiti's top beauties, had requested their death from the loas.

One of the heads was that of a handsome Belgian white man who had used her mother sexually in every conceivable way when she was totally involved with him. He had robbed Zeeda to marry a white woman in Port Au Prince.

Helene stared at the heads that had been severed by her voodoo priestess mother after their death. Their graves were invaded by Zeeda and her friends. The heads were severed and the bodies reburied. The heads had been inherited from Zeeda along with the power and knowledge to commune with the loas.

Helene dumped a mix of secret powders into a metal pot that sat on a short tripod. She threw a lit match into the pot. A geyser of blue, smokeless flame erupted. She chanted: "Oh, beloved loas, keepers of my soul and life, please rid my life of Sabina Jones. Please! Your servant can't endure the torture of her continued life. Please help me! Save me from the possible disgrace and misery of prison for her murder."

Zeeda had recounted for Helene the history of her voodoo lineage all the way back to ancient Africa where voodoo was born. Zeeda told her how her grandmother Zala had conspired with the loas to bring about the death of the Belgian roue within six months in an automobile crash.

She felt a spastic seizure of joy that shook her being as always when she made contact with the loas. She was elated at the promise of death for Sabina by the loas when she heard the sibilant voices of the loas intone. "Patience, patience: Your enemy will die soon." Her joy vanished as the voices went on. "But so will the man you love. Be strong. You will face much pain. Isaiah breathes, speaks, and makes love. But he is already dead. You must not have sex again with a dead lover. You must start to build strength. You can't, with sex. Love him fully without sex for the short time he has before the earth claims his body."

She collapsed on the floor. She rolled and wept as she tore out clumps of her long hair. She screamed over and over again. "Oh please! Don't let him die." Finally, she extinguished the flame and locked the closet door. She was so exhausted by the rites that she fell to the bedroom carpet in a trance of grief and worry about Isaiah.

At 8 P.M. she sat at dinner in the dining room with Baptiste and Isaiah. She looked lovely in a silk peach skirt and frilly low-cut white blouse.

Near the end of the meal of veal chops, scalloped potatoes, green peas, and Helene's delectable butterscotch cake, she cleared the table. She left the men to wash the dishes and wait for Isaiah in her living room. Baptiste said, "If and when you split from Sabina, you and Helene can live here rent free when I go to Sugar Hill."

Isaiah sipped coffee. "Pops, that's a beautiful idea... but I'm still trying to figure out how to cut Sabina loose and keep Eric."

Baptiste grunted. "I hope you don't think you're still in love with her."

Isaiah exclaimed, "Hell no... I've stopped having sex with her since Helene and me have been seeing each other. But Pops, I confess, I can't get Sabina's body out of my head. I feel like a dope fiend, kinda uptight kicking his jones."

Baptiste said, "You'll kick the habit. You're doing great."

Helene, eavesdropping in the kitchen near the dining room door, turned sadly back to the dishwashing machine. She had heard the truth from Isaiah's mouth. It hadn't been just her imagination. Isaiah had been bringing the white witch into her bed. Poor Isaiah, he's dead and still in love with her who will soon fall into her own grave.

Helene went to the living room in her quarters to wait for Isaiah. She sat down on a beige sofa, fully dressed, to watch TV. She usually changed into sexy lingerie for Isaiah. But now she had the problem of denying him sex while preserving their friendship. She had never and would not defy an admonition of the loas. She couldn't have sex with Isaiah even when she knew her total being would ache for his entry into her body.

She smiled as she thought, "I've got a big jones for him I've got to kick."

Isaiah came to sit beside her on the sofa. He took her into his arms and kissed her passionately. She felt her vulva quiver. She pulled away. "Oh, look darling, at that cute brown baby in the commercial."

He said, "The kid is beautiful and so is his mama... Why ain't you in one of your sexy outfits?"

She gave him a quick kiss. "I don't feel too sexy, I, uh, guess I'm just a bit tired and..."

He cut her off. "Baby, don't tell me you got a headache. Please!" They laughed. "No, not a headache. Let's go to bed and take a rain check on lovemaking tonight. Okay, darling?"

He said, "Yeah, baby, okay." He stood and picked her up into his arms. As he carried her into the bedroom, he baby talked, "Sweet baby is not feeling well. Daddy is gonna undress you and hold you in his arms until you fall asleep."

Her eyes sparkled with tears as he undressed her and put on her gown. She lay in his arms for a long time before she fell into ragged sleep, haunted by the sibilant voices of the loas.

Isaiah was disturbed by her writhing and fearful muttering, "Please, no! Please!" He got only a few hours sleep.

Next morning at breakfast on the patio with Baptiste he picked at his ham and eggs. "Hey sport, you look dragged out... You have a fight with your sweetie?" Isaiah pushed his plate away.

"No, Pops, everything is okay with us, but I'm worried about her. She wasn't in the mood for sex last night and when she went to sleep she had bad nightmares that jerked her around for most of the night."

Baptiste laughed. "There's nothing to worry about. All women sometimes don't feel like sex. Since she's only 28, it can be a change of life. Nightmares? Everybody, even dogs and cats, have them. She's all right."

Isaiah patted a napkin against his lips. "Pops, give me a rundown on her background. All she's really told me about herself is that she was born in Haiti and her parents are dead."

Baptiste said, "After her mother Zeeda died she came to live with her Uncle Oscar, her best friend since boyhood in Haiti. Her father split from Zeeda when Helene was 2 years old. He drank himself to death in Harlem

15 years later. Oh yeah, Zeeda was a priestess of voodoo and no one dared to offend or cross her in Haiti. Helene was 25 and one of the most beautiful girls in Harlem when Oscar got sick with leukemia. He died a year ago and Helene was alone. He called me a week before he died and told me to look out for her. I invited her to come out here as my permanent guest. Her Haitian pride wouldn't let her accept a charity set up like that. She insisted that she would stay here only if she could be my cook and housekeeper. You're her only boyfriend since she moved to Beverly Hills."

Isaiah reached for the phone. "Thanks, Pops. I'm going to call Eric." Isaiah rang his apartment twice in the next fifteen minutes without an answer. He called the gym. Alonzo told him be hadn't seen Eric.

Isaiah got to his feet. "Pops, I'll see you later. I'm going home. I'm worried about Eric."

Baptiste followed him to his Thunderbird in the driveway. "Call me soon as you find Eric," Baptiste said as Isaiah drove away.

He took the freeway home. Within 25 minutes he went into the gym which was resonating with the sounds of young boxers punching bags and each other in the ring. He approached Alonzo, seated at ringside. "You see Eric yet?" Alonzo shook his head.

Isaiah left the gym. He took the elevator to his apartment. He went in. "Eric! Eric!" he called out as he went through the living room into the dining room. He looked in the kitchen before he went into Eric's bedroom. He stood in a paralysis of alarm. Eric lay on the bed, dressed in the jeans and shirt he had worn the day before. He lay motionless, his face starkly white. A crack pipe and a half-filled vial of crack lay on the bed beside him. He looked dead.

Isaiah rushed to the bed. He felt for, and found, a faint pulse. Isaiah gave him mouth-to-mouth for a couple of minutes before he called 911.

Within several minutes he buzzed the paramedics into the security building. They came to Eric's bedside & gave him an injection and put an oxygen mask on his face. One of them, the black paramedic, said as he nodded toward the pipe and vial, "Looks like he od'd on crack... We'll have to report this to the police." They put Eric on a stretcher and Isaiah held the living room door open for them. "Where you takin' him?" he asked as they went toward the elevator. The white paramedic said, "The emergency room at Daniel Freeman. He's in a coma."

Isaiah took the pipe and vial off the bed. He dropped them in a drawer of Eric's dresser. He went to pick up the living room phone to tell the police about Sabina to bust her. He replaced the receiver. What if she, the compulsive liar, told racist white cops that it was his stash? He could wind up busted.

He went to the gym to tell Alonzo what had happened. He then went to his car and sped to Daniel Freeman. Two nurses and two doctors had Eric hooked up to breathing and monitoring machines in an Intensive Care room. A nurse seated Isaiah in the emergency room. "Your son is in Intensive Care. He's getting the best attention possible. Please be calm. I'll have a doctor inform you as to his condition in a few minutes." She gave him a form to fill out and sign. After he had completed the form, the nurse came to get it.

Then he started to sort out the details of the tragedy. He was sure Eric had found Sabina's crack stash and smoked, maybe for the first time. He'd find a way to make certain it was her pipe and dope. Then he was going to kill her, bury her body in the desert as he had fantasized.

A uniformed white cop approached him. "Are you Isaiah Jones, the stepfather of Eric Jones?" Isaiah stood up. "I am." The cop took a notebook and pen from his pocket. "Do you have the pipe and, uh, substance that was involved in this incident?"

Isaiah lit a cigarette. "No, that crap is at home." The cop scribbled in his notebook. "Are you or your wife users of any illegal substance? Are you getting along well with her?"

Isaiah hesitated. He couldn't tell the cop that Sabina was a crack freak & their marriage was the pits. When she came up missing, if her remains were found, he'd be a class A suspect when her murder was investigated. "No officer, we don't use anything. We don't even drink, except for an occasional light wine with dinner.

Our marriage is wonderful… Eric brought that crap to his bedroom from the street." The cop finished scribbling. "Mr. Jones, detectives will visit you to get the pipe and drugs." The cop left and Isaiah sat down.

A doctor approached him. "Mr. Jones, your son is still in a coma on life support assistance. It may be hours, even days, before he revives. It would be better for you to wait at home." Isaiah rose from the chair. "Thank you, doctor. I guess you're right."

Despite his strong effort not to, tears poured from his eyes as he drove home. He went into the apartment and sat on the living room sofa. He chain-smoked for an hour before Sabina came in from an early shopping spree on Rodeo Drive. Her arms were full of fancy wrapped boxes.

As she went past Isaiah he said, "I found your stash." She dropped the boxes on the carpet. She spun around, her face red with anger. "So what! You've got no business poking around in my bedroom. I'm a fuckin' adult." She rushed into her bedroom. He followed her with his jaw muscles twitching ominously. He entered her bedroom. He stood watching her on her knees, darting her fingers into shoes in a canvas rack on the closet door. "Bitch, I took your stash." She sprang to her feet. "Nigger, where's my fuckin' shit?" He grabbed her wrist and violently flung her against the dresser. She fell and lay stunned on the carpet. He kneeled beside her & gripped her throat with his giant hands. His face was maniacal as all of his pent-up rage, pain, and hatred exploded.

Her blue eyes popped wide as she made choking sounds. She went limp and her eyes closed. He kept his grip on her throat.

The doorbell chimes jolted him from his murderous fugue. He stood up and staggered to the front door with his hands shaking and sweat dripping from his face. He opened the door to Alonzo.

Alonzo looked questionably at Isaiah, then said, "Hey man, I'm glad you're back from the hospital. How's Eric?"

Isaiah held a palm to his throbbing head. "Thanks for ringin' the bell, man… Eric's in bad shape. He's in a coma."

Alonzo said shakily, "I'll beat the nigger to death if I find out who gave Eric that crack. My car won't start. Let me go with you when you go back to the hospital." Isaiah said, "Yeah, I'll take you." He shut the door and went into Sabina's bedroom. She was still on the carpet gasping for air and rubbing her throat.

He grabbed her arm and snatched her to her feet. He rammed his face into hers. "You low life stinkin' dope fiend tramp. Eric found your stash. He od'd. He's in a coma at Daniel Freeman. I could have given the cops your stash and got you busted, but I don't want them to know I was dumb enough to marry a low life bitch like you." He seized her throat again: "I'm gonna kill you if you're still here when I get back. Get out bitch!"

He left the apartment for the hospital. Sabina stood shaking in front of the dresser mirror. Panic seized her when she saw the ugly bruises on her throat. Her throat hurt a lot. It felt like his hands were still choking her. An icy chill shivered her spine.

She called Lisa. "Hey kiddo, you got strep throat or what?" Sabina heard the hoarseness in her own voice when she said, "No Lisa, the crazy Jap just tried to choke me to death — I have to move out before he gets back. I..."

Lisa cut her off. "Kiddo, I've got a guest room waiting for you. I'll have Donald come to get you and Eric and your things."

Sabina burst into tears. "Oh, Lisa angel, thank you. I have someone to move me out. Eric is in the hospital. I'll tell you about it... He's going to be fine. See you soon." She hung up. She called Freddy. His line was busy. She feverishly started packing her chic, large wardrobe into suitcases on the bed.

Freddy and Junior had finished eating lunch in the living room. Mother Esther brought in a homemade lemon cream pie for dessert. Freddy hung up the phone and cut the pie in half. He cut a slice and put it on a plate for Junior and put half the pie on a plate for himself.

"Daddy, can we go see the Dodgers next time they be playin' at home? Can we Daddy?" Freddy's thin image mumbled with a pie-filled mouth.

"Sure, baby boy. You got it." The phone rang. Freddy picked up to Sabina. "Get somebody over here to move me out right away. This is an emergency, Freddy. The square ass clown tried to kill me."

Freddy spat a mouthful of pie into a napkin. "I'll be right over baby, and move you and check you into a hotel. I..."

She shrieked. "No! No! He'll kill us both if he comes back and finds you here. Send a couple of your flunkeys. Will you?"

He hesitated. "Okay, I don't want to kill that nigger anyway. Where you goin'?"

Her voice box faltered. For a long moment nothing came out when her lips moved.

"I'll call you and give you my girlfriend's guest room phone number."

Freddy hung up. He called two homeboy brothers who idolized him. Their mother answered the phone. "Hi, Mrs. Jacob, is B.J. or Idus home?"

"They washin' my car. Which one you want Freddy?"

"B.J."

Shortly, the 19-year-old body builder and gang member came to the living room phone. "Hey, my man, what's happenin'?" Freddy whispered so Junior, and his mother, sitting at a sewing machine in the corner, couldn't hear him. "My woman has to move out and split her pad right away. You hip to that big apartment building across from the Kentucky Fried Chicken joint?"

B.J. whispered because his constantly worried mother sat across the living room watching him as he talked. "Yeah, me and Idus will take the van. What's your lady's pad number?"

Freddy's mother stopped the hum of the sewing machine. She stared at him. "Look for the Jones button and she'll buzz you in, homey. I'm gonna lay some righteous bread on you and Idus. Come by here when you get back." Freddy hung up. Junior left the table to play in the back yard. Freddy had created a complete playground of swings, teeter totter, and a miniature locomotive that junior could ride on tracks that circled the perimeter of the expansive back yard.

Esther took Junior's vacated chair. Her seamed brown face was somber. "Freddy, you whisperin' on the phone worries me so much — I been havin' bad dreams about you — like the ones I had before your brothers were shot down in the street. Please baby! Don't go back to doin' no devilment. You got a nice business. Ain't no reason to be no fool and wind up in the cemetery. I pray for God to keep you safe. But sometimes he punishes evil doin' no matter what anybody prays. Tell your mama you ain't doin' wrong."

Freddy threw his palms into the air. "I swear Mama, I ain't doin' nothin' wrong."

She got up and hugged him from behind his chair. "Mama, I was whisperin' 'cause I was talkin' sexy to a girl. You ain't got nothin' to worry about." Esther went back to her sewing machine.

Freddy went to the back yard to play with Junior.

At Sabina's apartment, huge B.J. and string-bean Idus were taking down to their van the last armloads of

139

Sabina & Eric's possessions. Sabina left the apartment. Idus drove the van away for West Hollywood.

In the emergency room at Daniel Freeman, Isaiah and Alonzo sat with great anxiety. "Man, I jus' know, ain't no way Eric is gonna die. He ain't gonna die!" Alonzo said as he gripped Isaiah's arm.

"No, he can't die... God couldn't be that cold."

A doctor approached them. The grim expression on the tall, blond doctor's face almost stopped Isaiah's heart. "Mr. Jones, I'm very sorry... we did everything we could... your son expired a moment ago. I..."

Isaiah sprang from the chair and dashed across the room through a door into the intensive care section. He searched a row of white draped partitioned cubicles occupied by critically sick patients. He found Eric. He wept as he took Eric's limp body into his arms and held him close to his chest. "Oh, Eric! What am I gonna do without you? I'm sorry I let you down. Please God, forgive me. I..."

Several nurse's aides and two uniformed security guards took Isaiah back to the emergency room. Alonzo was weeping. "Let's split man, before I crack up." Alonzo led Isaiah to the Thunderbird and drove them away.

In front of Isaiah's building he said, "I'll see you later man." Alonzo got out. Isaiah drove away to a liquor store.

He bought a fifth of scotch. He used a pay phone outside the store to call Baptiste. "Eric's dead and I'm going to kill that nigger Freddy for giving Sabina the crack that killed him. I..."

Baptiste hollered to cut him off. "Shut up! Listen, if the nigger did, he needs killing, but you gotta make plans first. Get over here right away so we can talk like intelligent people. Okay?"

Isaiah sobbed. "I'll be there... after I get drunk as a skunk." He hung up.

In West Hollywood, B.J. and Idus got in their van, parked in front of Lisa's building, and drove away.

From a guest room in the penthouse, Sabina called the hospital. She was told that Eric had passed away. She sat on the side of the bed in shock for several minutes before she screamed piercingly. Lisa rushed into the bedroom. She sat beside Sabina and took her into her arms. "What happened?" Sabina's body shook with sobbing. "Eric died... some fuckin' Asian kid gave him crack and he O.D.'d. Oh Lisa, I want to die!"

Lisa got up. "Kiddo, I'll be right back."

Sabina called Freddy. She waited until Esther brought him in from the back yard. "Yeah, baby, is everything cool?" She sobbed, "No, Eric died. He O.D.'d on crack that one of those street niggers gave him. Here's my number." She gave him the number and hung up just as Lisa returned.

"Here, take this so you can relax and maybe sleep." She gave Sabina a seconal capsule and a glass of water.

Sabina swallowed it and washed it down. Lisa removed her shoes and helped her to prop herself against the headboard. "Who were those black guys who moved you in?" Sabina rubbed her temple. "Just some flunkeys that work at a warehouse in my neighborhood ... You got any rock?"

Lisa shook her head. "Sorry, I'm fresh out. But I have some nose candy." Sabina nodded vigorously. Lisa said, "I'll have to go to a house down the street to my stash... be back in 15 minutes." Lisa left the room.

Drained, exhausted, Sabina soon fell into a jagged seconal sleep.

———

Isaiah put B.B. King on the stereo and sat down on the living room sofa. He opened the fifth of Cutty Sark and filled a water glass from the bottle. He had raised the glass to his lips when the phone rang. A deep voice with a Southern accent said, "Buzz us in. We're police."

Isaiah pressed the number 9 on his phone to unlock the outside door. He cracked the apartment door and sat on the sofa. He gulped down half of the whiskey in the glass.

Two tall beefy white detectives in wilted, light colored tropical suits came into the room. They stood before Isaiah, staring down at him with cold eyes. The older cop, with a weasel face, said, "I'm Stephen Forrest, LAPD narcotics division. You're Isaiah Jones?"

Isaiah lit a cigarette. "Yes, I am officer."

The other cop, wearing his dirty panama hat at a rakish angle on his silvered blond head said, "I'm Paul Janik, same division. We want all drugs and related paraphernalia in the apartment."

Isaiah said, "This ain't no drug den... my stepson o.d.'d on crack somebody gave him in the street."

"Where is the pipe and vial of crack that the paramedics saw?"

Isaiah got up. "Have a seat. I'll get them." They followed him into Eric's bedroom. He opened the drawer. Janik roughly pulled him away. Isaiah said testily, "Hey, don't rough me up."

Janik stared at a picture of Sabina on Eric's dresser. "A pretty broad... Your wife?"

Isaiah nodded.

Forrest rummaged in the drawer & brought out the pipe and half-filled vial. "Are you some kinda tough guy?" Janik said as they went into the living room to sit on the sofa with Isaiah between them. "No, but I'm a stone man."

"Do you abuse any other substance besides alcohol?" Janik said as he stared at the fifth of scotch.

"Man, I'm an athlete. That's the first hard booze I've had in 10 years." Janik horse laughed.

"We're jive proof boy... You got a sheet?"

Isaiah widened his eyes in fake puzzlement. "A what?"

Forrest said, "Come on, now, stop the bullshit. Everybody with crack in his house in the ghetto knows what a sheet is."

"Jones, have you ever been arrested?" Janik said. "We can go to 77th to check you out if you don't want to answer."

The whiskey was spinning Isaiah's head. "I've never been arrested. I live a clean life. Now, if you don't mind, I've got business to attend to — like calling the morgue about my son's body."

They stood. Isaiah walked them to the door. Janik said, "We'll be back to talk to your wife. When will she be home?" Isaiah shrugged. "As soon as I can reach her and get her back. She drove to Texas to visit relatives!"

Forrest said, "When she gets back, have her ask for me or Janik." They went into the corridor. Isaiah went back to the scotch.

Chapter 8

Wade Jackson, custodian of Freddy's stash house, along with three of Freddy's trusted aides, lived in a large house in South Central. There were three Uzi's and several automatic pistols in the house to protect the large amounts of cocaine that were usually stored there. It was after 4 P.M., a week from the day that Portillo promised Freddy the delivery of 200 keys.

Burly savage-faced Wade paced the living room floor. "Motherfuckin' Colombians are almost an hour late."

One of the men, Whitey Ferguson, at a front window, said, "They just pulled into the driveway."

Wade went to the window. He watched Emilio and Frank in Sears uniforms get out of a fake, exact replica Sears truck. They unloaded a giant used refrigerator in a new packing case from the rear of the truck. They put it on a dolly and wheeled it down the driveway to the back door. They hauled it into the kitchen. They stood and watched as Wade and the others ripped away the packing case and took out and counted the kilos.

Whitey Ferguson, a nearly white creole, tested a kilo. "It's righteous!" he exclaimed. Whitey was an O.G. who had been Freddy's trusted friend since boyhood. Freddy had also selected him to go with Sabina when she made the deal with Leeds.

Emilio and Frank put the junkyard refrigerator on the dolly and hauled it to the truck then drove away.

Emilio said, "I wonder if those two DEA tails are still waiting for us to come out of that downtown movie." Frank laughed, "They won't even see our dates, Bertha and Liz, come out. They'll split out of a back-fire door like we did."

Inside the stash house Wade called Freddy at a market pay phone. He had parked beside it and put an out of order sign on it. He had been waiting for over an hour. "I got the money order a few minutes ago. Thanks, my man." Freddy hung up and got into a Ford Escort that he used when he lugged really heavy green.

He drove to Portillo's estate. The paunchy yard guard and Rottweiler handler opened the steel gate electronically to pass Freddy through.

A DEA tail duo parked a block away to wait for him to come out.

Freddy drove down the long winding driveway to the front of Portillo's lavish white stone house. He got out and removed two large suitcases from the trunk. Portillo himself stood smiling at the open front door. "Hello, my friend. You're on time as usual."

Freddy followed him into the den. They sat on the sofa. Freddy shoved the bags on the carpet close to Portillo's feet. "There's two mil there. Mr. Portillo gonna count it?"

Portillo laughed. "I trust you my friend... besides, Emilio and Frank are not here to feed the counting machine. How is little Freddy and your mother?"

Freddy picked up a cookie from a tray on the coffee table. "They're fine and dandy."

Portillo said, "I've decided not to check out that Anglo guy Leeds... We don't need to do business with even an apparently legit white socialite — who can tell what he is? A hound in a tuxedo perhaps?"

Freddy stood. "Mama is expecting me home to play checkers with her. I been tryin' for six months to beat her. Talk to you soon."

Portillo followed him to his car. As Freddy started it, Portillo said, "I almost forgot to ask you about the all-American girl. Is she still in or out?"

Freddy frowned. "Mr. Portillo, I don't plan to cut her loose today or tomorrow. Okay?"

Portillo smiled. "I understand. A wise man takes good advice and finds good luck. A sucker ignores it and finds bad luck. Be careful, my friend."

Freddy peevishly gunned the Ford away down the driveway.

Next day at 11 A.M., Wade carried five keys in a flat case to a Kentucky Fried Chicken outlet on Crenshaw. The place was loud and crowded with young blacks shucking and jiving and eating chicken. He went to the counter and ordered several drumsticks. He paid and took the order to a rear booth. He shoved the bag beneath him on the floor. He ate and left the restaurant, leaving the bag.

Wade got in his car and headed toward his mother's house in Inglewood. He wouldn't go to the stash house for several days. His brother Bumpy would take over. When he did return to the stash house it would be without a tail. He knew how to shake even a DEA tail. He didn't know that Sabina had one.

Sabina parked in the lot with Whitey and went in the restaurant when Wade came out. She got a coke and sat in Wade's vacant spot in the booth. Minutes later she left, followed by agents as she drove toward Nelson's mansion in the hills.

Otis Lee the investigator parked across the street and witnessed the whole incident from the time Wade went in and Sabina came out with the bag. He saw a DEA car follow her and Whitey. It didn't take an ex-vice cop long to figure out what was going down. He drove quickly to his office to hold an urgent conference with Stokes. He went into the inner office and sat down beside Stokes' desk, his long yellow face a portrait of gloomy agitation. "Reggie, we got a big problem."

Stokes, a rock hard pragmatist, blew cigar smoke. "Like what, Otis?"

"Sabina is on the way to a DEA bust. She picked up a dope bag left by Wade Jackson in a restaurant. She had

Whitey Ferguson with her. Nelson, aka Stanford Leeds, has sprung the trap and she's headed for it."

Stokes threw his cigar into an ashtray and picked up the phone. "Freddy, this is Stokes. Get over here immediately. The investigator's report on Leeds just came in." He hung up and picked up his cigar. "Now here's how we handle Freddy. We tell him everything. We…"

Lee hit the desk with his fist. "Reggie, are you losing it? We could be charged with conspiracy to obstruct if we tip Freddy that Leeds is DEA. You know Freddy. He'd do something crazy to save his broad a bust and get that dope back."

Stokes ebonic face looked completely composed. "Freddy will be here at any moment. He owes us two grand for two unpaid days plus another three grand for expenses for the seven days. How long ago did Sabina and Whitey leave?"

Lee ran his tongue across his dry lips. "Ten, twelve minutes ago."

Stokes closed his eyes in deep thought. "She's probably on her way to Nelson's rented mansion in the hills… You've been here 10 minutes. It will take another 15 minutes after Freddy gets here to give him an oral outline of the report. I'll save Leeds' DEA masquerade to lay on him as the last info. We gotta get paid before he goes crazy. In any case, he'll be too late to block the bust. So, how can we be charged for obstructing anything? Oh, by the way, maybe I can milk him for another five grand."

Lee's brow wrinkled in puzzlement. "How?"

Stokes leaned forward. "As ex-cops, we can express a great reluctance to reveal a secret about Leeds that he, Freddy, should be concerned about. He hired us to find out if Leeds was gay, but nothing else. Right?"

Lee nodded with a big smile on his face. "He's on the turn so I'll go back to my desk. I'm not one of his favorite people." Lee left.

A moment later, Freddy rushed into the outer office, past the startled receptionist into a chair across from Stokes. "Freddy, my man, my investigator has worked hard for a week to find out if Leeds is gay. He even took a suite in the Beverly Hills hotel. He managed to meet Leeds and have a drink with him. That night he was invited to a party at Leeds mansion. He…"

Freddy said sharply. "Hey, Reggie, is the motherfucker gay?"

Stokes, killing precious time, searched a desk drawer for a fresh cigar. Finally, he lit one. "The investigator, a really attractive young white man, looks a lot like a young Clark Gable. He came onto Leeds when they were alone. Leeds punched him in the mouth. Freddy, Leeds is not gay, and he has a secret that I am sure you would want to know. But even for say, five grand, I'd be somewhat reluctant to violate my principles as an ex-cop. Here's a full report, minus the secret, of course."

Freddy took the several sheets of paper. Stokes said, "The unpaid portion of your bill is two grand for two days plus three thou for expenses."

Freddy counted out 5,000 dollars. Stokes gave him a receipt. Freddy studied the papers for several minutes, which pleased Stokes very much. The Sabina bust was probably going down at this moment, he thought. "Hey Reggie, it says here that she went to Leeds' pad the first of the week and stayed for two hours. Is the secret you cracked got anything to do with Sabina?"

Stokes held out his palm. "It's got everything to do with your lady. Absolutely everything."

Freddy counted out another five grand into Stokes' palm. "No receipt for this, Freddy. Leeds is really George Nelson, a DEA undercover agent."

Freddy popped out of his chair like a giant jack-in-the-box. Sudden sweat lathered his brow. He stomped his size 14s against the hardwood floor. Miss Morris and Lee anxiously watched him. "Goddamn, Reggie! Gimme that phone!"

Stokes pushed the phone across the desk. Freddy frantically dialed Sabina's bedroom phone. On the eighth ring Lisa picked up. "Hello?"

Freddy hollered, "Gimme Sabina!"

Lisa, taken aback by the harsh black ghetto voice, stammered, "She's, uh, not, uh, in. May I, uh, take a message?"

He pressed. "Listen lady, tell me where I can call her. This is a nitty gritty emergency. Lay it on me."

She said, "I haven't the slightest idea where she is. Sorry." She hung up, wondering why Sabina had given her number to such a rough character.

At Stokes' desk, Freddy stood glaring down at Stokes. He waved the papers. "Is that peckerwood's address in this shit?"

Stokes shrugged. "Freddy, everything you paid for is there. Cool off so you can think straight and solve any problems that the report has given you."

Freddy said, "Fuck yourself, Reggie," before he stomped out of the office.

Lee came to stand at Stokes' desk. "Damn, I was worried. He may try to hit Nelson for screwing Sabina and busting her."

Stokes smiled and nodded toward a .357 Magnum pistol in an open drawer. "Otis, I wasn't worried at all. I'll put in an anonymous call to Nelson's pad and tip him that Freddy may try to hit him."

Racing for the Hollywood Hills, Freddy had second thoughts. He u-turned and drove back toward his home.

———

In the Hollywood Hills Sabina & Whitey Ferguson sat in the drawing room watching Nelson drop a bit of their coke into a vial of liquid, which instantly turned blue.

"Sabina, we've got a deal." He took a large valise from the carpet by the sofa where they were seated. He put it on Sabina's lap. "Here's 210,000 for seven keys."

Whitey took the valise & opened it. He rifled through the stacks of big bills. "I'm an honest man. It's all there."

Whitey looked at Sabina. "It's all right. We don't have to count it. I trust him."

Whitey stood with the valise. "Let's get out of here."

Sabina said, "I'll jingle you soon, Stanford." He rose from the sofa and followed them to the door. "It's always a pleasure to hear your voice, Sabina. I'm…"

Four DEA agents burst into the room. One of them hollered, "You're all under arrest!"

Whitey galloped away for an open glass door. An agent fired over his head as he ran to a balcony railing and jumped over it to the ground. The pursuing agent shouted from the balcony. "Stop! I'll shoot."

Whitey stopped, turned, and drew a pistol from a shoulder holster. He leveled it at three of the agents now on the balcony. They all fired at him before he could squeeze off a round. Whitey tumbled down an incline with fatal bullet wounds to his head and chest. The green contents of the valise littered the hillside.

The agents handcuffed Sabina and Nelson. One of them called Wiggins to inform him of the bust and also to inform local authorities of the almost certain death of Whitey Ferguson.

The agents put Nelson and Sabina in the back of a steel barred van before they retrieved the litter of bills and ascertained that Whitey was indeed dead. They left in the van. One agent stayed to wait in his parked car for the coroner's ambulance to arrive.

Sabina sat in a daze, staring at the floor of the van as it headed for the temporary Federal lockup facility in downtown L.A.

Two hours later anxious Freddy sat in his bedroom on the side of the bed. He had called and awakened an LAPD narco cop who worked the graveyard shift. He took money from Freddy for info when any of Freddy's homeboys were hot.

"Yeah, who is it?" he barked sleepily.

Freddy said, "Stanley, this is Freddy. My lady Sabina Jones got busted by the Feds. Check, and jingle me."

Stanley Woods cleared his throat, "Okay, Freddy." He hung up. Five minutes later Woods called, "She's in the Feds lockup downtown. She was busted selling seven keys of coke. She can get big time… Whitey Ferguson was shot to death by the Feds that busted your girl."

Freddy groaned. "Thanks, Stanley. I won't forget this favor." He hung up and dialed Jimmy Coglin's office. He was a black, former L.A. prosecutor. He was famous in private practice for winning criminal cases for his clients against all odds.

"Mr. Coglin, this is Big Freddy. I got a problem — my lady Sabina Jones got busted by the Feds with seven keys of coke. Will you go and talk to her and let her know I hired you to represent her?"

The rich baritone voice of Coglin replied, "Sure, Freddy, within the hour." Freddy said, "By the way, tell Sabina that I found out that Leeds is DEA." The lawyer replied, "Will do," and hung up. Freddy hadn't needed to explain to super-shark Coglin that Sabina was his, Freddy's agent, in the dope deal. Coglin would persuade her, con her, do everything to keep her from putting a finger on Freddy.

Freddy lay across the bed in street clothes and worried about Portillo's reaction when the news hit about Sabina's bust with Leeds. He should have taken Portillo's advice. He'd been stone stupid to trust Leeds. Now he was facing the joint if Sabina flipped. Guilt for Whitey's death rode his aching head like a ton of lead. He wasn't confident at all that paranoid Portillo would not put out a contract on him for the Leeds mistake.

His mother Esther, who had been visiting a sick friend, knocked on the door. "Yeah, come in." She came in. "Late lunch is on the table, Freddy. You must be starvin'." He managed a light-hearted laugh, "No, Mama. I ain't hungry. I've decided to miss a meal here and there to lose some weight"

She studied him. "You ain't lyin' to Mama? Ain't no trouble took your appetite?"

He shaped a gleeful grin. "Shoot no, Mama. I told you, I ain't doin' no wrong." She left to eat with Junior.

Ninety minutes later, Coglin requested and was given a chance to talk to a distraught Sabina in an anteroom of Federal lockup. A Federal marshal stood outside the door peering at them through a square of glass at the top of the door.

Gray-suited Coglin, a hawk-faced dark-skinned giant, with crinkly white hair, sat across from Sabina at a small table. She was still in street clothes, but she looked as wilted and bedraggled as her clothes.

"I am Jimmie Coglin. Mr. Evans has retained me as your counsel... Have they interrogated you?" She shook her head. "How long will I have to stay here?" He placed his hand on her wrist. "A day or so before you are arraigned. A judge will set your bail and you will be released. I will be at your side in all court appearances. Freddy cares deeply about you and you can depend on us all the way... Do you have a police record of any kind?" She hesitated, averted her eyes. "No, I've never been arrested." He knew she was lying. He half-whispered in the tender manner of a father. "You must tell me the truth. They'll send your fingerprints to the FBI in Washington to check them... It's not a hideous crime to have a police record. I almost did growing up in South Central."

She sighed, "Okay, I have a rap sheet in Austin, Texas for theft and prostitution, nothing else." He squeezed her wrist. "That's good news. Everything is going to be all right for you. Refuse to answer any questions about the case unless I am present. All right?" She started to cry. "Forgive me, but so many bad things have happened to me... I'm afraid I can't keep it together unless I get out soon. My son died today. I don't know what I can do about his body while being locked up here."

Coglin picked up his briefcase off the tabletop. "My deepest sympathy. Freddy will handle everything that concerns you." He leaned close to her face. "Mr. Evans told me he found out that Leeds is DEA." Her face drained of color. He stood. The marshal unlocked and opened the door. "Get strength from the fact that Jimmie Coglin is your attorney and friend. Don't forget, Mr. Evans has no limits to what he will do to help you get an early release." He went out into the corridor.

The marshal took Sabina to a cell shared by three other young women. One of them, a hard-faced black woman, seated on the top of one of the double deck bunks said, "Girl, you been cryin' — bad news?"

Sabina climbed onto the top bunk on the other side of the cell, shaken by the news about Leeds. She said, "No, I got good news. My lawyer, Jimmie Coglin, told me I'll be walkin' soon." All three looked surprised.

A tall thin white woman in a red mini exclaimed, "You're lucky. He's one of the best there is." The black woman laughed. "You either rich or you opened up some guy's nose that's got long bread."

Sabina dried her tears with toilet paper. "My man is a rich neurosurgeon." She stretched out on the bunk and closed her eyes, all the while knowing she would not sleep this night.

In the same building Nelson relaxed in quarters where DEA agents and U.S. Marshals took breaks. Several DEA agents played cards. A pair of marshals shot pool. Nelson sat on a cot in one of the adjoining rooms. He would sleep here tonight. Tomorrow, a DEA attorney would take him into court to be arraigned on charges of buying an illegal substance. A Federal judge, informed of his undercover status, would set a minimal bond which would be posted by his agency. He'd go back to the mansion and remain undercover. Nelson had no idea that Big Freddy knew he was heat.

At that moment in South Central, Freddy parked his Rolls on Avalon Boulevard. He went to the door of a decrepit wood frame house. He knocked. Nina Ferguson, a 30ish petite woman with a pretty brown face marred by ghetto stress lines, opened the door. She was wearing white short shorts. Freddy noticed that she kept her sexy body in shape as he took a seat beside her on a worn leather sofa. The racket of her four children playing in the back of the house could be heard in the living room.

"Can I get you a Pepsi or something, Freddy?"

He shifted on the sofa. "No thanks, Nina… I ain't stayin' long — I got bad news, real bad news."

She grabbed his arm. "Nothin' happened to Whitey. Tell me nothin' happened to him!"

Freddy looked at the floor. "He got shot to death several hours ago. He…"

She burst into tears and pounded his barn door shoulder with a tiny fist. "He worked for you, the king of the homeboys, and you couldn't protect him?"

He slid himself away from her. "No homeboy did it. The Feds wasted him in a shootout when they busted a lady makin' a dope deal. He was guardin' her. He, uh…"

She jumped in his lap and glared into his face. She blubbered bitterly. "Tell it like it is, Freddy! He was killed guardin' your white bitch and your dope."

He shoved her off his lap onto the floor. He stood and looked at her as she rose from the carpet. Did she know enough to hurt him? Should he kill her? He reached into the pocket of his black silk leisure suit. He took out a wad and peeled off several thousand ink notes. He tried to stuff the money into her bosom. She slapped his hand and backed up. "Freddy Evans, I don't want anything you've got. Get out!" He gritted his teeth. "You crazy bitch, you ain't got no sense talkin' to Big Freddy like that. I'd bust your motherfuckin' head wide open if I didn't care so much about Whitey." He walked to the door, opened it. "You ain't got the bread to bury him. I'll give this bread to Angelus Funeral Home." He stepped out quickly when she picked up a heavy glass ashtray from the coffee table. She hurled it. He heard it crash against the door. He went to his car and drove to Angelus Funeral Home to make arrangements for Whitey.

At 6 P.M., Portillo sat on the den sofa with his wife Bianca. She was stretched out with her head on his lap as they watched the 6'o'clock news on TV. Shortly, a male reporter started to recount the details of the Sabina bust and the death of Whitey Ferguson.

Bianca felt a sudden tension in Portillo's body. "Oh, Ernesto, that woman and the drugs are connected to you... Tell me that some day we will live without fear and tension. Ernesto, we would be so happy." He lowered his head to kiss her temple. "Yes, my love, one day we will live free of the hounds. I promise." She sat up. "Are you in immediate danger of big trouble?" He laughed. "Of course not. There's no need to worry. Everything will be brought under control." She stood. "I'm going to the kitchen to tell the cook we want to eat dinner early. I'm hungry." She kissed him and left the room.

Portillo summoned Emilio and Frank by intercom. They sat beside him. "Our dumb ex-friend Freddy and his all-American girl have gotten into a big mess with the Feds which threaten us all. They..."

Emilio interrupted. "We know, Mr. Portillio. We heard it on TV. Should we eliminate Freddy right away?"

Portillo said, "Eventually, but for many reasons, it would be a mistake to end his life while she is in lockup. I have a plan to get them both when Freddy gets her released. Excuse me, I have to go to the bathroom." He left the den. Emilio & Frank went back to their bungalow in the rear of the mansion.

In Beverly Hills, Baptiste, bleary-eyed Isaiah, and Helene had watched the TV news segment about Sabina's arrest. Helene sat between the men on the living room sofa. Isaiah clapped his hands. "Hooray! She deserves all she gets & more. One important thing needs to be done."

Baptiste said, "I've called the funeral home in your name to make arrangements to pay for the body of poor little Eric to be picked up after the coroner autopsy and for his funeral."

Isaiah's face was grim. "I appreciate that Pops, but I meant that the killing of Big Freddy was unfinished business. He gave Sabina the dope that killed Eric."

Helene said softly, "Isaiah, I hope that is the real reason you want to kill the man... Excuse me, I'm going to prepare our dinner." She left the room.

Baptiste took a salt free cracker from a dish on the coffee table. "Isaiah, Helene can be trusted. But please don't crack Freddy's murder to anyone else. I would advise you not to risk your life and freedom. Chances are, Sabina will flip on him and he'll get life in the penitentiary for using her to sell all that dope."

Isaiah sipped black coffee to sober up from the scotch binge. "I can't wait to kill that nigger. There ain't no cinch he'll go to the joint. Jimmie Coglan could find some technical shit in his case and beat the system... I'm killing him this weekend."

Baptiste looked worried. "You mean in the street? With witnesses?"

Isaiah drew himself up on the sofa. "Pops, I ain't crazy. That investigator's report on Sabina and Freddy you have in your safe gave me the perfect way to do it."

Baptiste shook his head. "It's no good son. Freddy is probably under 24-hour watch by the DEA."

Isaiah chuckled, "Ain't no DEA gonna be with us or see me kill him. I can't let that fat tub of lard live past the weekend."

Baptiste's face contorted with sudden pain in his hip. "I'll be back. I've gotta get a morphine tablet for my arthritis." Isaiah started to rise. "Where is it, Pops? I'll get it." As he walked away Baptiste said, "Thanks, but I need to get some exercise."

———

At 8 that night Sabina was taken from her cell to talk to a Miss Nancy Philbin from the Federal Prosecutor's Office. Sabina faced the tall brunette, a greying former Miss Arizona of 1960, across a conference table.

"I don't know why you wasted your time bringing me here. I've been advised by my attorney Mr. Coglan not to discuss my case."

The horn-rimmed glasses of the former beauty queen caught light and shimmered as she ruefully shook her head. "We know that Freddy Evans sent you to sell his dope. My dear, you are a lovely white woman who has been used and victimized by a notorious black criminal. Save yourself a stiff sentence by helping us and the DEA to put him in prison for life. For God's sake, you're intelligent enough to save yourself, aren't you?"

Sabina shook her head. "I'm not talking about the case. I want to go back to my cell." They stood. The prosecutor gave Sabina a card. "Call me if you change your mind after your release on bond." Sabina took the card. "I'm not going to lie and send an innocent man to jail." They left the room. A marshal took Sabina back to her cell.

Next day at noon, Nelson was released on $50,000 bond posted by the DEA. An hour later Sabina was arraigned on a charge of selling the kilos and conspiracy to engage in a continuing criminal enterprise, that of Freddy Evans. She was released on a $500,000 bond posted by Freddy through a bondsman.

Sabina took a cab to Lisa's building. Two of the DEA agents in dark suits who had busted her got out of their car and stood at the door of the building's foyer. They blocked her entry. "Mrs. Jones, we want to talk to you."

She said harshly, "Get out of my way. I'm not talking to you."

The shorter agent said, "Don't talk. Listen. We are prepared with the approval of the Federal Prosecutor to offer you a nice downward reduction deal in charges and possible sentence, if you will help us take down Freddy Evans. Well?"

She spat on the sidewalk. "Get the hell out of my way. I'm not buying any deals from you snakes." They stepped aside. The taller one said, "You'll be sorry," as she went into the foyer.

In the penthouse Lisa took her to the den for a lunch of roast duck and mixed vegetables. Sabina was depressed and her stomach was too upset with nervous tension to eat much. "Lisa, I'm going to have to move. Two of the DEA pricks that busted me were waiting outside your building to offer me a deal. You could get busted from the heat on me. All your phones are probably tapped."

Lisa smiled, "Kiddo, I want you to stay. I haven't dealt anything out of this place since you got busted. I'm not a fair-weather friend. We can use Tracy's phone on the 5th floor for private calls. I'll call and tell her you may want to use her phone."

Tears welled in Sabina's eyes. "You're the best, Lisa… Oh yes, don't do any business with Stanford. He's DEA."

Lisa's mouth popped open. "Are you certain?" Sabina laughed mirthlessly, "As certain as I am that my baby's dead. Can I have a bottle of booze to take to my bedroom?" They stood. "Sure. Champagne or Jack Daniels?"

Sabina went to a bar in the corner of the room. "Jack Daniels for me," she said as she took a fifth and a tall glass off a mirrored row of shelves on the wall behind the bar. She went to her bedroom.

Ten minutes later Nelson called. "Hello, beautiful. I've been worried about you and very frustrated because I wasn't free to hold you in my arms and comfort…"

She hung up on him. She called the morgue. She was told Eric's body had been picked up by a mortuary at the request of Baptiste Landreau & Isaiah Jones.

In the drawing room of Nelson's home, he looked at the two agents who had propositioned Sabina. He shrugged. "She's brighter than I thought. She apparently suspects that I'm heat... Why don't we bust her when she dates Freddy again. I'd bet she'll be dirty with some crack when she leaves him. Maybe she'll change her mind and cooperate. She'll be locked up again for a week or so. It will take that long for arraignment on possession charges and another bond hearing."

John Martinez, the taller agent said, "George, won't they be leery of meeting so soon?"

Nelson chuckled, "She's hooked on a fast buck and crack. He's hooked on a fast buck, crack, and her body. They're a cinch to meet soon. Did crazy Rita Suarez make that million-dollar bond?"

Bob Reed, the shorter agent said, "No, she's Randolph's case. We were talking about her this morning. She's so paranoid and violent that she's put two of the women prisoners that shared her cell in the hospital. Five or six of the others got no sleep and had to be moved out. Rita is an animal. You wouldn't..."

Nelson's hands writhed in his lap. "I would. I want that painted maggot put in with Rita when you bust her. I want Big Freddy!"

The agents stood. Martinez said, "George, won't her lawyer, Coglan, argue that we lacked probable cause and committed illegal search & seizure when we busted her?"

Nelson said, "Sure, he'll have to make that argument in court. In the meantime, she sweats in jail."

Martinez said, "Sounds good. We'll get on it right away." They left.

Nelson went to take a shower. The phone turned him back to the drawing room. "Mr. Leeds, Big Freddy may put a contract out on you." The caller, with a heavy Mexican accent, hung up. It had been Stokes the investigator.

Chapter 9

In West Hollywood, Sabina disconnected her phone. She didn't want to receive a call from Freddy on a phone that was probably tapped. She had vomited the pint of whiskey she had drunk. She tried, and failed, to focus her mind on something other than rock. She had never been so depressed. "You've been nothing all your miserable life," she told her wild-eyed reflection in the dresser mirror. "You're never going to live like a socialite. Know why? Because you're too stupid and you're a fuckin' tramp. You're worthless. The only good thing you ever did was to bring Eric into the world so you could kill him. Oh Eric! Please forgive me." Tears flooded her cheeks as she went toward an open glass door leading to a small balcony enclosed by a four-foot concrete wall. Her electric blue eyes gazed up at the twilight sky. A molesting wind whipped back her long hair which flew like the wings of a golden bird. The wind plastered her transparent silk gown against her outrageously sexy body. Trancelike, she climbed to the top of the wall. She teetered as she glanced down at miniaturized people and cars 20 stories down. She stood straight and tall, with her eyes fixed on the sky. The white stone balcony was like a ship sailing in an ocean of blue twilight with Sabina an ancient Viking queen fearlessly taking her soul to Valhalla.

"Big guy, I can't con you. You know I haven't seen the inside of a church or prayed since I was a little girl when my Papa took me and taught me how to pray. I want to be with Eric. Please big guy, let me be with my son." She held out her arms and closed her eyes for the plunge. She felt exhilarated, joyful.

The instant before she was going to step into space, Lisa grabbed her around the waist and pulled her off the wall. They fell to the balcony floor.

"You crazy bitch, what the fuck are you doing?"

Sabina gasped. "Why did you stop me?" Lisa got to her feet & pulled Sabina to hers. She put an arm around her waist and led her into the bedroom. Sabina collapsed on the bed and closed her eyes. Lisa sat on the side of the bed and silently studied Sabina's face for several minutes wondering how she could help, short of calling in men with white coats to take her away.

Sabina opened her eyes. "Do you have any kind of dark wig?"

Lisa looked puzzled, "Sure, red and black."

Sabina sat up. "Will you loan me the black one and your car? I've got to make a call and score some rock to get myself together."

Lisa stood up. "I'll get the wig, but I can't let you take my car. You're sizzling & my car could be confiscated if you got busted in it dirty. Do you have the bread for a cab."

Sabina got out of bed. "Thanks for the wig. I've got bread for a cab... Bring me some of your makeup."

Lisa went to get the wig. Sabina started to bobby pin her long hair flat against the back of her head.

Lisa returned with the makeup and a long black silky wig. "Kiddo, are you all right now? Please be careful. I'm going to be so worried until you get back. I called Tracy downstairs. She said you could use her phone."

Sabina put on the wig. "Thanks, honey, for everything. I'll be all right." Lisa left.

Sabina transformed her pale white skin with Lisa's makeup to complement the black wig. She dressed in a dark blue linen suit. She went to ring Tracy's bell on the 5th floor.

Tracy, a tall redhead model, opened the door. "Hi, you must be Sabina. I'm Tracy. Come in." Tracy led her into a plush living room. "Make yourself comfortable," Tracy said as she left the room.

Sabina sat on a lemon velour chaise. She took a phone from the top of a cocktail table & dialed Freddy.

"Big Freddy here." She half-whispered, "Meet me within an hour at that dump motel, the Sweet Dreams on Hoover. You know the spot?" He hesitated, "Yeah, I passed it a thousand times... Maybe it ain't cool for us to meet. Coglan told me to stay away from you until the case is settled."

She started to cry. "Listen, I'm on the edge. Fuck Coglan! I've got to have some medicine... I'm in disguise, and I'm taking a cab."

He snorted, "Hey ya dumb bitch. I bet Leeds sweet talked ya and fucked ya before he busted ya and took my stuff. Maybe I don't wanna meet you."

She was breathing hard. "I'm facing some heavy shit alone for you. I didn't know Leeds was DEA and I never went to bed with him. Do you want in on the rap? Meet me!"

He said, "Baby, you know I wouldn't let you down. See ya." He hung up.

She went to hail a cab in front of the building. Martinez and Reed sat in a blue Ford a half block away. Martinez put his binoculars on Sabina when she left the sidewalk and walked to the curb to flag down a cab.

"That broad with the black hair is Sabina. I remember her walk." Reed started the Ford.

A minute later a cab stopped and Sabina got in. Twenty minutes later the cab let her out in front of the Sweet Dreams motel. Martinez and Reed parked a block away.

Interracial hookers paraded past them in loud shorts and micro-minis. Some of them got into cars with black and Hispanic tricks.

Sabina paid and got out of the cab. She rented a room for two hours. She sat and pushed back shabby drapes to stare out of a grimy window as she waited impatiently for Freddy. Finally, she saw him drive his mother's Ford Escort into the parking lot. She unlocked the door and stood in the doorway.

He came in wearing house slippers and a white sweater over his black satin pajamas. He embraced her for a long moment. "Baby, I 'preciate the way you stood up after you got busted." She pulled free. "You bring the medicine?" He took off his sweater. "Yeah, but it's straight rock without China White."

He gave her a glass pipe and two vials. She propped herself up in bed still fully dressed. He sat on the side of the bed as she hit the pipe. "Baby, why don't you take off your threads?" She gave him the pipe. "Take off my shoes and hang my suit coat in the closet." He did.

He stretched out beside her in the bed. "How about the rest of your threads?" She moved close to him. "Freddy, just this one time, let's don't have sex. Hold me."

He cradled her on his chest with his penis tenting his pajama pants. They smoked for a half hour. "Baby, can I have a taste, just a light taste, of your righteous head? Okay?" Sabina began to kiss her way down Freddy's body.

Fifteen minutes later he left. She called a cab and waited in front of the motel for it to arrive.

Tricks, thinking she was a working girl, stopped and waved to invite her to their cars. Her cab arrived. She got in and the cab drove toward West Hollywood.

Martinez and Reed u-turned to follow. At Hoover and Adams Boulevard they cut their Ford into the path of the cab to force it to stop. They went to the cab and told the startled Armenian driver, "We're police." Reed noticed Sabina slip something beneath the rear seat.

Martinez told the driver, "We're putting your passenger under arrest for possession of narcotics."

Martinez pulled Sabina out to the street. Reed got a full vial and a quarter-filled vial of crack from beneath the seats.

Martinez handcuffed her and with Reed led her to sit in the back of the Ford beside Martinez. She said angrily, "You dirty bastards! You've got no case. I don't know anything about those vials. Maybe your partner had them in his hand when he came to the cab."

Martinez laughed, "You're right in a way. Maybe we've got a case and maybe not. But that was your dope & you're going back to the Federal lockup downtown."

They drove her to the lock up on Alameda. Fifteen minutes later she was led to crazy Rita Suarez's cell. The heavyset tall Puerto Rican sat on the bottom of a bunk bed. Hard rock spewed from a row of speakers on the cell house wall. Rita's mean, jive-tinted face was hideous with suspicion when a marshal locked Sabina into the cell.

"I want to make a phone call to my lawyer."

The tall black marshal said, "Yeah, later." He walked away down the tier.

"Hello" Sabina said as she climbed to the top bunk.

Rita grunted. Sabina stretched out on the bunk. She thought, "Will these nightmare events never end? Why couldn't she have jumped seconds before Lisa saved her for this?"

173

Ten minutes later, Rita stood suddenly and put her black, curly topped fright face close to the side of Sabina's head. "Open your eyes. You can't fool Rita. You're a fuckin' C.I. for the feds. I ain't gonna tell you shit about my case or my old man. I think I'll break your motherfuckin' neck. I may drown you in the john."

Sabina jerked erect on the bunk. "Are you nuts? What the fuck is a C.I.?"

Rita snatched off Sabina's black wig and threw it into a corner. "It means confidential informant, as if you didn't know — fink! I'll…"

The marshal making a cell count interrupted Rita. "Behave yourself, Rita," he said as he moved down the tier. Rita shot him a hateful look and went to sit on the toilet. The cell soon stank like rotten garbage.

Sabina waited in vain to be taken to a phone. Several marshals passed the cell until lights out. Everyone told her, "As soon as I can."

She lay in the bleak shadows of the cell with only the pallid light from a row of tiny bulbs that line the cell house wall. Rita's heavy masculine voice stage whispered, "I'm gonna get you when you go to sleep C.I." Rita laughed long and loud like she had told herself a very funny joke.

Sabina got no sleep. Several times, during the long night, Rita would get up and peer into her face.

Next morning Sabina was a mental and physical basket case. At 8 she went and sat on the john to urinate. She stared at the floor.

Rita jumped off her bunk and punched Sabina's jaw with her fist. Sabina, stunned, fell to the floor. Rita lifted her off the floor and dunked her head into the toilet. She dropped her body across Sabina's shoulder so she couldn't pull her head out.

Sabina was near drowning when a marshal, on mourning count, opened the cell and pulled Rita away. "Rita, I'm going to put you in the dark downstairs if you screw up any more today."

Rita's dark eyes rolled in terror. "Oh, please, don't do that. I'll be cool."

The marshal watched Sabina vomit and retch into the john. Then she doused her head and face with water in the cell wash basin. He took Sabina to the small conference room where she was fed a breakfast of oatmeal, orange juice, & toast. She drank the orange juice and ate half the oatmeal. She dozed for an hour before a tall brunet, Nancy Philbin from the U.S. Attorney's office, came in and sat across the table.

"You look a mess, Jones. I heard what Rita tried to do to you... Why does an attractive and intelligent woman like yourself go on making bad decisions and taking punishment? You want to get out of here? I'm here to help you walk now."

Sabina pressed her palms against her aching head. "Help me? Walk now. You don't know I've got a possession charge? You people won't let me call my lawyer, and you put me in a cell with a fuckin' lunatic. Stop the bullshit lady."

Philbin said, "It's not like that; you can walk within the hour... under certain circumstances of course."

Sabina stared at her for a long moment. "Like what circumstances?"

Philbin said softly, "Like your full cooperation to take down Freddy Evans. The possession charge will be withdrawn and you will be released on your continued original bond. Want to deal?"

Sabina knew she couldn't go back to Rita's insanity. She was so tired and drained anyway. Her voice broke, "I'll take it."

Philbin stood. "Mr. Martinez and Mr. Reed will come in to give you details in a few minutes."

Shortly, Martinez and Reed took seats at the table. Martinez lit a cigarette. "We're sorry about the way you forced us to handle you. You're a streetwise, tough cookie. You were involved at a key level in a racket that threatens us all, and generations of our children. Need I give you painful mention to the death of your son?"

Reed said, "Does anyone know that you were arrested yesterday?"

She laughed bitterly. "No, I wasn't even allowed to call Mr. Coglan."

Martinez removed his tan straw hat and put it on the table. "That's fine for the case, Mrs. Jones."

She gave him a dirty look. "You mean finely illegal *&* probably unconstitutional?"

Martinez shrugged. "All is fair in this war... You can't tell Coglan about the bust yesterday, or about anything we discuss here today. He..."

She interrupted him. "He's my lawyer. I need him to defend me in court... I don't know whether I should make a deal with you people or not."

Reed looked irritated. "Freddy Evans is our immediate target. Coglan has been his lawyer and friend for 10 years. Whatever you tell Coglan, Freddy will know. We're going to guarantee you, with the approval of the U.S. Attorney, a downward reduction in charges and sentence. I think you'll get no more than probation and a fine if you take our deal. Coglan will press, in court, for what you already know you've got. He'll be delighted to take credit for getting you off lightly. You understand everything I've said?"

She nodded. "You want me to wear a wire and talk to Freddy about the seven keys?"

Martinez shook his head. "No. When he gets the 20 keys to you, we'll bust you and Freddy's guard. We'll write you when he raises you on bond. He'll be a red-hot bomb and make our case. He'll badmouth you for pushing him to make the deal that blew so many keys. He may even suspect that you're working with us, but we'll protect you. You'll be safe. You will also testify against him in the seven keys case for which a federal grand jury has just indicted him."

Reed said, "Does Freddy know that you and Lisa Lundgren have been close pals since you both were young girls in Austin?"

She looked upset. "Say, leave Lisa out of this shit."

Reed said, "Lisa is already an unindicted seller of cocaine to a DEA agent."

Sabina's lips curled. "You got that right. The goddamn agent is Leeds."

Martinez threw up his hands. "We are not here to discuss Mr. Leeds. He will have his day in court. If you make and keep our deal, your pal Lisa will never be tried for anything. Now here's the plan. Meet Freddy in a couple of days. As I said, you won't need a wire for this meeting. You will need to put a big romantic dream inside his head."

She guffawed. "Put a romantic dream inside an original gangster's head? He's a sex freak but he isn't romantic at all. You guys can't be serious."

Reed looked pained. "Sabina, let us guide you into the mode of thinking necessary for you to play Freddy properly. He thinks he's in love with you. Whether he really is or is even capable of real love for any woman beside his mother is a moot question. You play him like you're both in love. You tell him you want to be his wife after your upcoming divorce from your husband. Tell him you're certain that Coglan will get you probation. Do what you do best, lie, and describe the rapture of a honeymoon in Paris and the thrills of riding down the Champs Élysées together. Tell him how exciting it would be to visit the famous ruins of the Colosseum in Rome. Tell him how much you want to be the mother of his son since you lost yours. Feed the big dream into his head before you tell him that your trusted, loving friend Lisa has received a large inheritance and she wants to make an investment in 20 keys. A friend of ours at the *L.A. Times* will run a short account of Lisa's good fortune, courtesy of a rich relative who died in Texas. If he..."

She cut him off. "You guys have a hearing problem. I refuse to involve Lisa in heavy shit like that."

Martinez's olive face was a portrait of aggravation. "Sabina, you apparently have a hearing problem of your own. Lisa won't be really involved in the 20-key deal. In fact, don't tell her anything about it. l told you she's safe from prosecution under the terms of our deal. Does Lisa have a middle name?"

Sabina looked puzzled. "No. Why?"

Reed said, "Lisa Lundgren in *The Times* will have a middle name. Lisa will have to assume that it's a similar name to her own if it comes to her attention. If Freddy balks when you request the kilos, take a hard line. Convince him that he might lose you on this issue if he doesn't care enough about you to let you make the deal with Lisa. Before you leave him, pressure him to give you his decision within a couple of days. That is, if he doesn't promise the kilos when you ask him. Any questions before you go home?"

They stood.

"No, I understand everything," Sabina said as she followed them into the corridor. Martinez gave her a card. "Memorize the phone number and destroy this card. Good luck."

She went to the street to catch a cab for home. The day was bright and clear of smog. She filled her lungs with air and felt better. But she needed some crack in the worst way.

When she got to the penthouse Lisa was furious. "Sabina, have you heard about a fuckin' invention called the telephone? I couldn't sleep worrying about you last night. What happened?"

Sabina kissed her cheek. "Lisa, you're so precious. I'm sorry you worried and didn't sleep much. I didn't get much sleep myself until almost daybreak. Billy made passionate love to me all night and I woke up an hour-and-a-half ago. Like me, he's optimistic about my case since Coglan is handling it."

Lisa followed her to the bedroom. "Donald's in New York, probably with some tramp... I really don't care anymore what he does. I'm fucking a rich living doll corporate executive. He's in a marriage that's on the way down the toilet."

Sabina laughed. "Sure it is." Lisa shrugged and laughed. "So he's conning me. He's got the prettiest dick in my memory and he makes magic with it. He gladdens the heart of this ex-hooker with gifts of money and jewelry. I'm happy in the affair. You want to eat?"

Sabina took off her shoes. "No thanks. I ate breakfast at Billy's place. I'm still tired... think I'll take a nap." Lisa yawned and went to take her nap.

———

The following weekend on Saturday morning Freddy met Sabina in the Sweet Dreams Motel. They lay nude in bed together after sex and rock smoking. Sabina caressed his chest and belly with airy fingertips. She said sweetly, "Freddy, I have something very important to tell you... I'm certain that I've fallen madly in love with you. Will you marry me when I get my divorce in a few weeks? I'm so sure that Coglan will get me off."

He squeezed the breath out of her. "Baby, you got my nose open too. Shit yes. I'd marry you today."

She lay on him with her fat sex trap pressed against his crotch. Her huge blue eyes danced as she kissed the tip of his nose and gazed into his face. "You've made me so happy darling — we can honeymoon in Paris — see the ruins of the Colosseum in Rome together. Let's live an exciting, full life together and really enjoy having money. I need to be a mother to your son. It would ease the pain of my loss of Eric. Freddy, I love you and I love my best friend Lisa. I'd trust her with my life. We've been friends since grammar school." Sabina reached and got her purse from a chair near the bed. She took out the phony *Times* mention of Lisa Handsberry Lundgren's inheritance of five million from an oil-rich Texas relative. Freddy read the clipping. "She's lucky as a shit house rat."

Sabina laughed. "She wants to make an investment in 20 keys if she can get them at 20 thou a key she…"

He groaned and popped up out of bed and sat on the side of it. "Baby, I can't do no more dealin' through you."

She pouted. "You mean you don' t trust me? Or is it just Lisa you don't trust?"

He flung his arms in the air. "l trust you… I ain' t got no trust in no white people. I don't know about doin' a big deal with one of them after Leeds. I'm sorry baby." He got to his feet and went into the shower. He came out a few minutes later. Her face was grim. As he dressed, he said, "Ain't no need to be salty baby. Maybe after Coglan cuts you loose, I'll let you sell her the keys."

Sabina said sternly, "If I don't get those keys by next Saturday, I'm not seeing you any more Freddy. I can' t marry and live for the rest of my life with a man who refuses to do a favor for my best friend. I'll call you in two days to find out if you've changed your mind."

He stared at her. "I'll make up my mind in a couple of days… here's some medicine." He threw a vial of rock on the bed, kissed her forehead, and left the room.

She went to a window and watched him drive the Ford Escort off the lot. He wouldn't say no to her when she called. He was stone hooked on her like Isaiah had been, she thought. She felt powerful, excited as a principle player in one of the most dangerous of all games. How did she really feel about Freddy? She told herself she felt absolutely nothing for him except a secret loathing of his rough and clumsy lovemaking.

She showered and dressed. She drove to West Hollywood in her red Excalibur convertible. The wind whipped through her hair and she felt free of tension, except for the ghost of Eric, which haunted her mind. She felt almost happy since she and the DEA were partners instead of enemies.

Sabina went to Tracy's apartment the following Thursday to call Freddy for his decision about the keys.

"Baby, I'm gonna do it, but we gotta talk so I can run down the plan to deliver. I won't have 20 keys until two weeks from now. Sorry, Lisa will have to wait. Call me this Saturday. Tell Lisa to get 400,000 together for delivery in two weeks. Talk to ya." He hung up.

Sabina called the number on the card Martinez had given her in the lockup. A woman answered and assured Sabina that she could take confidential messages for Martinez. Sabina gave her a complete report of what was happening with Big Freddy. She then went back to the penthouse.

She was laying across the bed smoking crack when something hit her mind. She looked at her watch. It was 1:30. She had forgotten Eric's funeral at noon in the chapel at Angelus. Without makeup, in jeans and a blouse, she dashed to her car and drove dangerously fast to

Crenshaw Boulevard. She parked on the street in front of the funeral home. She was too late. A lead limousine moving behind a hearse passed her. She looked directly into Isaiah's hostile, tearful eyes. He was on the rear seat with Baptiste, Helene, and Alonzo. A procession of a dozen cars, driven by Eric's friends, followed the limousine on the way to Rosedale cemetery just two miles away.

Sabina felt so guilty and frustrated that she sat for half an hour staring at the fast traffic on Crenshaw before she drove away.

At home Freddy relaxed on his bed after a heavy lunch. The sound of Billie Holiday's old recording of "Gloomy Sunday" came barely audible from a stereo. He had stalled Sabina on the Lisa deal deliberately. He also had never liked for a woman to manipulate him or control him. Freddy Junior's pretty mother Heather had that flaw before she died of cancer in her pussy he thought, when Junior was three. "I've got to stay away from Sabina for a week or so," he told himself. "I gotta find out if I can do without her. If I can't, I'll risk the deal with Lisa and marry Sabina. Shit, I wouldn't mind seein' Paris and Rome with a beautiful white woman. And she told me she needs Junior. Maybe he needs her. Mama's gettin' old. Maybe Sabina could relieve her with Junior. Damn, I know it ain't gonna be easy to kick my jones for her body. But I sure will try hard as I can. I gotta call Mr. Portillo in the next couple of days." Junior knocked on the bedroom door. "Yeah, it's unlocked." Junior opened the door and stood on the threshold. "Hi daddy, you goin' to sleep?" Freddy held out his arms. "No baby boy, I was just thinkin' about you."

The kid, dressed in jeans and a tank top, came and lay on Freddy's arm. "Daddy, what was you thinkin' 'bout me?"

Freddy shoved his crack pipe and a vial under a pillow. "I was thinkin' 'bout sweet grandma Esther maybe gettin' old and tired. We don't want her to get sick and die. Maybe you need a new mama. She's a beautiful white lady I know. We was talkin' about gettin' married. What you think?"

The kid stared at the ceiling in deep thought. "Is she prettier than my real mama Heather that went to heaven?"

Freddy lied. "No, Junior. Sabina is pretty but no woman could be prettier than Heather."

Junior toyed with the face of a gargoyle carved on the mahogany headboard. "You like Sabina?"

Freddy thought out his answer. "Yeah, a lot, but not as much as I cared about your mama. I was really nuts about her since we was kids in school."

They heard Grandma Esther at the backdoor yelling. "Junior, Junior! Grandma baked you somethin' good."

The kid jumped to the floor. "I like Sabina, Daddy, since you like her," he said as he skipped toward the door. He stopped and turned with a devilish grin. "Daddy, you got my okay to marry Sabina. Righteous?" He vanished into the hallway.

Chapter 10

The next weekend, on Saturday at 9 P.M., Baptiste and Isaiah sat on the patio after dinner. "Pops, tonight is the last night for Big Freddy."

Baptiste shook his head. "Young people like you are oblivious to the glorious essence of youth and life. You want to risk everything — your freedom, even your precious young life — to kill a worthless louse. Don't do it, son. I think you & Helene can put something beautiful together... You could try for a son. Let the system punish Freddy. We know Freddy is guilty of giving Sabina the dope that killed Eric. But I read an article in the *Times* that mentioned Ernesto Portillo, who lives in a walled estate in Baldwin Hills, as the probable source of the dope in South Central."

Isaiah shrugged, "I ain't got no way or time to scale walls." He looked at his watch. "I'll be splittin' to do my thing in an hour or so. So, Pops, I can't take your advice this time. If I don't get back, ship my body to my Aunt Melba. I want to be buried in Georgia with my mother and father & brothers and sisters."

Helene joined them, bringing black coffee for Isaiah and grape juice for Baptiste.

Baptiste said, "I'm just sorry you don't value or appreciate your life. I really can't condemn you because I was a lot like you in a different way when I still had some youth. After Opal's mother was killed in Spanish Harlem, I threw away the last of my precious youth for nine years with promiscuous dog-ass sluts on a sexual binge. They were Hispanic, white, and black. I tell you, when I think about how stupid I was to waste my time and potential that way, I could cry and tear out the hair I've got left. Why shit, I could have become a doctor or even a psychiatrist in 9 years. I was a fool and you're a fool if you risk yourself to kill Freddy. That's all I have to say."

Isaiah looked surprised. "Pops, I could never have guessed that you ever were a hit and run stone stud — again, thanks, but I guess I'm too angry and stupid to take your advice."

Helene sat down and stared at Isaiah.

"Hey baby, why are you lookin' at me like that?"

She dropped her eyes to the silver water pitcher. "I'm sorry darling. I've been worried about you a lot."

He threw an arm around her shoulder, "Baby, nothing is gonna happen to me."

An hour later she followed him to his car. She kissed him long and passionately. She felt this was the prediction of the loas of his death and she would never see him again.

"Baby, why did you kiss me like that? I'll be back after midnight, okay? Nothing is going to happen to me." He got in the car. "That kiss was because I love you so much." He drove away. Baptiste went painfully to bed.

Freddy was playing ping pong with Junior in the den. Predictably, the nimble young kid had beaten his ponderous opponent four games in a row. He needled Freddy. "Hey, Daddy, am I gonna be your age before you beat me?" He laughed and boogied around the table, as sweaty, exhausted Freddy collapsed into a chair.

"Hey comedian, if you don't go to bed and stop messin' with me, I'll put some fire in your caboose." The kid broke out into gales of laughter. "Baby boy, don't wind up a dumb, nothin' nigger like me with no real book learnin' and a prison record." The kid looked confused. "But Daddy, you gotta be pretty smart. You rich!"

Freddy's face was pained. "I ain't got no respect from many black peoples and no peace of mind. Ain't nothin' more righteous than them. You gonna hang tough and stay away from gangs & dope, even pot, and get respect from all black peoples?"

The kid nodded vigorously, "Daddy, I promise with my whole heart."

"Baby boy, I know you'll keep your word." He studied Junior's face, so innocent and vulnerable. He sat Junior on his lap. Junior put an arm around Freddy's neck. "Promise you won't drop outta school like me and go to college. I already gave Grandma the bread to put away to send you. I might not be around to remind you so I'm gonna trust you to go." Junior looked surprised. "Daddy, where you goin'?" Freddy put an arm around his waist. "All kinds of peoples, young and old, die every day. Now hit the sack." Junior kissed Freddy's face before he scooted away for his bedroom.

The phone rang. It was Sabina. "Baby, that new car dealer that's tryin' to get you that car said he'd let me know when he gets the one you want from Detroit by this Sunday comin'. We can meet on Hoover at 8 o'clock to discuss it." Freddy hung up. He took a shower and lay down to relax on the bed in shorts until midnight. Then he would go to check receipts and to close his Chicken Shack.

At ten to midnight he got up and dressed in dark trousers and a white shirt. He strapped on a shoulder holster to carry his .357 Magnum. He believed there was a slight chance that some out of town chump stick-up man would try for him when he closed the Shack. He slipped on a light sweater to cover the holster and put a black cap on his head.

He went to the garage next to the house. He pressed a device in his hand and the garage door swung up and open. He decided to drive his mother's Ford which was parked beside the Rolls. He drove out of the garage and closed its door with the hand-held device.

As Freddy drove through the mean streets, his gutter Camelot, remorse and sharp pangs of self-hatred assailed him. He wished for the thousandth time that he had stayed in school so he could rap smooth, perfect English jive like the big white movie stars that conned beautiful blonds into their beds. He pounded the steering wheel with his fists. Why couldn't his mother Esther, who was a brown-skinned cutie when she was young, have married a handsome young, half-white dude like Whitey Ferguson, the creole? Why did she have to marry his ugly ass father Silas who got in the wind after he was born. He would be light skinned and handsome if he hadn't been born ugly and black. Self-pity flooded his eyes with tears. Why had he been so stupid not to finish school and become a muckety-muck doctor or lawyer? He wouldn't have Portillo in his life to stress him and haunt his sleep. He wished he had never known a single homeboy. He was tired *&* sick to his soul of all of them and of the dope he used and that they bought from him.

He had been tempted several times in recent months to put the muzzle of the Magnum against his temple and escape all the pressure and fear in an instant. But then he'd always remember how much Esther and Junior needed him.

He pulled the Ford into the parking lot of his business. Dwarfish Payback Shorty Thomas, an O.G. *&* the manager, was about to secure the front door after the last customers left. Shorty had served a prison bit with Freddy when they were juveniles.

Shorty held the door open for Freddy. As he entered the place, there was the pungent odor of frying grease *&* a residual meld of cheap perfume worn by the women who had sat in the booths to eat. Shorty followed him to the cash register. Freddy's reddened, damp eyes had caught Payback's attention.

"My man, you been cryin'... who died?"

Freddy managed to laugh. "Shit no, I jus' ate some hot chili from Mexican Philippe's joint that I had in the frig."

Shorty said, "See ya, my old lady is waitin' for me in the lot."

As Shorty left the place, Freddy stopped counting the receipts and went to lock the front door and to move a steel security grate over the front door. He then finished checking the receipts. He put the money in a safe in a rear room. He set an alarm system before he stepped out the rear door into an alley. He locked the heavy metal door and walked around the building to the Ford. He held his hand close to his holstered pistol as he darted wary eyes into the shadows. He got in the car and drove toward home.

Twenty minutes earlier, Isaiah had punched a hole in a locked swing-in window in the rear of Freddy's garage. He had unbolted it. Then he had climbed through and crouched behind the Rolls. He waited with a tire iron for Freddy.

Freddy drove into his driveway. He swung the garage door open from inside the car.

His mother had seen the flash of headlights for an instant on the living room wall as she read the Bible while waiting for him to come home.

Freddy drove into the garage.

191

A block away a DEA agent parked his blue Pontiac after tailing Freddy from the restaurant.

Isaiah crept up behind Freddy as he got out of the Ford. He raised the tire iron high with both hands to deliver a killing blow to the top of Freddy's head.

Freddy caught a flicker of motion in the corner of an eye. He jerked his head around. The blow broke his right shoulder blade. He yelped in pain and staggered backwards. He drew the Magnum and aimed it at Isaiah.

Before he could squeeze the trigger, Isaiah lunged and broke his gun wrist with a crunching blow of the tire iron. The gun clattered to the concrete. Freddy groaned and started to turn away to flee. Isaiah picked up the gun and kicked Freddy hard in the belly. He doubled over and crashed to the concrete.

Isaiah stood and fired at his head. In the dim light of a full moon he saw blood spurt from Freddy's head. He was certain Freddy was dead or dying. He wiped the gun clean of his fingerprints and tossed it beside Freddy. He went through the window and out to the alley behind the garage.

He hurried through two deserted blocks to his car. He got in and drove toward Beverly Hills.

Esther wondered why Freddy hadn't come in the house. She had heard a muffled shot. She went out the front door to find Freddy. She saw the open garage door. She went in and screamed at the top of her lungs when she saw him in a pool of blood.

The DEA agent roared into the driveway. He went into the garage where Esther was cradling Freddy's bloody head in her lap. She was pleading over & over. "Oh, sweet Jesus, please don't let my baby die!"

The agent rushed to his car and called for an ambulance on his car phone. He went back to press a handkerchief hard against the deep scalp wound to keep Freddy from bleeding to death.

Eight minutes later, the paramedics arrived to give Freddy's wound a temporary pressure bandage, an injection, an I.V. and oxygen before they loaded him into the ambulance. Esther locked her front door and got into the ambulance to ride beside Freddy. The paramedics took him to the emergency room at Daniel Freeman.

In Beverly Hills, Baptiste and Helene waited in the living room for Isaiah and watched TV until the late news came on. Would they hear that Isaiah had been killed or arrested for murder?

Fifteen minutes later Helene saw Isaiah's car at the gate. She buzzed him through. She met him at the door and led him into the living room.

Baptiste noticed a splatter of blood on Isaiah's shoes and on the bottom of a trouser leg. "Did you get hurt? Did you…"

Isaiah fell onto the sofa between Helene and Baptiste. "I ain't got a scratch. But tub o' lard is history."

The late news came on TV. They watched a long segment of film clips on Saddam Hussein and the Saudi

193

Arabian standoff. After that the reporter started to give the local news, accompanied by film clips; a hostage situation in a McDonald's in Bellflower; an attempted robbery of an armored car in downtown L.A. earlier that morning; then a film clip of Freddy being taken out of the ambulance and carried into the emergency room. Esther went in behind them weeping. The reporter said that Freddy had been shot by an unknown assailant. Freddy's condition was serious from shock and loss of blood, but he had been given a transfusion and was expected to survive the attack.

Isaiah leaped off of the sofa. "I didn't kill that mother-fucker!"

Helene took his arm. She started to take him to her quarters to comfort him and help him to cope with his rage and frustration. Baptiste said, "Don't go home. Stay here until we can sort out this mess. Freddy wants to kill you. Tomorrow or the next day Alonzo can bring you some clothes and other necessities."

Isaiah nodded. He left the room with Helene. Baptiste went to his bedroom to take a morphine tablet and go to bed. He lay sleepless. He knew that Freddy would put out a contract on Isaiah very soon. Finally, he drifted into a terminally sick man's ragged sleep.

The next morning in Lisa's penthouse, Sabina heard an account of Freddy's plight on TV. She got up and picked up the phone to call Martinez's office to tell him what had happened. She cradled the phone. The DEA had probably known about Freddy minutes after he was shot. She wouldn't call or visit Freddy at the hospital. That would surely not be good since he had shown that he was reluctant to make the Lisa deal. She would just have to wait until he got out of the hospital.

At the hospital two days later Payback Shorty stood at Freddy's bedside. A profusion of flowers in vases sat around the room. One of them, a giant bouquet, had been sent by Portillo.

Freddy turned his still bandaged head to watch a nurse leave the room. He half whispered, "Shorty, tell Buddy Sims and Big Time Slim I want Isaiah Jones hit. Tell 'em where he lives. You know, that big apartment building 'cross from the Kentucky Fried Chicken joint."

Payback nodded. Freddy went on. "Tell 'em I'm payin' 25 thou a piece to do the number — you got any bread in the damper?" Shorty hesitated. "Yeah, a chicken shit 10 thou or so I'm savin' to buy a crib when I get married."

Freddy said, "Give them five thou a piece. I'll give you the bread back plus five thou when I get out of here on the weekend."

Shorty gently patted the cast on Freddy's broken right wrist. "I'll take care of business, homeboy. Don't worry about..." Esther and Junior entered the room to interrupt him. He smiled, said "Hi," and started to leave. He came back to the bedside & said to Freddy, "Whitey Ferguson's funeral is today."

Freddy said, "Take that big bouquet that just came in a few minutes ago to the funeral. Take that card off and put a nice card on and sign my name."

Shorty said, "You got it," before he left the room.

Esther & Junior kissed Freddy's cheek. They stood back when a doctor and two nurses came in to check Freddy.

Buddy Sims and Big Time Slim were late teen gang members. They sat in the living room of Bertha Sims' home playing chess. Payback called, "Hey Buddy, can you meet me right away 'bout you and Slim makin' 50 thou?"

Buddy hit Slim in the chest with his fist. "Yeah. Where?"

Shorty said, "In that park at Vernon and Crenshaw at noon."

Payback hung up. Heavyset handsome Buddy grinned. "Pal, I got good 50 thou news."

Tall, husky Slim said, "Nigger, do you have to punch me when you get good news?" They left the house and got into Slim's blue Mercedes. Mother Bertha Sims, an attractive brown skinned woman, watched them drive away. She hoped they weren't going to do something that would put them in prison or the cemetery.

In Baldwin Hills, Portillo sat in the den in conference with Emilio and Frank. Portillo, dressed in a brocaded white silk lounging robe and matching pajamas, said, "You sent the nice flowers, Emilio, to our ex-friend?"

Emilio nodded, "I should have sent him a bomb in a package."

Portillo smiled, "That would not be good even if he'd be able to open such a package himself. I have put together a smooth plan to get rid of the all-American girl and Freddy." He paused. His black eyes gleamed in recognition of the genius of his plot. "Freddy, not we, will kill himself and the cunt that caused his downfall."

Frank's mouth gaped open. "Mr. Portillo, are you certain you can make it go down like that? I don't see how…"

Portillo scowled to cut him off. "You doubt Ernesto Portillo? Leave my presence at once!"

Frank slunk out of the room followed by Emilio.

Portillo went into his bedroom to smoke some rock and polish his plot to exterminate Freddy and Sabina.

In the small park on Crenshaw, Payback Shorty sat on a bench in the park which was crowded with black and Hispanic adults with their children.

A small group of homeless young black men shucked and jived on the grass near Shorty. He watched the fast parade of motorists joy riding up & down Crenshaw on this bright Sunday. A clean cut, neatly dressed Muslim hawked bean pies on the corner across the Boulevard.

Ten minutes later Buddy Sims and Big Time Slim joined Shorty on the bench. Slim said, "Run down who and where." Shorty took a hit from a stick of grass. "You know the big nigger with the muscles that runs the gym behind that big apartment buildin' 'cross from that Kentucky Fried Chicken place?" Buddy took the joint and drew on it. "Sure, he's Isaiah Jones. He fought a couple of pro heavyweight fights back in the early 80s."

Shorty nodded. "Good, my man. Do you all know the dude that flunkeys for Isaiah?"

Slim said, "Sure, he's big like Isaiah & drives an old Buick with KAYO on the plates. His name is Alonzo."

Slim took the joint. Buddy said, "You want 'em both hit? It's gonna be easy to find 'em."

Shorty shook his head. "No, just Isaiah. Do it your way soon — now don't get salty, but I think Isaiah is gone into hidin' after leaving Big Freddy alive. I thought of an easy way to find Isaiah. Wanna hear it?"

Slim laughed. "We ain't got no closed minds. Run it down."

Shorty said, "Alonzo is Isaiah's best friend. He's gonna meet Isaiah to keep him hip to what's happenin' in the gym & in that building that Isaiah manages for the rich old black dude in Beverly Hills. I'm gonna give you five thou now. Say, do you know where Alonzo parks his car? Maybe you could pay some dude you can trust to park and watch Alonzo's car for 50 bucks a day."

Buddy said, "I got a big van that's real nice inside and out. It's got thick carpets, a cot, and other goodies. We'll park in the block where he parks his Buick and live in the van until he takes us to Isaiah. And hey, there ain't no parkin' limit on the west side of Crenshaw."

Shorty counted out 5,000 to each. "This is down payment bread. You get 15 thou a piece comin' when you do the number on Isaiah. Look for Isaiah's 87 Thunderbird comin' and goin' from the garage under the building. He's gone into hidin' if you don't see it at all, and he don't answer that telephone that you call from at the security door." They nodded, stood, and exchanged high fives before they left the park. Shorty left a moment later.

At Daniel Freeman a moment later two black LAPD detectives entered Freddy's room. The tall gaunt one showed crooked yellow teeth. "Hi, Freddy, my man... you got at least one enemy. Who tried to waste you?"

Freddy groaned and used his left hand to lift to a new position, his right arm in a heavy cast up to his neck. "Ross, he jumped me in my dark garage. He didn't say nothin' & he had on a mask. Ain't no way for me to know who the nigger or dirty white cop is who fucked me up."

The paunchy, shorter cop said, "Come on, Freddy. You gotta have some idea about who might have done it. Think hard."

Freddy moaned, "Cecil, my head hurts too much for this shit. I ain't got an enemy I'm hip to. Man, I'm sick."

The cops looked at each other and left the room. Freddy watched them leave and realized that he wouldn't have been attacked by Isaiah if he hadn't met Sabina. He reviewed the early April day when he saw her for the first time. He had put several items in a shopping cart. He was in the fast checkout line. Sabina was directly in front of him waiting to get nine or ten items checked out. She wore white silk shorts and a white lace blouse. Sexy calf-length leather boots encased her tiny feet.

Freddy was fascinated as he eye-swept her mane of golden blonde hair which shimmered nearly to her center-fold waist, her breathtaking sculpted round behind & straight, long curvaceous legs. Was her face a match for the rest of her, he'd ask himself. She reached the checkout stand and faced the clerk at the register. In profile, he knew when he saw the elfish tip tilted nose that her face was irresistibly pretty like the faces of several of the buxom blondes in magazines. In his early teens in jail he had gazed at the paper sexpots while he whipped his dick to an orgasm.

He checked out and rushed to the parking lot to hit on her. She had gotten to the family Thunderbird. He wheeled his cart to the driver's side. He softened his original man's face. "Excuse me young lady... I'm Big Freddy and I'm gonna make a citizen's arrest on you."

She looked startled, "Arrest me? Why? Are you out of your alleged mind." She started the car. He laughed. "I ain't crazy... I'm arresting you for being so beautiful. Gimme your phone number. I gotta lot of sweet things to say to you."

As she started to move the car away she said, "I'm married." He unlocked his Rolls parked two spaces away. He was putting his groceries on the front seat when she saw his Rolls in her side view mirror.

She'd backed up parallel to the Rolls. She said through her open window, "I'm Sabina, Big Freddy. It's a pleasure to meet a man with your style and wit." She leaned and gave him a lavender calling card. "Call me between 10 A.M. & 3 P.M. weekdays. If my husband or little boy answers, hang up. Okay?"

He grinned. "Okay, baby, I understand." She had driven away and he'd sat visualizing what it was going to be like freaking off with such a heavenly package.

Now, an ugly female white nurse came to his bedside to interrupt his bittersweet reverie. "I hope you're feeling better Mr. Evans," she said as she stuck a thermometer in his mouth.

In South Central, on Crenshaw, Buddy Sims and Big Time Slim parked Buddy's huge van in the block where Baptiste's five story building stood. The pair watched Alonzo's Buick with the KAYO letters on its license plate parked in front of the building.

In early evening Isaiah called Alonzo at the gym. "Hey man, look in the safe in our office. There's a big ring of numbered keys for all the apartments. Take mine and get me a couple suits, some shirts, shoes, and my shaving stuff and toothbrush in the bathroom."

Alonzo said, "You lucky you caught me. I was just splittin' for home when you called."

Isaiah said, "Call Marcy and tell her you and the family are invited to have dinner with me and Baptiste."

Alonzo laughed. "Dinner in Beverly Hills? My old lady's gonna faint or think I'm jivin'. I'll bring the stuff & see ya around eight. Ain 't that when you all rich niggers eat?"

Isaiah laughed. "Okay, pal, eight is cool... thanks a lot." He hung up.

Alonzo went into the small office in the corner of the gym. He spun the dial on a medium sized old safe to get Isaiah's front door key.

Buddy went to Isaiah's apartment phone at the security door. He went back to the van when there was no answer. Buddy and Big Time watched Alonzo come out of the building with a large suitcase and get into his Buick. They followed it to Alonzo's modest home on Martin Luther King Boulevard. They parked the van a half block away and waited.

In West Hollywood, Sabina started to get ready to see a play with Lisa and her corporate exec beau. Donald, Lisa's live-in lover, was supposedly in the Big Apple freaking off with a sexy teenage tramp. The phone rang. Sabina picked up. It was Jimmy Coglan. Her lawyer said, "I have good news, Sabina. I just left the U.S. Attorney's office. I was virtually assured that when you go to court in September that the prosecution will not oppose my request for your probation. The condition is that we plead *nolo contendre* to the charge."

Sabina said, "*Nola* what?"

He said, "It's merely legalese for a plea of guilty... In the meantime, don't see Freddy and don't get into any kind of trouble — not even reckless driving. Promise?"

She laughed, "I'm not stupid. I don't want to blow a good break. Thank you." He hung up.

Donald Kusik, gambler/gigolo and once Lisa's doll-faced obsession, had come back from a romantic month in the Big Apple. One of his female pals had called him in New York to tell him that Lisa was cheating on him with a business exec named Brad.

The object of Donald's slavish infatuation was 17-year-old Skye Larson, a statuesque Swede with saucer-light blue eyes and a radiant mane of waist-length platinum blonde hair. Unbeknownst to Donald, she was also a closet-nympho freak prostitute. Donald and she had taken a limo from LAX to West Hollywood. Now he was checking her into a hotel down the street from Lisa's building.

As Donald registered, Skye, posing a few yards behind Donald, in a pink silk micro-mini, bumped her awesomely sculpted behind against the bell captain's crotch. The bell captain directed a bellman to take the couple's luggage to their room.

Donald kissed Skye. "Bye, sweet thing. I'll call and move in with you in a couple of days." She showed TV ad teeth. "You just better do that. I won't be able to sleep without you beside me."

Donald went to Lisa's building. He took the elevator to the penthouse. As he stepped into the entrance hall, he saw a stylish man's straw hat on a rack. He looked into the living room. He went down a hallway toward her closed bedroom door. She wouldn't dare to cheat on him, he thought. He put an ear to the door and heard erotic sounds of lovemaking. He carefully cracked the door and peeped inside.

He saw Brad, the corporate exec and Lisa in bed engaged in an enthusiastic 69. Donald went to his room and got a .22 handgun. When he got back the couple had concluded. Brad had gone into an adjoining bathroom. Donald opened the bedroom door. He pointed the gun at Lisa and fired twice over her head. "You dirty sneakin' tramp. Where is he?" Lisa stood and stared at him with mouth agape.

Sabina was at the mirror making up her face when she heard two muffled gunshots. She rushed out of her bedroom and moved cautiously toward Lisa's room, peeked inside, and saw Donald holding the gun.

Inside Lisa's bedroom, Lisa burst into tears and the wary Romeo locked the bathroom door from the inside. Donald waved the gun. "I'm going to kill you for this."

Sabina lunged into Lisa's bedroom and bear hugged Donald's waist from behind. They tumbled to the carpet. Lisa leaped into the fray. She stomped on his gun hand and, as he lost his grip, snatched the gun. Donald struggled mightily to free himself from the clutches of the women. Lisa hollered, "Brad, help us!"

The tall muscular ex-cop unlocked the door and took the gun. He wore only a bath towel tied around his waist. "Let him up." They did. Brad aimed the pistol at Donald's head with his arms fully extended, holding the weapon in the fashion of a cop. "We're going to your room. You're going to pack your stuff and leave this apartment forever. Make one false move and you're dead. This is your guy, and I could make a citizen's arrest and get you thrown in jail. But if you're a nice boy, I'll let you leave in one piece."

Donald gave Lisa & Sabina a venomous look before he went down the hall to his bedroom, followed by Brad. Brad watched him pack two enormous suitcases. Brad commanded, "Give me your keys to the inside door of the foyer and the key to this apartment."

Donald reached into his pocket and gave Brad the keys. The weight of the suitcases staggered Donald as he went to the elevator. Before he stepped into it Brad said sternly, "Buster, I'll hunt you down and kick the shit out of you if I hear that you bothered those women or returned to this apartment."

Donald glared at him and stepped into the elevator.

At 7:30 P.M., Alonzo and Marcy were in their Buick heading for Beverly Hills with their two children, Alonzo, Jr., five, and Carol, seven. They were followed by Buddy & Slim.

At three minutes to eight the Buick reached the gate at Baptiste's home. Helene buzzed Alonzo through it.

Buddy pulled past the house as the Buick pulled into the driveway and parked beside Isaiah's Thunderbird. They saw Isaiah's car through the steel gate. Slim said, "Ain't we lucky. That's Isaiah's ride in the driveway."

Fifteen minutes later, everyone was seated at the dining room table. Helene had prepared barbecued ribs, mac and cheese, and sweet potatoes topped with marsh-mallows. There were three kinds of salad and home baked applesauce cake with ice cream for dessert.

After dinner the children went into the den to watch a Disney special on TV. The adults stayed at the table sipping after dinner beverages. Baptiste gave Alonzo an envelope. "Alonzo, this is a small token of my apprecia-tion for the great help and friendship you have given Isaiah and the kids at the gym. There's a grand there and I'm going to pay you 300 a week to keep the hallways vacuumed and to look out for my tenants. You know, take any complaints and call in a plumber if someone has a problem you can't handle. Do you want the job?"

Alonzo said, "Sure. Thanks. Me and Marcy can han-dle everything jus' fine. Thank you, Baptiste, and thank you, Helene, for all this righteous food."

Helene said, "I'm so happy you enjoyed it. Thank you."

Shapely pretty mulatto Marcy said, "I don't know when I've enjoyed myself so much. I'm sure Alonzo and I can do a good job."

Isaiah said, "Alonzo what do you think about thumb-tacking a note on that bulletin board near the elevator?

206

Let it say that you are the temporary manager. Sign it and just write that you can be found in the gym."

Alonzo smiled, "That's a good idea. I'm gonna take care of business."

In the van three quarters of a block away Buddy said, "Let's split and come back later when the neighborhood goes to sleep."

Slim lit a crack pipe. "Yeah, ain't no doubt Isaiah is there and that's where the rich black dude lives. We don't want the cops out here to spot us."

Buddy u-turned the van and headed back to South Central. At midnight they picked the door lock and hot-wired an '89 Ford in the garage of a bachelor they knew. He was in the hospital recovering from an accident that happened on his construction job. They drove to Beverly Hills. They parked a half-block away and walked to Baptiste's gate. They peered through the steel bars to see, in the light of a full moon, that Isaiah's car was still parked in the driveway near the house.

They quickly slipped on Dracula & Freddy Krueger masks. They pulled themselves over a six-foot stone wall and dropped into the yard. They wore black shirts, sneakers, trousers, caps, and black cloth gloves. Both carried an automatic pistol with a silencer. They glided like sinister apparitions across the yard toward the big two-story brownstone house.

They went to the back of the house. Five minutes later, they had picked the lock on a heavy back door on the patio. They moved silently through the immense kitchen. They cut the cord of a wall phone. They cat-footed into the dining room.

Helene had left the gleaming white damask table-cloth on the long dining room table. She had cleared it after the dinner with Alonzo's family. She and Isaiah were fast asleep in her quarters.

"Dracula" and "Krueger" crept into the living room. They cut the phone cord there also. Their killer eyes shone eerily through the hideous masks. They decided first to search the second floor for Isaiah. They eased up the long, winding, carpeted staircase. They went down a hallway. They opened the door of Deanna's shrine, then moved on to Baptiste's door. "Krueger," Buddy Sims, turned the knob and opened the door. Baptiste was snoring; he was lying on his side with his back to them. His white hair shone like burnished silver in the pale glow of a night light. "Dracula," Big Time Slim, raised his pistol and aimed it at the back of Baptiste's head.

Buddy whispered, "Don't. He's good and too old to be a problem. He let my sick mama and me stay in a pad in one of his buildings no rent for three months when I was a kid." They noticed the butt of a pearl-handled pistol sticking out from beneath a pillow. Slim stuck it in his waistband. They cut the phone cord before they went to search the other rooms on the second floor. They went down the stairway into the living room. They went through a door off the living room into a long hallway.

It was lighted by a row of amber bulbs in simulated candles mounted on the wall.

They went to the end of the hall and opened the door to Helene's living room. They saw an open bedroom door. They moved to it and peeped inside.

Isaiah was asleep holding Helene in his arms. The interlopers saw Helene stir and mutter excitedly something weird, like a holy roller speaking in tongues. "Yoo la oh loas!"

The bedlam of the voices of the loas invaded her sleep. "Wake up! Wake up!" Helene bolted out of Isaiah's arms and sat upright in the bed. She stared at the monster figures in the doorway leveling their guns. Isaiah sat up, rubbing sleep from his eyes. "Hey, you guys, what the fuck…"

Slim's silenced gun made a sound like a giant snake's hissing. The bullet made a round hole in the center of Isaiah's forehead. Tiny rivulets of blood ran down his astonished face. As he slumped backward, Buddy shot him through the heart.

Helene screamed and sprang off the bed to attack them with her long fingers clawing air. Slim sidestepped her and smashed the barrel of his heavy pistol against the side of her head. She fell to the carpet and lay still as if she had been poleaxed.

Slim leveled his gun at her head. He pulled on the trigger. He tried harder to fire the gun. The trigger wouldn't budge.

Buddy grabbed his arm. "Don't do it, Slim! She's too pretty, and she's black."

Slim aimed at a wall and sent a round into the wall. He said, "I don't understand why the trigger fucked up. This piece has never failed before." They cut the bedroom phone cord and quickly left the house.

They took off their masks. Slim dropped Baptiste's pearl handled pistol into some shrubbery near the wall. They went over the wall and walked casually down the deserted street to the stolen Ford. Buddy drove the car to a garage in South Central.

Four minutes later Helene got groggily to her feet. She couldn't look at Isaiah. He was a crumbled, blood-soaked heap in the bed. She ran, with blood streaming from her head, to Baptiste. She shook him awake. He recoiled from her blood-stained head and gown.

"Isaiah's dead!"

Baptiste felt his ailing heart jolt his chest. His elevated blood pressure almost knocked him out. He sat up with his chest heaving. "Who? Where are they now?"

Her legs gave way. She sat on the side of the bed. "They wore monster masks... I think they've gone."

Baptiste picked up the phone on a nightstand. He banged it down. "They cut the phone lines. Are you sure Isaiah's dead?"

She burst into tears. "They shot him in the head, and I think in the heart."

Baptiste cradled her bloody head against his chest. "Was one of them a big fat slob?"

She groaned in pain. "No. One was big, husky, but not fat."

"Helene, can you walk across the street to wake up the Blankenships?"

She nodded yes.

"Then go tell them what happened and to call the police."

Helene stumbled several times as she hurried from the house. Baptiste reached under a pillow for his pistol. Realizing it was gone, he went to the dresser and took a .38 from a drawer. He then went slowly down the staircase.

Outside on the street Helene talked to two Beverly Hills uniformed cops. They had been driving toward her on routine patrol when she opened the gate to cross the street. The officers drove with her through the open gate to the house. Baptiste was on his knees beside Helene's bed. He was pounding the floor with his fists and weeping wildly. "I promise you son, I'll kill that fat bastard for this," he blubbered.

One of the cops used his car phone to call for an ambulance before Helene took them to her bedroom. The paramedics arrived one minute later. One of them, a slender woman with short brunette hair, lifted Isaiah's wrist to find a pulse. She shook her head. "He's gone."

One of the cops leaned and stared at the hole in Isaiah's head and the hole in his pajama top at the heart area. "Don't touch anything. This is a case for homicide."

The other cop left to go to the patrol car to call it in.

Baptiste struggled and tried to slug the paramedics and the cop when they moved him from the bedside. The woman paramedic injected him with a sedative. The cop and the other paramedic half carried Baptiste to his bed.

Within 45 minutes, murder in Beverly Hills had drawn a curious crowd and TV camera crews to the street outside the house. Homicide and police photographers were taking shots of the crime scene.

Helene had returned home after being taken by the paramedics to the hospital for stitches and attention to her head wound.

The coroner's death wagon would soon come to take Isaiah's body to the morgue for an autopsy. A detective took notes in the living room as he questioned Helene.

Two hours later the house was quiet and Isaiah's body had been removed. Helene lay with her head bandaged staring at the ceiling beside sedated Baptiste.

Chapter 11

Freddy was released from the hospital the following Saturday morning, a week to the day after Isaiah shot him. He lay in his bed feeling weak and sick. The long cast was still on his broken right wrist and shoulder, all the way to the base of his neck. His head wound still had a medium bandage.

At 11:00 A.M. Esther took Payback Shorty to Freddy's bedroom. Shorty sat down on the side of the bed. "Buddy and Slim took care of the Isaiah business fine and righteous."

Freddy nodded. "I got hip to it on TV. Bring me that leather shoulder bag outta the top drawer of the dresser."

Shorty went and brought back the bag. Freddy counted out 40,000 for the hit, plus 15,000 for Shorty's 10 grand outlay for the down payment on the contract.

Shorty put both wads in his jacket pocket. Freddy counted out another 10,000 on the bed. "I want a guy named Leeds hit."

Shorty said, "Who is the dude?"

Freddy replied. "He's just a white dude that was busted with my lady. This is the down bread, and tell Buddy and Slim they got 15 thou apiece comin' when they hit him."

Shorty scooped up the bills. "Where's his pad? And rundown somethin' on him." Freddy started to reply when Esther knocked and opened the door. She scolded, "Shorty, you said you jus' wanted a second with that boy. He jus' got home and he's weak. Will you please come back later next week."

Freddy waved his good left arm. "Okay, Mama, he's leavin'."

Shorty stood up and Esther left the room. Freddy got Stokes' report on Leeds from the shoulder bag. He gave it to Shorty. "Everything is in those papers about him — don't give the papers to Buddy & Slim. Tell 'em what they need to know. I'll lay a coupla grand on you after they…"

Shorty said, "I go for that. See ya," before he left the room.

Twenty minutes later Portillo called. Sweat dampened Freddy's palms when he heard the low, steel-edged voice. "Hello, my friend. I have been much concerned about you and your health. It is very urgent that I see you here Sunday, tomorrow morning, at 11 A.M."

Freddy said, "Mr. Portillo, my right arm is in a cast. I'm…"

Portillo hung up on him. Freddy lay in a sudden welter of hot sweat. Had Portillo decided to kill him when he went behind those walls? Did he have to obey Portillo's command? No, he thought, if he was ready to lose the source of dope for the homeboys and the big bucks he got from them. He told himself no, if he was ready to risk a bloody visit in the night from Emilio and Frank that could leave Esther, Junior, & himself dead. He had to go to Portillo. He'd have to risk it and kiss Portillo's ass black and blue to try to survive. He wouldn't have any power. He couldn't stay king of the ghetto if he lost the loyalty and dependence of the homeboys. He'd be just another fearful resident in the crossfire of gang war.

Big Time Slim was finishing dinner in the early evening after Freddy was visited by Payback. He and his woman Lois were at the table in the kitchen of their tiny but neat apartment on Figueroa Street in South Central. Lois, a pretty, tall, curvy, dark-skinned teener, held Slim's 8-month-old son on her lap as she breastfed him.

"Baby, you stayin' home tonight with us?" she asked with pleading eyes.

Slim, seated beside her, leaned and gave her a long, passionate kiss. "Yeah, sweet and beautiful, we goin' take care of some righteous bed business tonight."

She gave him the baby and got up to clear the table. The phone rang on the wall. She picked up. It was Buddy Sims. "Hiya, Lois. Put Slim on." She frowned and took the baby. "Buddy wants you."

Slim went to the phone. "What's happenin', Buddy?"

Buddy chortled, "Man, we so lucky, it's unreal. Meet me right away at my house. Shorty just left five thou down apiece for a new job, and 15 apiece after we do it." Slim hung up and kissed Lois, seated at the table, giving baby Leonard seconds from her breast.

Slim looked at the floor. "I gotta go, Lois."

"When you gonna get back?"

He grinned. "Maybe a couple hours… maybe longer… maybe sooner. Baby, Daddy's gonna take you out of this dump in a month and move inna fine pad on the west side. I love you." He went toward the front door. He said, "Bye, Cinderella," to a grey hamster with a white front foot who was running on a wheel in its cage. He left the house and gunned his Mercedes away.

In the Hollywood Hills, Leeds, aka George Nelson, had just finished a conference with DEA agents Martinez and Reed. Nelson walked them to their car. Martinez said, "George, I'll call you if anything dramatic develops…" He paused to look at his watch. "Uh oh, we're already 15 minutes late to relieve Grigsby and Constanza on Sabina. Grigsby foams at the mouth when we don't show on time."

Nelson laughed. "I know, Grigsby was my partner for a year. Take care."

Reed drove away. Nelson went into the house and stopped in the hallway leading to his bedroom to activate an alarm system of invisible infrared beams of light that would sound a strident alarm in his bedroom if anyone came onto the premises.

Two swiveling TV cameras were mounted in tall oak trees at the front *&* back of the house. One of the TV screen monitors was in the bedroom. Nelson lay in bed reading a new publication — *Analysis of the Criminal Mind.*

At midnight, Buddy *&* Slim drove to the Hollywood Hills. Inside his bedroom, Nelson had fallen asleep.

"There's the dude's white jag in the driveway," Slim said as Buddy drove the stolen Ford past Nelson's house. Buddy parked 200 yards away. They got out and put on their monster masks. They wore the same black outfits they had worn when they hit Isaiah. They swiftly moved into Nelson's front yard. The alarm woke him.

Nelson got up and took his .357 Magnum from the dresser. He stood and watched the invaders on the monitor screen go around the house holding their guns, to the rear of it. He watched them break a glass patio door near the lock and come into the house. He pressed a button that blackened all the TV monitors throughout the house.

Nelson then went into a closet across the hall from his bedroom and shut the door. In the darkness several minutes later, he heard their feet on the hardwood of the hallway when they went to look into his bedroom.

"Maybe he ain't home. Rich white folks got two and three cars. Maybe he's drinkin' champagne and suckin' some society bitch's pussy," Nelson heard Slim say as they passed.

Buddy said, "Yeah, let's go to the front room and smoke some dope while we wait for…"

Nelson stepped out of the closet and leveled the Magnum at their backs with both arms extended. "Drop your guns and hit the floor on your bellies, facing me."

The pair froze for an instant before they both spun around to fire at Nelson.

Nelson's gun fired five times in rapid succession. Slim fell dead with a bullet through his right eye. Buddy fell, fatally wounded by a bullet into his aorta.

Nelson kicked away their guns and stooped beside them. He stripped off their masks and saw they were so young. He shook his head and went to the phone to call the LAPD homicide division. Then he awakened Wiggins at home to inform him of the incident.

In Lisa's penthouse, Sabina sat in the living room with Lisa & Brad, who had evicted Donald at gunpoint several days before. Brad drained his champagne glass and looked at his watch. He stood. "It's after 1 A.M. I'll have to leave you lovely ladies." Lisa walked him to the private elevator. They kissed before he stepped into it. "Call me tomorrow sweet daddy long legs," Lisa said as the elevator closed and started its descent.

Lisa staggered as she went back to join Sabina on the sofa. Sabina studied her face. "Lisa, are you sure you've gotten over Donald?"

Lisa poured champagne into a glass. "Absolutely. Why?"

Sabina hesitated. "I saw him a couple of times going into that hotel down the street." Lisa leaned toward Sabina. "So what? Was he alone?"

Sabina lit a cigarette. "No, he had a young thing with him."

Lisa laughed too loudly. "How, uh, old was she?"

Sabina giggled. "Lisa, you're not over him completely."

Lisa waved a hand in the air. "That's nonsense. I'm just curious."

Sabina let her sweat it out for a long moment. "She was 17, maybe 18, and so pretty I hated her guts when I saw her."

Lisa got up. "You know Sabina, you're so much fun, I've got a headache. I'm going to bed." She left the living room.

Sabina sat drinking champagne and thinking about Eric & Isaiah. Soul-deep guilt triggered a flood of bitter tears.

In his hotel room down the block from Lisa's building, Donald sat on the side of the bed. He was about to pitch a big buck scheme to Skye, his teenage sweetie. She sat up in bed in black panties & bra. Her big blue-green eyes sparkled as she gave him her complete attention.

"Do you know what a fence does?" he asked.

She replied rapidly. "Sure, they buy stolen stuff."

He toyed with her pink garters. "Do you realize how beautiful you are?" She giggled. "Of course."

He looked into her eyes. "You're too beautiful to turn tricks like you were doing when I met you. I've got a smoother, cleaner angle for us to get some big bucks."

She looked puzzled. "How? Donald, I'm not gonna help you rob banks. I'm allergic to jail."

He smiled and took a vial of chloral hydrate capsules from his shirt pocket. "We'll be moving so fast the cops won't have a chance to bust us. Every one of these capsules can bring us a 15 thou Rolex watch or big cash and credit cards."

She stared at him, completely puzzled. He said, "I've got a list of bars and restaurants in Malibu and Beverly Hills where big shot middle-aged guys hang out. You play the innocent little square & let them pick you up. Then you let them con you into a hotel or motel room. Naturally, you suggest taking champagne. You undress and rattle their brains to distract them. You drop one of these quick dissolving capsules into their glass."

She frowned and interrupted him. "Stop it, Donald! I could go to prison for crimes like that... Go try to score for some coke."

He patted her leg. "I'll go in a few minutes. As I was about to say, after you give them the capsule, they'll stay out for hours. You strip them of cash, jewelry, and credit cards. I can sell the jewelry to a fence and the credit cards to a group that will buy furs and jewelry with the cards and pay us a percentage. Most of the guys you'll meet will be married & won't be inclined to make a police complaint. It's foolproof, beautiful. You won't go to prison... Will you do it for us?"

She leaned and kissed him. "I think so. I'll let you know when you get back with the coke."

He put on his tan, tropical suit coat and left the room. On the elevator he thought about his skimpy 500-dollar bankroll. He needed her to start playing the knockout drop game as early as tomorrow.

He went to his rented white BMW convertible. He drove toward Sunset and Vine to score for cocaine.

Immediately after he left, Skye called the bell captain in his room at her hotel. He answered sleepily, "Yeah? Larry here."

Skye said, "This is Skye. Come up here right away." He hung up.

Three minutes later she let him in, wearing pajamas and robe. She kissed his cheek and took his hand. She led him to the sofa. They sat down. "What's wrong doll?" he asked as he cupped her hands in his.

"I'm leaving my boyfriend. I need to make some bread. You got any ideas?"

He thought for a moment. "I could move you into a room upstairs. My uncle is on the desk from 11 to 7 in the morning. He knows a lot of johns. Kermit, the guy on the desk when my shift starts from 7 to late afternoon, sometimes until 6, knows a lot of johns. I know a few myself. I could send customers to you that would pay 50 to a 100 bucks for a quickie. You give me 25 percent and we got a deal."

She said, "We got a deal." She scribbled a note to Donald. "Sorry love, to split like a coward, but I just can't risk prison, even for a dreamboat like you. Skye."

Within minutes they had packed her things into suitcases and she was installed in an upstairs room. Larry kissed her and said, "I'll call the bell stand and desk to give instructions to the two night bellmen to tell your boyfriend that you took a cab for LAX."

Larry left. She went to bed.

An hour later Donald keyed into his room. He sat on the side of the bed waiting for Skye to come out of the bathroom. He noticed and picked up the note. His hand trembled as he read it. He sat for several minutes like a statue before he called the desk. "Did my wife leave the hotel?"

Kermit, the old man said, "Your wife left for the airport more than a half hour ago." Donald hung up. He had never been more depressed and panicked. He had only 400 dollars after scoring for the coke. His shoulders slumped like he was an old man as he got up to go into the bathroom. Heavy stress always gave him diarrhea.

He came out and picked up the phone. He called his mother Victoria collect in Boston, Mass. Donald heard the long-distance operator say it was a collect call from Donald Kusik. A familiar butler's voice answered, "Mrs. Victoria Kusik will accept... One moment please."

A moment later Victoria came to the phone. "Oh, dear boy, I've been so worried about you. It was simply cruel of you not to call me for the last three months. You're not in jail, are you?"

His eyes filled with tears. "No, mother, I've had a run of bad luck. I'm coming home to stay."

She exclaimed joyfully, "Oh, you angel! Hurry! Should I send you airfare?"

He sighed, "No, I have enough money for that. I love you mother."

She said softly, "I love you very much." They hung up.

He packed his bags and called LAX. There was a flight leaving for Boston at 3 A.M. He called the car rental agency and told them to pick up the BMW in the hotel parking lot and bill him at his mother's address.

He called for a bellhop to get his bags. Fifteen minutes later he was in a cab to LAX. He was happy to be leaving West Hollywood, the supermarket of broken hearts and dreams.

Chapter 12

In Baldwin Hills at 10:45 the next morning, Portillo, Emilio, & Frank waited for Freddy to arrive. As Esther and Junior helped Freddy into the Rolls she pleaded, "Freddy, come back in the house and go to bed. Why do you have to go out in the shape you in?"

He kissed her cheek. "I gotta go, Mama. I jus' gotta go."

Junior said, "Daddy, grandma's right. Stay home and I'll read to you."

Esther shut the car door. "When you gonna get back?"

He started the car. "I dunno. I gotta see a lady after my first appointment … I guess I'll be back 'roun three. Bye, Mama, bye Junior."

They waved as he backed out down the driveway to the street. They watched the Rolls disappear.

He drove with his good left arm to Portillo's house. Emilio and Frank were standing outside in front of the house. They helped him out of the car. Emilio said, "Freddy, you look like you got hit by a fuckin' train."

Frank goaded, "I hope the husband of the all-American girl didn't cut off your pecker." They howled at that crack as they led Freddy into the den.

Portillo sat with a bland expression on his face. He wore red satin lounging pajamas. Freddy studied his face as he sat down beside him. Emilio and Frank left them. Portillo gave him a big smile, too big. And Portillo's eyes were cold. "My friend, it grieves me to see you in this condition. I tried to save you much misery. But you…"

Freddy looked like he was about to fall to his knees and beg to be forgiven. "Mr. Portillo, I was an asshole dummy not to take your advice on Leeds. I hope you will find it in your ticker to forgive me. I'm ready to do whatever you tell me to get outta this mess."

Portillo scooted to him & embraced him for an instant. "Freddy, dear friend, I've already forgiven you. Have you had any ideas about how to solve your problems?"

Freddy said, "I ain't been thinkin' my best since I got banged up. Tell me what to do."

Portillo smiled. He was going to throw verbal garbage and con Freddy's way to relax him and make him feel sure that no harm would come to him. Then, at the end of their conversation, Freddy would ask for rock laced with China White heroin, and Portillo would give him rock laced with mellow China White and crystallized cyanide. "Freddy, I'm very optimistic about Sabina."

Freddy's tight face relaxed. "You ain't kiddin, Mr. Portillo?"

Portillo crossed his legs. "No… Maybe she is loyal and cares about you. Perhaps the hounds can't persuade her to turn against you. Perhaps…"

Freddy cut him off. "I got it! If I married her, she couldn't testify against me."

Portillo slapped his palm against Freddy's back. "That's precisely what I was going to say."

There was a long silence as Portillo threw his head back and stared at the ceiling, apparently in deep thought. Portillo sighed. "It is not a good idea after all. Some Anglo women, in my opinion, are good fucks... Many of them are good and loyal, but how do you know apples that are only rotten inside from a big barrel of apples? To risk marriage to one of them is unthinkable, even in your case. My friend, most of the adultery and painful divorces in this country occur among Anglos. The bad Anglo broads are greedy for money and will marry, suck, and fuck the devil for material things. Blacks should marry Blacks, Anglos Anglos, and Latinos should marry only Latinos. I would advise you not to risk torture as the husband of Sabina Jones. Think about where the late Mr. Jones is now and how he got there."

Freddy looked very confused. "What should I do?"

Portillo took a .38 from beneath a sofa cushion. He wiped it thoroughly with a handkerchief. He extended it on the handkerchief on his palm. He said, "Be patient and use this to get rid of her. It can't be traced." He shrugged. "As I said, she may stand up to the hounds for you... but can you gamble on that? Think about it and take action." He stood. Freddy put the pistol in his waistband as he struggled to his feet. He shook Portillo's extended hand.

"Thanks, Mr. Portillo. I'm gonna do the do on her when I get the chance."

Freddy thought about Sabina. She was going to want some rock with China White. Portillo walked with Freddy to the front door. Just before Freddy stepped out, he said, "Mr. Portillo, you got any of that special rock you can spare?"

Portillo took the deadly vial from his pajama pocket. "This is top quality. It's just a little, the last I have. So, save it and smoke it with her to relax her. Maybe you can do it then if she isn't wired and she assures you she's lost any tail."

Freddy put the vial in his coat pocket. "Thank you, Mr. Portillo," he said as he went to his car. The right sleeve of his white tropical suit flapped. Emilio and Frank helped him into the Rolls. Freddy drove through the gate, opened by the paunchy yardman who also handled the pack of killer Rottweilers.

Freddy knew that he wouldn't kill Sabina as he drove through the balmy first day of September. He had bought the dream she had put into his head. He was going to marry her. He couldn't dump her. He needed her. He was in love.

He would quit dealing Portillo's drugs and go to Paris and Rome with Sabina after Coglan got her cut loose on probation. He'd agree to make the 20-key deal with Lisa to please Sabina. Then he'd slip the 8-carat diamond ring in his pocket on her finger and ask her to marry him.

He'd bought the hundred grand ring from a black bandit for five grand. The bandit's M.O. had been to

follow wealthy couples from fashionable restaurants &
rob them at gunpoint when they drove to their homes in
Malibu and Beverly Hills. The bandit had been shot to
death while fleeing police. Sabina would never have to
pawn the ring so there would be no reason to rundown
its hot history.

In Beverly Hills, ailing Baptiste and Helene left for
South Central in a rented, inconspicuous dark blue
Ford. They were going to collect rent money from the
tenants in the dozen buildings Baptiste owned. Helene
would be the permanent collector of monies when he
left soon for Sugar Hill to live with Opal. They had not
mentioned Isaiah's name to each other since the day before when he had attended crowded memorial services
for him before Angelus shipped his body to his Aunt
Melba in Georgia.

Baptiste carried a gun as he & Helene moved through
the ghetto collecting money.

Freddy drove into the parking lot of the Sweet Dreams
Motel. Sabina watched him arrive. She went to help him
get out of the car when she saw his bandaged head and
right arm in a cast and sling.

He fell into a chair inside the room. "Freddy, are you
all right?" she asked with genuine concern since the
kilo deal was dangling.

He was out of breath. "Sure, I'm jus' weak... Take off
your threads. I ain't in the mood for sex. I jus' wanna pin
your fine body."

She took off her clothes and did a cute pirouette before him. He gazed at her nude splendor. She wasn't wearing a wire, he was glad to notice. She hadn't and wouldn't flip on him.

He put her on his lap. "I'm gonna have someone deliver the keys to you tomorrow in that grocery lot where we first met, at noon... Drive to the Crenshaw Mall parking lot near The Broadway. Leave it and go into the mall and buy makeup and some other little shit. Slip out a door on the opposite side of the mall from where you parked and walk to a ride one of my homeboys is gonna park on Marlton, a side street. There'll be a piece of cardboard taped on the inside of a corner of the windshield. The DEA will be waitin' and watchin' your parked ride in the mall lot. Then you drive to the grocery lot. Got that?"

She pecked his face with kisses. "Darling, that's brilliant."

He reached his good left hand into his pocket and slipped the fiery ring on her finger.

She exclaimed, "Oh my God! It's magnificent!"

He whispered into her ear. "Baby, will you marry me, soon?"

She kissed him with fake ardor. "I will! I will, darling... soon as Coglan cuts me loose."

He stroked her pubic hair. "I been wantin' to hook up with a package like you since I was a kid."

She couldn't resist saying, "Well heah I is honey chile."

He pinched her thigh hard. "You some kinda racist bitch? Don't fuck me over like that." He went on, "When we get back from seein' all that stuff in Paris and Rome, maybe we can make some kids... A whole house full together. Is that righteous with you, baby?"

She forced a smile. "I'd love it, darling." She leaned to the bed and got her purse. She took out her pipe. "Did you bring any special rock so we can celebrate?"

He took his pipe from his coat pocket with the vial of Portillo's deadly rock. She put a rock in their pipes & lit them. They inhaled deeply and greedily. Seconds later, sweat drenched their bodies. They rolled agonized eyes at each other. They fell to the carpet. Their bodies jerked spastically. They vomited and made horrible choking sounds. Minutes later they lay still, their mouths agape, dribbling vomit as their dead eyes stared at the ceiling. The hot diamond on her blued finger shot pastel skyrockets of light in the dim sleaze of the room. Their infatuation with the most vicious of assassins — cocaine — had really brought them down.

DEA agents Martinez and Reed had sat in their car parked a half block away for an hour and a half. Martinez said, "She should have been out by now... He's in no shape for sex. Something's wrong."

Reed got out of the car. "I'll have the motel clerk knock and find out what's going on." He went to the bulletproof glass at the office window. He showed his badge and said to the Asian clerk, "Go to the pretty blonde's room and knock. If you don't get an answer, go in and check the room."

The clerk took a passkey off a rack and went to the room. Reed watched him knock three times before he keyed into the room. A moment later the old man came out excitedly waving his arms.

Reed went into the room and saw the bodies. He told the clerk to shut the door. He went back to Martinez, stuck his head into the car. "Our case against Freddy is dead in there. They're both dead." The agent called Wiggins and the LAPD on the car phone before they went back into the death room.

In Malibu, a beach town near L.A., an affluent colony of movie celebrities, big shot producers, and business moguls lived in very expensive homes. Bradford Hansberry, Lisa Lundgren's current heartthrob, lived in an imposing two-story white brick home near the Pacific Ocean.

It was several hours after Sabina and Freddy had been found dead. Bradford lounged on the sofa in the den in candy-striped pajamas and an indigo satin robe. He didn't feel up to par. He was still somewhat hungover from drinking at a party in Lisa's penthouse the night before. He was glad he didn't have to drive into downtown L.A. to his office.

He headed a company that marketed picture books for the blind. On the first page of the books was a braille touch index of substances that felt like sand, cloth, wood, and even water. There was also a color chart of raised dots and dashes to let the blind see the various colors of the pictures.

Sue Hansberry, Brad's once shapely wife, sat beside him spooning rocky road ice cream into her cute mouth, the last thing about her face that was still attractive except for her violet eyes, like Liz's. She finished the ice cream, picked up the TV remote control. She got a late afternoon newscast. She got up. "Brad, you want me to bring you something?"

He shook his head. "No thanks, honey. I'm trying to lose a couple of pounds." She gave him an odd look. "You look just perfect to me... I'm the one that needs to get back the figure that I had when we met, remember?"

"Sure, you had the most luscious figure in all of our high school. You're still beautiful to me at any weight."

She took her ice cream dish to the kitchen for a refill. He watched her thick legs and thighs bulging white shorts. Her bobbed hair was prematurely snow white. He cared for her deeply, but the flame of his sexual desire had been almost extinguished. He was 52 and she was a year younger. She looked like she could be his mother. His eyes were suddenly riveted to the TV screen. A TV anchorwoman's voice-over was explaining how Sabina Nilsson Jones and a notorious black gangster and dope trafficker had been found dead in a South Central L.A. motel. A videotape played of their corpses in body bags being lifted into a coroner's ambulance.

Brad sat there, stunned, when Sue returned to sit beside him. He had been fooled completely by Sabina. He'd thought she was a clean-cut, well-bred young lady like her best friend Lisa. Dead in a South Central motel with a nigger, he thought. He shuddered and his hand shook as he lit a cigarette. Sue stopped spooning ice cream into her mouth. "Bradford, are you all right?"

He struggled to smile. "I'm okay... I just remembered that I promised an important client I'd play a few fast holes of golf with him." He glanced at his watch. "It's only 4 o'clock. I've got time to keep my word." He got up and went into his bedroom to dress casually in blue cotton slacks, knit short-sleeved shirt, and white cap. He brought his golf bag with him into the den. He kissed Sue's forehead. "Be back shortly, dear."

She burped. "Hon, bring me a dozen chocolate donuts." "How about three donuts," he said. She pouted. "All right." He left the house and went to the garage. He drove his black Porsche away from Lisa's penthouse. His ex-cop's reflex reasoning was that the probability of guilt by association applied to Lisa. If Sabina, her best friend since girlhood, fucked niggers, then hadn't, couldn't Lisa be fucking one now? The thought that he had been so naive to be taken in by the Texas sexpots enraged him. Lisa had sat on his face during their unin-

235

hibited sex parties. However, he would be cool and quiz her skillfully. There was a slight chance that she was innocent of sexual coupling with black men. He thought of his only child, twenty-five-year-old Dawn. He had disowned her when she had married a black man five years ago.

Brad parked near Lisa's building. She was in her bedroom when he rang her bell. She said into the intercom speaker, "Yes, who is it?" He said, "Brad." She buzzed him in and wondered if she heard something in his voice she hadn't heard before.

He came into the bedroom with a smile on his movie-star handsome face. He sat on the side of the bed and leaned to press his mouth against hers for an instant. She noticed a subtle tenseness in his body and his green eyes had a frigid overcast even as he smiled. She put a palm to her mouth and yawned. "I'm hung over... but the fun we had last night is worth less than a wonderful feeling today."

She picked up the phone and dialed Sabina's room. The operator said the phone was off the hook or out of order. She hung up. "Brad, would you mind going to Sabina's room. Tell her to put her phone on the hook and ask her to start some coffee."

His penetrating eyes bored into hers. "She isn't in her bedroom, Lisa... she was found dead around noon in a South Central motel with a notorious black dope dealer."

Lisa shook her head vigorously. "Brad, it's someone else with her name. Sabina's in the guest room." She started to get out of bed. He shoved her back to her pillow. They showed a mug shot of Sabina taken at the Federal lockup. "She got busted the week I was in Mexico on business. Why didn't you mention it when I got back? Didn't you know she had a seven-kilo case pending?"

Lisa's eyes hardened. "Yes, I knew, but why are you asking me all these questions? I wouldn't gossip to you or anyone about my best friend." Tears rolled down her cheeks. "Poor lovable Sabina... what happened?"

His cop mentality was rapacious. "They found a vial of rock cocaine poisoned with cyanide. She's married to a black man who was recently killed... have black men ever come here?"

Lisa was getting angry. "No, Brad. Not ever. Let's talk about something else, okay?" He shaped a grotesque smile. "I want to know how a young lady of your apparent class *&* high morality could claim a dog like Sabina as best friend. You've got to somehow be involved in her lifestyle. Have you ever been in bed with a black man?"

She lost it. "Listen, Saint Bradford, so what if I fucked every black man in South Central? Let's talk fuckin' morality. Have you got a married jerk's kind of goddamn license to get in my bed, fuck me, and commit adultery?"

He opened his mouth to speak, but Lisa cut him off. "I heard from a friend who knows that you're a murderer. You shot an unarmed black juvenile when he talked back to you. You didn't quit the LAPD, Brad, you got kicked out. Don't let me hear your mouth say Sabina's name ever again. Maybe you should get laid by someone in your age category — a nice moral senior citizen bitch. You..."

The intercom panel lit up and buzzed. "Yes, who is it?" A gruff masculine voice said through the foyer speaker, "Wilson & Browning, homicide officers." She buzzed them into the building. Brad got to his feet. "I've got an appointment. You're the one with all the information they want." He left the room.

The elevator opened and the two middle-aged, heavy-set white detectives in dark suits stepped out. Wilson, the rather nice looking one, walked with a slight limp, a souvenir of a bank robber's bullet, gotten when he was a robbery detective. He stepped in front of Brad so he couldn't enter the elevator. "Who are you?"

Brad said, "I'm Bradford Hansberry, an acquaintance of Lisa Lundgren's."

Browning, the evil-faced one said, "Did you know Sabina Nilsson Jones?" Brad hesitated, "No, not really. I saw her twice here at parties."

Wilson said, "Show me some I.D., Mr. Hansberry." Brad showed him his driver's license and credit cards. Wilson stepped aside... "We may want to talk to you in the near future." Brad gave them his office card. "I'd appreciate it if you contacted me to talk at the office."

Browning smiled slyly. "You're married, you rascal." Brad laughed shakily as he stepped into the elevator.

Lisa stood in the hallway wearing a robe, waiting to lead them into the living room to tell them what she knew about Sabina's secret life — practically nothing.

Freddy's mother, Esther, and Junior sat on the living room sofa. They stared through a window at the street waiting to see Freddy's car pull into the driveway. The phone rang on the coffee table. Esther picked up. One of her elderly friends was calling. "Esther, this is Sedalia, and I been prayin' for you and Junior and for Freddy's soul. The Lord sometimes takes our loved ones from us for His mysterious reasons. We just gotta have faith that he knows best."

Esther said loudly, "You heard somethin' bad happened to my son?"

Sedalia was silent for a long moment. "I'm so sorry, Esther. I thought you had heard that Freddy was, uh, found, uh, with a young white woman, dead."

Jolts of intense pain hammered Esther's chest. She gasped. "Sedalia, how you know it's true about Freddy?"

Sedalia sobbed, "Oh, Esther, it's true. I heard it on TV a few minutes ago. They showed 'em takin' out the body bags from a motel on the way to the morgue. Esther, I wish I hadn't tole you first. I'm comin' to pray with you."

Esther dropped the phone and fell to the carpet clutching her chest. Junior kneeled beside her. "What happened to Daddy, Grandma? Grandma, are you havin' another heart attack?" She waved a trembling hand toward the phone. "Call 911!" In confused anxiety, he misdialed twice before he reached the clearing facility for emergencies in L.A. county. A crisp female voice answered, "This is 911, what's the problem?" Junior was weeping, "My grandma is havin' a heart attack." The voice said calmly, "Someone will come right away. Give me her name and the address where she is now." Junior gave the information.

Esther was unconscious on the floor and her breathing was raspy and uneven. Junior was sure she was dying. He looked in Esther's phone book for Sedalia's number. He dialed it and got no answer. A moment later the doorbell rang. It was stooped 75-year-old Sedalia and her son Willie, a tall graying man of 50.

Junior let them in. Willie lifted Esther to lie on the sofa. Junior said, "I called 911. I hope Grandma don't die before they get here... What did you tell Grandma about Daddy?"

Sedalia and Willie looked at each other. Willie put his arm around Junior on the sofa. "Your dad got a very bad break. They found him dead in the Sweet Dreams Motel with a white woman... Junior, it's hard to face, but you gotta be strong because life ain't fair all the time."

Junior wept uncontrollably against Willie's chest. "Who killed Daddy?" Willie held him close.

"They don't know yet for sure what happened."

The keening of an ambulance could be heard coming from a block away. Shortly, it pulled into the driveway. Two white male paramedics came through the open front door. They quickly examined Esther and gave her an injection and placed an oxygen mask on her face.

"Where you takin' her?" Junior asked.

One of the paramedics said, "Midway Emergency." They put her on a stretcher and wheeled her out to the ambulance. They drove away fast with the siren keening. A small crowd of neighbors went back into their homes after the ambulance left.

Willie and Sedalia stayed to comfort and pray with Junior.

In Baldwin Hills, Portillo sat in the den with Emilio and Frank. They had heard the newscast about Freddy and Sabina. Frank said, "Mr. Portillo, you're a genius. All our problems are solved."

Portillo frowned, "You're wrong, Frank. Sometimes a solved problem gives birth to new problems. The hounds won't really buy a theory of double suicide after the autopsies. They'll know that someone gave them the cyanide rock... proving who did will be impossible, of course. But the intensified attention of the hounds is not a good thing for us. Also, we do have another problem after Freddy's departure."

Emilio piped up. "I know what that is, Mr. Portillo." Portillo smiled, "Tell me Emilio." Emilio said, "We need a replacement for Freddy in South Central to supply the street dealers."

Portillo said, "You're right. Any ideas about who could fill such an important position?"

Emilio's deep thinking stalled a quick response. "Well, uh, since Whitey Ferguson is dead, maybe Wade Johnson would fit the spot. I've always seen him sober, and he's a fast thinker. He's got no broad problems and he lives with his mother. Freddy put him in charge of his stash house a couple of years ago."

Frank said, "Wade's a strong, stand-up guy. He's a serious dude."

Portillo said, "He may be our man. However, I never make the same mistake twice. If I decide that Wade is in, you both will make all business arrangements with him. I don't want to meet him at all. He could find himself an all-American girl like Freddy and make me vulnerable to the hounds again... Go through an extra tricky routine before you meet with Wade to lose any hound that tries to tail you."

The pair left to go to their bungalow to plan strategy and procedure for a private meeting with Wade without DEA intrusion.

In Beverly Hills, Baptiste and Helene sat in the living room on the sofa after watching the newscast about the Sweet Dreams Motel incident. "Baptiste, I'm so glad you didn't have to kill Freddy."

He said, "Helene, I'm glad Freddy is dead, but his boss, the bastard that had to give the okay for the hit on poor Isaiah, is still alive and living better than well in Baldwin Hills. He's got a young girlfriend in Bellflower according to that investigator's report that Isaiah left with me. She's got a French name. I'll call the information operator to get her address. I'll look at the report for her name after I polish up a plan to make Portillo pay for Isaiah's death."

Helene looked shocked. "Oh Baptiste, please don't try to kill Portillo. You're not well and he has body-guards with guns, I'm sure."

Baptiste chuckled. "I don't ever try, Helene, to do anything. I do it!" He got up and went to his bedroom to take a morphine tablet and relax to plot how to kill Portillo. It was the last important business he had to attend to before he went to Sugar Hill to live with Opal.

Chapter 13

Two days later George Nelson sat with Wiggins in his downtown office evaluating the current situation. His tall blonde 40ish secretary gofer came out of her glass-partitioned cubicle in a corner of the large room. She put a faxed-in coroner's autopsy report on Wiggins' desk. He studied it for a moment. "Well, George, Big Freddy and his gorgeous inamorata died from cyanide asphyxiation... and our chances to take down Portillo are just as dead."

Nelson smiled and shook his head. "Chief, I'm not that pessimistic. There must be a crowd of ambitious homeboys eager to take king Freddy's place. Portillo will have to select one soon. Our C.I.'s in the ghetto will tip us who, when the lucky punk is chosen — we put him under the same intense scrutiny we applied to Freddy. Down the line he'll make a mistake and we'll bust him. Maybe he'll flip on Portillo to get a downward reduction deal."

Wiggins leaned back in his chair with an almost cheerful look on his cherubic pink face. "George, your analysis of our prospects is excellent and reassures me very much. It would have been a major loss for our organization, and a personal, deeply felt sorrow for me had those hit men killed you. George, be careful. Others may try for you. Now here's some good news. Central has given me permission to let you go to Seattle to spend a couple of weeks with your family."

Nelson beamed. "Thanks, Chief, for the kind sentiment, and for the vacation. I moved out of that house into a hotel in Burbank…" He paused to laugh. "The monthly rent was due today."

Wiggins lit a cigar. "George, I understand we plan to bust Lisa Lundgren for those gram sales to you."

Nelson looked at his watch. "Yes, Martinez & Reed are on her. She's going to memorial services for Sabina in the chapel at Hollywood Forest Lawn. Lisa arranged and paid for cremation and the rest of it. We've had a tap on the phone of Lisa's connection. He's a 50-year-old Mexican national, Jorge Mendoza, with a rap sheet in Mexico for murder and smuggling. He's an illegal who slipped into the country a year ago. He's just an ounce dealer, but he's agreed to deliver to Lisa a pound of coke for 15 thou."

Wiggins said, "He's gouging the hell out of her. As you know, a key is two and a half pounds and goes for 15 to 20 thou."

Nelson stood. "In Jorge's deal Lisa obviously thinks the product is good enough to cut and make a profit. She's imaginative. It was her suggestion that he make the delivery at the funeral home when he refused to make it to the penthouse as usual."

Wiggins stood and walked with Nelson to the door. They shook hands before Nelson stepped out into the corridor.

———

Lisa had just finished dressing in a black silk dress and wide brimmed black straw hat. She wore black elbow-length cotton gloves and black sling pumps. She looked at her reflection in the dresser mirror. She could be taken for Hispanic, and she could speak fluent Castilian without an American accent.

She took 15,000 dollars from a closet stash. She put the bills into an envelope and dropped it into her large black kidskin shoulder bag. She went to the living room and sat on the sofa. She snorted up several lines of coke off the glass-top table. Her dope-spurred mind sprinted through her plan and moves she'd make within the next few days. The tension and fear of the DEA hammer coming down on her for the sales to Stanford Leeds had become unbearable.

She sat and looked around the beautifully furnished living room. It had taken so much care and money to put together. She sighed. She was alone and the bright bubble of her penthouse gaiety, prestige, and comfort had burst. She would have one of numerous buyers of expensive furnishings to come in and make her a reasonable offer. She'd go underground and deal off the pound she'd get today, after she had cut it to make two. She'd only sell to wealthy people she knew. She could get a 150 dollars a gram from them and make a nice profit.

She had also found a stash of 30 thou in Sabina's room before she gave the homicide detectives permission to search it for clues to her death. In total she would have, including money in her bank account, almost a quarter of a million dollars. Tomorrow she would sell her Rolls for 90 to 100 thousand. She was confident that when she went to Mexico, she'd have no problem hooking up with some rich handsome man. She'd rent a villa and buy an elegant car.

She thought about her father, Tim Lundgren, who was in prison for life for shooting her Spanish mother, Laura Esparza, to death. She had watched him do it when she was 13. She had then disappeared into the underground world of the homeless in Austin, Texas.

She looked at her watch. She was late. Services for Sabina would be almost over. She hurriedly left the penthouse and went to the garage. She drove her beige Rolls to the parking lot of a Forest Lawn chapel. The lot was nearly full with luxury cars belonging to Sabina's and Lisa's friends and acquaintances.

Lisa got out of the car and exchanged a look with Jorge Mendoza seated in his rust-colored Cadillac. Lisa entered the chapel building and went directly to a ladies room near the wide chapel door. She went in the restroom and saw that the wastebasket near the wash basin was almost empty of used paper towels. She tore off hands-full from a roll above the basin. She crumpled them and threw them into the wastebasket. She put the envelope with the money at the bottom of the basket. She left and went into the crowded chapel.

She took a seat in the back row. A small urn containing Sabina's ashes sat on a mahogany pedestal before the pulpit. A pasty-faced cadaverous short, balding staff minister was ending a final prayer for Sabina's soul. "Christ Jesus, we have faith that you will forgive any and all sin and take Sabina Nilsson Jones' soul to your bosom for everlasting peace and freedom from the mental and physical suffering on this mortal coil. Thank you, Lord. Amen and Amen."

Mendoza went back to his car after he had picked up the money from the wastebasket and left the coke. He then drove away.

Two DEA agents on the street forced him to stop at gunpoint and took him and his car into custody.

A woman from the mortuary brought the urn and gave it to Lisa.

Lisa left quickly and went to get the coke. She walked to her car with a group of somber-faced men and women friends of Lisa who had met and liked Sabina. An agent walked behind Lisa to see that she didn't pass the coke to anyone.

Martinez and Reed were parked on the street waiting for Lisa. They were certain she was dirty with the pound of coke after hearing the tape from Mendoza's tapped phone when the delivery plan was made.

Lisa drove into the street and spotted Martinez and Reed instantly. She remembered them from Sabina's description of them the day that, outside Lisa's building, they propositioned Sabina to flip on Big Freddy.

Lisa stomped on the gas pedal. The Rolls hurtled away from the undercover Pontiac that Reed had just started up. Reed turned on his siren and gunned the Pontiac after her at 60 miles an hour. Reed miraculously escaped from near collisions with cars pulling into traffic from parking places. He narrowly missed collisions with cars crossing through intersections on the green as he rammed the Pontiac through red lights.

The Rolls was roaring away toward a freeway entrance several blocks away. Martinez said, "She's gonna get away."

Reed gritted his teeth and pushed the Pontiac to 70 miles an hour. Pedestrians and cars gave way, to leave a hazardous path through which he threaded the Pontiac.

Panic and coke distorted Lisa's perception. Too late, she realized she had driven at high speed into an exit ramp of the freeway.

Reed stopped the Pontiac at the exit ramp. The agents listened to the racket of sudden braking and honking of horns. Martinez said, "She's not going to stay pretty out there."

Now she was in a horrific din of honking, irate motorists as they swerved and flashed past her at freeway speed. Lisa was terrified, drenched with sweat as she somehow drove 200 yards in the dulcet thunder of a stream of vehicles. She screamed and threw her hands across her face. A gargantuan trailer-truck towing a rack of new cars screeched its brakes as it loomed only 50 feet away. It couldn't stop. On impact with the Rolls the explosion of sound was like a sky tall giant had crushed a house-sized kettle with his foot. The crumpled Rolls burst into a fiery mass and skidded across the road to stop on a shoulder. It had sideswiped and narrowly missed fatal collision with other cars.

The truck driver was unconscious, but alive, behind the wheel. The truck had massive damage to its front end.

Within ten minutes, Highway Patrolmen had closed the freeway section all the way to the exit-entrance ramps a half mile from the accident. Firemen and police arrived shortly. The firemen extinguished the flaming hulk of the Rolls. Lisa lay on the front floorboards. Her lipless mouth gaped open. She had almost been incinerated by the flames. The urn containing Sabina's ashes lay shattered on the front seat. Lisa's clothes from Rodeo Road and her shining mane of black hair were gone.

The coke package had ironically survived. A cop picked it up from the road. It had been thrown from the Rolls when the car tumbled off the freeway.

Next morning in Beverly Hills, Baptiste lay in bed after an almost sleepless night. He had been in severe pain. He had begun to worry about the devastating effect on Opal if, in his rapidly declining health, he himself would be killed when he ambushed Portillo. His eyesight was poor, and he wasn't sure he could drive himself to Bellflower at night to kill Portillo when he visited Lisette Fontaine. He wasn't eager to have Helene drive him because he didn't want to jeopardize her life and freedom if something went wrong. Maybe he would not kill Portillo. Perhaps he and Opal would be better off if he left for Sugar Hill a week sooner. Revenge for Isaiah's death was the root reason he wanted Portillo dead, he admitted to himself.

Were there other reasons he asked himself? Yes, a more important reason than selfish revenge. Portillo dead would mean that the dope pipeline into South Central would be broken, at least for a while — perhaps permanently. Thousands of young black people, like the ones who were a part of the Center that Alonzo ran, would be saved from cocaine destruction. He couldn't go to Sugar Hill and leave Portillo alive, he finally decided. He was going to kill him even if he lost his own life.

He got out of bed to dress. He & Helene had to go to Baldwin Hills to collect rent from two tenants. After that he would go to the gym, say goodbye to 50 of the kids and the parents Alonzo would have assembled there.

After breakfast with Helene on the patio she said, "Baptiste, you look very tired and weak. I can go to collect that money. Stay here and relax."

Baptiste smiled. "I have to go to South Central anyway. I'm going to say goodbye to Alonzo's kids and their parents. I may not be well enough a week or two from now."

Helene got up and started to clear the table. At 11 A.M. they went to the four-car garage. Helene got into her '76 Mustang to start it and back it out. It wouldn't start. She got out and told Baptiste. "Maybe we should drive the Rolls to the agency and rent a car."

Baptiste said, "We haven't time for that. You drive the Rolls."

Helene got behind the wheel of the ancient black car and drove toward South Central. They passed Angelus Funeral Home. The parking lot was clogged with expensive cars. Baptiste recognized several well-known gangsters. They were entering the funeral home an hour-and-a-half early.

Baptiste said, "Helene, I guess that services are going to be held for Big Freddy." She said, "You're probably right. Even a murderer has friends."

Helene drove to Baldwin Hills, overlooking the ghetto. Thirty-five minutes later the Rolls cruised through South Central and entered Baldwin Hills. Four blocks from the houses that Baptiste rented out, the Rolls approached Portillo's walled estate. Baptiste said, "Helene, behind those walls lives a man who is responsible for the imprisonment, misery, and death from crack, of young black people in South Central."

At that moment, Emilio drove through the gate behind the wheel of Portillo's Continental. He was taking the car to have the brakes adjusted. Baptiste made a mental note of the Continental's license plate number. Helene said, "Is that Portillo?"

Baptiste shook his head. "No. He's too young to be Portillo."

Helene went to both residences and got the rent money. Then she drove Baptiste to the gym. They parked the Rolls on the street in front of Baptiste's apartment building. They walked to the rear of it into the gym. About 50 kids and their parents, seated on folding chairs, crowded the huge room. They clapped when Baptiste entered. Alonzo helped him into the ring. Baptiste spoke into a hand-held microphone. "I'm very proud of the young people and their parents here today. You are a relative few of the good children and parents in South Central. There is the rampant misconception among certain white people that most black people have a genetic predisposition toward dope and crime. You and a majority of others are living proof that such a theory is garbage. My heart is heavy today because I'm here to say goodbye. I'm going to Sugar Hill in New York to live out the rest of my days with my daughter Opal. All of you will be in my thoughts and heart until I die. I feel so deeply about you all. I have the fullest confidence that out of yourselves and life you will get the very best always."

The room was cathedral quiet. His eyes filled with tears. "I want to share a secret with you... well, at least part of a secret." He flung up his right fist as Malcolm used to do. The sleeve of his suit coat slashed air like a blue silk blade. His impassioned bass voice shook the room. "I am going to take radical action against crack cocaine in South Central before I leave California... I hope I'll be successful, and the poisonous flood will stop, if only temporarily. Farewell, and thank you for giving me this day to remember forever. Goodbye, and my best wishes always."

There was a bedlam of applause and kids and adults shook his hand and touched him as Alonzo led him through the throng.

Alonzo put his arms around Baptiste's waist and walked with him to the car. Baptiste opened the rear door and sat on the rear seat. Alonzo said, "Pops, you gonna do a vigilante bit and knock off all the dealers?"

Baptiste smiled slyly. "Alonzo, you'll never know." Helene got under the wheel. She started the car. He said, "Helene, head south. I want to go to Bellflower now in daylight, to see where that French girl lives and what her neighborhood looks like." He leaned and gave Helene a piece of paper with Lisette's address on it. He lay down on the rear seat. "I need a nap... I didn't sleep much last night." She didn't pull the Rolls away. "Oh, Baptiste, shouldn't I take you home?"

He grunted. "Take me to Bellflower." She shook her head and drove south on Crenshaw.

Thirty-five minutes later, on the outskirts of Bellflower, she pulled into a gas station. She glanced at

Baptiste as she got out to give the station attendant a 20-dollar bill. She went to the rest room. She came out and got from the attendant directions to the street where Lisette lived.

Ten minutes later Helene cruised down the quiet residential block with attractive modest homes. She parked across the street from Lisette's pink stucco bungalow behind a white wood framed house. She shook Baptiste to awaken him. "We're here, Baptiste... she lives in that pink bungalow."

Baptiste sat up and studied the scene for a long moment. He noticed the house next door to the white house had a thick stand of shrubbery next to the walkway leading to Lisette's home. He also noticed an ornate custom purple Jag parked in the street. It belonged to Lovely Luther, Lisette's pimp.

Irma Witkowski lived across the street from Lisette, and it irked her that Luther came into her neighborhood. Now here were two more niggers she thought who were probably some kind of criminals. She jotted down the license of the Rolls as Helene pulled away for Beverly Hills.

Chapter 14

In a waiting area in Midway Hospital's intensive care section, Zenobia Witherspoon, Esther's older sister, sat anxiously with Freddy, Jr. Sitting beside her was tall, black-suited lawyer Coglan. He had been a friend and former employer of Esther's as a cook and baby sitter for his two children years before. She had worked in his home when Big Freddy was a pre-teener.

A tired looking female doctor with short graying hair approached them with a grim expression on her chubby face. "Unfortunately, we couldn't save Esther Evans... she passed away just a moment ago... I'm deeply sorry." The doctor turned and walked away. Junior and Zenobia clung to each other in tears. Coglan said, "Mrs. Witherspoon, do you have transportation?" She nodded her head. "Yes, by cab, the way we came. I'm going back to Esther's house to change clothes. Services for Freddy will be held in an hour or so."

Coglan helped her to her feet. "I'll drive you and Junior home and then to Angelus." He led them to his gold 90 Eldorado.

Fifteen minutes later he sat with Junior on the living room sofa. Zenobia quickly went into a bedroom and took off her slacks and put on a black dress. She came and sat on the sofa beside Coglan. She said, "There's quite a bit of time before services. Do you want some coffee or anything?"

Coglan said, "No, thank you."

She said, "Since you're a friend of the family and was Freddy's lawyer, maybe I need you to look at Esther and Freddy's wills..." She started off the sofa. "I'll get them." He waved her back to stay seated. "Mrs. Witherspoon, I prepared both wills. I have copies and am very familiar with them... you and Junior are now the beneficiaries of Freddy's considerable assets after the death of Esther today... but everything that Freddy owns will be confiscated under a relatively new law."

She looked at him for a long moment with her mouth open. Her dull, tear-reddened sable eyes peered at him, magnified by thick bifocals. "You ain't tellin' me there ain't nothin' goin' to Junior... not even the house?"

Junior said tremulously, "They gonna take even my train and swings and stuff in the backyard?"

Coglan nodded with his eyes fixed on the thick white carpet, Esther's pride and joy. Finally, he said, "Maybe the house can be retained... whose name is it in?"

Zenobia said, "In Esther's. Freddy gave her 200,000 in cash to buy it 9 or 10 years ago when he struck it rich. He moved her and Junior out of the projects."

Coglan said, "The way the house was bought I'm afraid makes it impossible to keep. Do you know when Esther stopped working? Has she received any large inheritance or big settlement from any lawsuit?"

Zenobia thought for a moment. "No, none of that. Freddy made her quit her job as a maid in Beverly Hills when he bought the house."

Coglan shook his head sadly. "That job she held in Beverly Hills was after she got sick for several months and my wife and I had someone replace her. We paid her well. I'm sure that she was paid a fair salary for her three years employment in Beverly Hills. I could try to save the house, but I don't see how I could show proof to a judge that Esther used her own money to purchase this house or that new Ford she owned. Only Esther's and Freddy's burial policies are exempt from seizure."

She looked incredulous. "You mean even after he died, they gonna take everything?"

Coglan said, "A young woman dope dealer was burned to death in her Rolls on the freeway a few days ago. All her money, everything she owned, was confiscated. Everything will be auctioned off. They will use some of the money, of course, to bury her. You see, Mrs. Witherspoon, the government uses these funds to finance its war against drugs." He paused. "They use the law to take all dope-tainted assets, even jewelry. It's just a reflection of a really outraged and vindictive society. I'm afraid we're out of luck. What do you plan to do?"

She sighed and hugged Junior close to her bosom. "I'm going to take Junior back to Mississippi with me."

Coglan said, "How are you fixed financially?"

She squared her shoulders. "I've owned a beauty shop in Vicksburg for 30 years, since my husband Abe died… I rent out six booths to women that stay busy all day, six days a week. I ain't rich, but I ain't poor neither. If you will take care of the legal part of things about Junior, I'll take care of Junior and see that he goes to college like Freddy and Esther wanted him to do."

Coglan stood. "I'll take care of everything, including arrangements for Esther." Zenobia walked with him to the front door. "She told me she wanted to be buried in the cemetery near our Mama and Papa in Mississippi. Freddy would want to be buried with Esther. How much do I owe you?"

He embraced her and said. "Not a cent. Let's go to the chapel. I'll send you a check for any money left from their policies."

Zenobia kissed his cheek. "Thank you, Mr. Coglan."

She and Junior followed him to his car. They got in and Coglan drove away.

In Bellflower, in Lisa's bedroom, Lovely Luther lay nude with Lisette. There was a knock on the door. She slipped on a robe. "Oh shit, who could it be?" He looked at his watch and smiled knowingly. He put on a robe and went to the living room. She looked through the front door peephole and opened the door on chain. "Yes?" she asked…

A male voice said, "We have a large package for Miss Lisette Fontaine."

She looked back at Lovely. "Let 'em in with the crate but don't look inside it yet."

She let two swarthy muscular men dolly a large object the size of a small gas range into the living room. The men wore logos on the front of their blue uniforms that advertised Creative Electronics of Hollywood. She signed a delivery slip and they left.

She stood staring at the cardboard encased mystery. "Let's go back to bed, baby. You'd never guess what it is."

She took off her robe and went to lie in his arms on the bed. She said, "I'm dying of curiosity. Lovely, what is it... a big screen TV?" They had banged heroin. Their eyes were dreamy. She rested her blond head on his chest. Her buttocks were tattooed with red welts. Luther had put them there with a straightened out thin wire coat hanger, doubled. He had used the whip as part of his foreplay that had preceded sex. His handsome, wolfish yellow face shaped a rare smile. He nodded his curly topped head toward the dresser top. He had brought her a pair of handcuffs and a rhinestone studded dog collar and leash. "Baby, those cuffs and the collar will be a gas for your freakish tricks. Cuff 'em and jerk 'em around the pad on their hands and knees before you whip their asses. Say shit like, 'Doggie, I'm gonna take your fuckin' ass to the pound and have you put to sleep if you don't move faster.' Run 'em into a sweat on the leash. Got it?"

She caressed his long, limp penis. "Yes, Lovely, I got it."

"I had a company that makes special shit for the movies make that item in the living room for you."

"Lovely, stop dangling me."

He said, "Okay. It's an electric chair with arm, chest, and leg straps like the real thing. You sit your tricks in the chair, then you drop a black hood over their heads. A battery in the chair bottom shocks the tricks' ass just enough to excite him. That will help to get the freak off faster."

She screamed in delight. "I love it, Lovely!"

He reached for his dope kit on the floor beside the bed. "Baby, let's do the do again. I'll rundown everything about the chair later."

Chapter 15

In Beverly Hills at the end of the next week at 7 P.M. on Saturday night, Baptiste sat on the living room sofa. Shortly, Helene joined him. She had been in her horror closet of shrunken heads in communion with the loas, her beloved voodoo gods. She had begged them for the dozenth time to make Portillo dead so Baptiste would not have to take the risk of killing him.

Helene watched Baptiste slitting slots in a thin leather belt from tip to buckle. Then he opened a package of single edge razor blades. He tightly fitted them into the slots.

Helene said, "Won't you risk a struggle with a man younger. He may be in better health than you."

He put the garrote aside. He took a .38 pistol from his waistband and an ice pick from his coat pocket. "Helene, it's true, I've got a gimpy leg and hip, but my upper body strength is very good for a man my age. The bastard could be as big and strong as Hulk Hogan. I'm going to put Ernesto Portillo in his grave or die trying. If I can't garrote him to death, if he somehow fights free of it, I'll stab him. If he's too tough to die after that, then I'll shoot him. I hope that won't be necessary. A gunshot in a quiet neighborhood like that would be bad. Neighbors could see me and call the cops to give a description of our car within minutes. We'd be stopped before we got to L.A. Instead of me taking that midnight train to Sugar

Hill, we'd be in a cell... Helene, I really don't want you to be a part of this. I can drive myself to Bellflower."

She looked very aggravated. "Baptiste, I loved Isaiah as much or more than you do in my own way because we were lovers. I want to go. I will go!"

He shrugged. "All right, Helene... Did you put my bags in the trunk of the car?" She nodded. He said, "I packed my big wardrobe trunk. Ship it to me by railway express in a few days. Any questions about your business duties for me?"

She said, "No. I understand everything I'm to do... What if he doesn't visit his French girlfriend tonight?"

Baptiste hesitated. "Then I'll know that God wants him punished at another time and place. We'll wait for him until 10:15. If he's no show, you'll drive me to the train station. I'll get on the train and forget about him. We'd better leave now."

They stood. She said, "How did you find out how to make a garrote like that one?"

He replied as they walked toward the front door. "A serial killer in Haiti used one like it to kill a half-dozen white men before you were born. He was killed by the police."

They left the house dressed in black and went to a black Ford. Helene drove toward Bellflower.

In his Baldwin Hills bedroom Portillo finished dressing in a white silk suit and pearl gray hat. He sprayed himself with Brut cologne. He stood for a long moment looking at his image in the dresser mirror. Damn, he thought, you get more handsome as you get older.

Bianca stood in the bedroom doorway in a pink lounging robe. She watched him with suspicious eyes. "Oh, Ernesto, will you go again this Saturday night without Emilio and Frank to guard you?"

He frowned, "Sweet flower, I must always keep my Saturday night appointments alone... The DEA agent who sells me weekly reports on his organization's investigation of me wants no one to witness our meeting." He threw his hat on the bed and sat next to it. "Sweet flower, I refuse to go to keep this important meeting. It will upset you too much. My life, my freedom perhaps, is not as important as your peace of mind."

She wrung her hands. "Please, Ernesto! Go! I'm sorry I'm no longer young and foolishly jealous. I trust you. I was just puzzled until you explained. Please forgive me and go."

He smiled and stood up. He took her into his arms. "Dear Bianca, there is nothing to forgive you for. I'm flattered that such a beautiful woman as you can be jealous of an old man like me. I love you." He released her and took his hat off the bed. He placed it on his head at a rakish angle. He kissed her lovingly before he left the house.

He entered his Continental and drove toward Bellflower. His heart was already pounding in expectation of seeing the cruel and excitingly beautiful Lisette.

Baptiste and Helene arrived on Lisette's block seven minutes after Portillo entered her rear bungalow. Baptiste went to lie down almost invisibly on the grass under the shrubbery near the entrance to the driveway of the front house.

Portillo's Continental was parked on the street near Baptiste. Baptiste held the lethal garrote and waited for Portillo.

Helene sat in the parked Ford near the end of the block. She stared down toward the middle of the block. She'd pick up Baptiste when he stepped into the street and waved.

Irma Vitkowski was in a drunken stupor on her living room couch. She had jotted down the license plate number of Baptiste's Rolls that sunny day when he and Helene had briefly scouted the block the week before.

Inside of her bungalow, Lisette entered the living room. Portillo's naked body was shiny with sweat. She had put the rhinestone dog collar around his throat and had roughly yanked him on his hands and knees throughout the house. He was panting from exertion and excitement as Lisette's doggie.

She wore her uniform — thigh-high black leather boots and nylon leopard print leotard. Her blonde mound of Venus shone through the nearly transparent crotch of the leotards. A wide slit would reveal her pink vulva when she would open her thighs after Portillo was seated and strapped into the chair. It stood in a corner behind a portable black silk screen.

She lashed his welted buttocks with her cat-o-nines. "You fuckin' doggie — I'm gonna put you in the pound and have you put to sleep if you don't obey my commands promptly."

She went to pull away the screen. His eyes were fearful as he stared at the ominous looking chair. "Sit in it, doggie shit ass."

He rolled piteous eyes at her. He crawled to peer behind the chair to see if it was wired to a wall outlet. She lashed his back and buttocks repeatedly as he climbed into the chair. "Stupid doggie. You think Mistress Lisette would kill an obedient slave?"

He whined, "No, merciless angel of heavenly orgasms. Forgive me."

She strapped his chest, legs, & arms. He was trapped in the chair. His sweaty behind was on sheet copper. A truck battery beneath the seat was rigged to send its voltage to the seat at 6-second intervals for 2 seconds. A switch at the side of the chair would turn it on.

Lisette approached Portillo with a black satin pillow case to put over his head. He cried out, "Please, no! Let me see your exquisite pussy, okay?"

She dropped the case to the carpet and hit the switch. His body surged against the jolt of current, which frightened him. At the same time, he felt a uniquely thrilling, nearly orgiastic sensation from his scrotum up his spine to the base of his ecstatic brain. He rolled his eyes in the painful sweet rapture of it all. Lisette was on the carpet at his feet. She spread her legs. He gazed into her pink snare, which she pulled wide. He had not had a hard on like this one, he thought, since he was a kid gangster in the streets of Bogota.

On the tenth jolt of current his penis gushed semen. Sweat covered his body. He sagged in the chair completely drained. He gasped. "Please wonderful Mistress of sweet agony, I've had enough."

She turned off the juice and unstrapped him. "Slave, would you like to take a shower before you dress?"

He shook his head no. He tried to embrace her. "No, I want to kiss you, beautiful brute."

She moved away and lashed his arm with the whip. "No slave kisses Mistress Lisette." She watched him dress. He took a diamond bracelet from his coat pocket. He slipped it on her wrist. "This is what I promised you a few weeks ago. Wear it and think of your slave."

She gazed at the sparkling bauble. "Doggie, I'm glad you appreciate your master."

He went out the front door at 9:30 P.M. on unsteady legs. Lisette put the screen around the chair.

Baptiste got to his feet when he heard Portillo coming down the walkway. An elderly white man came down the sidewalk and passed him without seeing him.

Portillo walked to his car. He stepped into the street to go to the driver's side. Baptiste crept up behind him when he reached the front bumper. He looped the razor-studded garrote around Portillo's throat. He made choking sounds as his long body jerked and pulled against the garrote. He and Baptiste fell to the street. Baptiste fell on Portillo's stomach. Portillo clawed at Baptiste's face, attempting to gouge out his eyes. Baptiste ducked his face against Portillo's chest. Portillo ripped a small clump of Baptiste's hair from his scalp.

Baptiste tightened the deadly noose. Portillo thrashed stoutly, but he was pinned down by Baptiste's 200-pound body. Baptiste twisted the garrote with his right hand and stabbed Portillo repeatedly in the side with an icepick.

Within three minutes Portillo lay still, with his blank eyes staring up at the full moon. Baptiste struggled to his feet and stumbled to the middle of the street. He waved toward Helene, parked at the end of the block, then returned to the cover of the shrubbery.

Helene started the Ford and drove to Portillo's Continental. She opened the passenger door and Baptiste fell into the car. Helene quickly drove toward the Amtrak train station in downtown L.A.

Baptiste changed into a tan leisure suit, shirt, and lightweight brown leather jacket. He stuffed the old blood-stained black suit into a garbage bag with the bloodied black gloves. Helene glanced at him, "How do you feel?"

Baptiste was still atremble from the death struggle. "Horrible. Helene, I hope you never have to kill anyone. It's not a pleasant experience at all. I wish he had never been born... then I couldn't have killed him."

Inside Lisette's living room, Lovely Luther, in magenta silk pajamas, came from his locked bedroom at the rear of the bungalow. Lisette waved the diamond bracelet before his eyes. "Give it to me," he said as he picked up Portillo's thousand dollars off the top of the coffee table.

She hesitated, "What will the trick think when he comes next Saturday night and I can't show it?"

Lovely laughed. "Shit, I'll get a dupe made, of cubic zirconia, from a guy on jeweler's row downtown. The trick won't know it from the real thing. How did the chair work?"

She took off the bracelet and gave it to him. "Daddy Lovely, you're a fuckin' genius. He got off in half the usual time and I only touched him with the whip." She moved to kiss him. He backed up.

"Not now sugar, get in the kitchen and make me some blueberry pancakes. Got that?"

She said meekly, "Yes, sweet Lovely, I'll do it right away." She hastened to the kitchen.

He put Stevie Wonder's "Isn't She Lovely" on the stereo. He sat on the sofa and waited impatiently for his favorite delicacy. He heard a woman's piercing scream from the street. She had spotted Portillo's corpse when she returned home from a movie with her husband. They owned the house on whose lawn Baptiste had lain to ambush Portillo.

Lovely closed his dreamy eyes and enjoyed Stevie's soothing voice.

Within fifteen minutes, a coroner's death ambulance, police vehicles, detectives, and uniformed cops had appeared at the crime scene. They strung a yellow tape waist high around Portillo's body and his car.

The headlights of police vehicles lit up the scene. A homicide detective kneeled beside the body and scanned it with the beam of a powerful flashlight. He removed a half-dozen strands of Baptiste's hair from Portillo's clenched right hand. He dropped the hairs into an envelope. He sealed it and put it into his coat pocket. He directed several uniformed officers to knock on doors of nearby houses on both sides of the street.

Ten minutes later a rookie cop knocked on Lisette's door. Lovely had eaten his pancakes and was kicking back on the sofa near the front door. He got up and looked through the peephole. Lisette came into the room as the cop knocked again, hard. Lisette whispered, "Is it the heat?" Lovely nodded. She rushed into the bedroom and got a small quantity of heroin and flushed it down the toilet.

Lovely opened the door. "Do you live here?"

Lovely said, "Yeah, officer, with my wife... What's goin' on?"

The officer's blue eyes stared over Lovely's shoulder at Lisette as she came into the living room. She was wearing her mistress uniform, with Lovely's lime silk shirt covering her upper body.

"A Hispanic man wearing a white suit was murdered on the street out front. Do you know someone like that?"

Lisette stepped in front of Lovely. "No, we don't, officer."

The officer took a step into the house. Lisette frowned and moved back. He looked down at Lovely on the sofa. "You guy, what's your name?"

Lovely forced a genial smile. "Lov, uh, Luther Williams. And that's my wife, Lisette."

The officer said, "I may be back," before he turned & went down the walk.

The senior detective stood getting nothing from the several other officers who had asked immediate neighbors if they had seen anything. The blonde rookie joined the group. "Well, Pete, did you find out anything from the occupants of the rear pink bungalow?"

He chewed his bottom lip. "Sergeant Limanski, there's a black man who looks kind of slick and, uh, you know — suspicious... he's living back there with a knockout blonde with a French accent... Maybe the guy's okay."

Limanski stroked his thick, auburn mustache. His mean face hardened. "Does this nigguh, black man, have crinkly white hair?"

Pete said, "No. He's a young dude... looks like a Creole or somethin', with curly black hair."

Limanski said, "Pete, you and Kenny take him into custody. He could be tied in some way to the killer."

The two cops went to Lisette's door and knocked. She peeped and opened the door. "Yes, officers, what is it now?"

Pete said, "We want to talk with your husband."

She called out, "Luther!" In a moment he came from the bedroom into the living room wearing a red silk robe. "Now what, man?" Lovely asked testily.

Pete and heavyset dark-haired Kenny stepped forward and seized Lovely's arms. "Hey, you gangsters can't do this!" Lovely protested as he tried to jerk free.

They threw him to the carpet face down. Lisette screamed. "I'll sue you cocksuckers for this!"

Pete said, "Shut up. Shut your sewer mouth, lady, or we'll take you with him." Kenny said, "Get him some trousers, jacket, and shoes."

She went and brought back the items in a couple of minutes. Kenny had his knees on Lovely's back. "Why are you arresting me?" Pete said, "For suspicion of complicity in that murder in the street."

Lisette hollered, "My husband hasn't left the house since noon today. This is some racist shit."

They let Lovely up to put on a tan sharkskin suit &
tan loafers. Kenny looked behind the screen. "Hey, Pete,
this guy's got an electric chair." He pulled the screen
away. Pete said, "Well, I'll be damned. Why do you
have this chair, Mr. Williams?"

Lovely thought fast and grinned, "Oh, that's just
somethin' I rigged up to sit in for videotaping. We were
gonna try to win one of those big buck prizes that the
TV show Totally Hidden Video is giving away."

Lisette hugged Lovely. "Daddy, you won't be in long.
I'll get in touch with Coglan and a bondsman right
away." They handcuffed Lovely and took him to an unmarked brown Pontiac. They seated him in the back seat
between them. Limanski moved the Pontiac away for
the Bellflower lockup.

A block from the Amtrak station at 8th and Alameda
Streets in downtown L.A., Baptiste said, "Helene, stop
and park. I'll take my bags to the station."

Helene parked & looked exasperated. "Baptiste, why
do you want to strain yourself carrying those heavy bags?"

He got out. "You can put the bags on the sidewalk."
She got out and opened the trunk. She lugged the large
bags to the sidewalk. He said, "Thanks, Helene, I'm going
to miss you." They embraced. "I miss you too, Baptiste...
take good care of yourself and give Opal my love. I'll
be calling you in Sugar Hill on business and just to say
hello." He hefted the bags. "Damn, they are heavy, but
I can carry them a block... Helene, dump that garbage

bag in a grocery or liquor store trash bin on your way home. I'm leaving you here because I don't want anyone around the station to see you driving me. Keep his car to run your errands. Remember, you may be questioned by police about my movements tonight before I took the train. Tell them you know nothing about where I went or how I got to the train station. Someone picked me up that was a stranger to you... Oh yes, in the morning, check the front seat for any blood stains. Goodbye, dear friend." She kissed his cheek and gave him a final hug. She watched the sick old man struggle down the sidewalk with the bags. She was relieved when she saw a redcap on the sidewalk in front of the station spot Baptiste. The porter hurried to take the bags and carry them into the station.

Helene drove away for Beverly Hills.

A half mile from downtown she dropped the bloody clothing into a liquor store dumpster. A porter led Baptiste to his roomette.

Baptiste dropped the neat and narrow bed from the wall and fell on it. At four minutes after midnight the train pulled out of the station for New York City.

A half hour later the gentle sway and low hum of the train wheels on the tracks was like a dulcet lullaby and sang Baptiste to sleep — sleep that was haunted by Portillo's face in the throes of death.

The morning after Portillo's death, Detective Limanski and other officers knocked on every door on the murder block. Irma Witkowski lived across the street from the crime. She had been too drunk to answer when police knocked on her door the night before.

Now the fat blob of a woman opened her front door to Limanski. "Hello, I'm Mrs. Witkowski, what do you want?"

"Mrs. Witkowski, I'm Detective Limanski. I'm investigating the murder that occurred last night across the street. Did you see anything that could be helpful?"

She pressed nicotine stained fingers against her mouth in deep thought. "No officer, I went to bed early last night... last week I saw a nigguh black girl driving an old Packard or some kinda old car. There was an old darkie with white hair on the back seat looking across the street like he was casing one of the houses to burglarize or something... you know how they are."

Limanski looked very interested. "Mrs. Witkowski, could you search your memory and tell me just what kind of old car it was."

She fluttered her heavily veined hands. "I don't know... they looked suspicious, so I wrote down the license plate number on a slip of paper. That should help you."

His mean face looked almost pleasant. "Dear lady, give me that slip of paper."

She started to search the top of the coffee table and then all around the living room. She sat down on the sofa. Limanski sat down beside her. "Where could it be?" he asked.

She shrugged. "My daughter straightened up the house a bit for me. I've got bad arthritis and I'm not able to clean the house like I did before my husband Hans died last year… she must have thrown that slip of paper in the trash out back."

Limanski stood. "Did you put out your trash for pick-up this week?"

She shook her head. "I haven't been well… the trash is piled up back there."

He took her hand to help her to her feet. "Let's go and look for that piece of paper."

She led him through the untidy home to several trash cans overflowing with beer cans, wine bottles, and rancid garbage. "What color was the paper," he asked as he started digging into the odorous mess.

She sat on the back-porch steps and watched him. "It's on pale blue notebook paper."

A sweaty half hour later he found the slip of paper. He said, "Mrs. Witkowski, I'd like to wash my hands."

She led him to the bathroom. He took off his jacket and washed his face and hands. He dried himself with a less than clean towel. He put on his jacket and straightened his tie. He left the house with the lukewarm clue. The hot one was Baptiste's hairs.

In his roomette on the train, Baptiste sat on the side of his bed polishing the completed manuscript of his autobiography. He had been absolutely candid about the good and bad he had done in his lifetime. He had included a detailed account of Portillo's murder and why.

Opal would not submit it to her agent friend for publication until after his death — which was soon, he knew.

If he could just make it to Sugar Hill and spend a few weeks with Opal, he would die happy. But he couldn't be sure of that because his faulty heart was pounding erratically with occasional frightening fluttering.

He put the manuscript aside and stared out the window. Grazing cows and birds flitting through the bright sunshine reminded him sadly of his boyhood in Haiti. How could all those years of his life pass so quickly he asked himself as he fell back on the bed and closed his eyes.

Chapter 16

Early Monday evening, almost 48 hours after Portillo's murder, Wiggins was in a conference room in a corner of his office. Martinez, Reed, and Nelson were seated at a long table. Brown plaid-suited Wiggins said, "Gentlemen, the Big Freddy-Portillo involvement in drug trafficking has given them the ultimate punishment. What are your thoughts about the present state of affairs relative to the impact of cocaine supply in L.A. and particularly in South Central?"

Martinez said, "A C.I. in South Central has told me that Freddy's replacement has already been chosen... the same C.I. tipped me where he thought Freddy's stash house was located. Reed and I, with several other agents, went to the location. The house was vacant."

Nelson said, "Wade Johnson, Freddy's stash house boss, is rumored to be Freddy's replacement."

Reed said, "Wade is slicker than a greased eel... wish we knew where his new stash house is located."

Wiggins said, "Since we're wishing, I'd like to know the location of Portillo's stash house — somewhere in L.A. county."

Nelson said, "Chief, that house could have tons of coke stashed in it. Also, the cartel will send someone soon to take over Portillo's very important position. Chief, is there any local police progress into the investigation of Portillo's murder?"

Wiggins studied a fax report from Bellflower. "Yes, last week a neighbor saw Baptiste Landreau casing her block. His black housekeeper apparently was his driver last week. Detectives will question her to find out if she drove Baptiste the night that Portillo was killed. A detective Limanski got Landreau's license plate number from a neighbor and white crinkly hairs from Portillo's clenched hand. They could be Landreau's. A young black man, Luther Williams, Lisette Fontaine's pimp, was arrested and released this afternoon by Bellflower police."

Nelson said, "Has the old man been arrested?"

Wiggins lit a cigar. "Not yet, but he will be when his train pulls into Grand Central Station in New York City."

At 9 A.M. Limanski pushed the intercom button at the gate of Baptiste's house. Helene heard the doorbell ring. She put on a pink robe over her bra and panties and went to the intercom speaker near the front door. "Who is it?"

Limanski's gruff voice replied, "Detective Limanski, Bellflower Homicide Division."

She buzzed his unmarked Pontiac through. He parked in the driveway near the house. He got out and stared into the garage at the Rolls, rented Ford, and Helene's Mustang. Helene watched him as he boldly, and perhaps illegally, went to open each of the car's front doors. He carefully scrutinized the seats and floors of the cars with his powerful flashlight.

Helene was standing at the open front door when he finished. "Detective, your actions are very puzzling... Why are you here?"

He followed her into the living room. They sat down on the sofa. "I think you know why I'm here."

She smiled scornfully, "That's amazing. I can read your mind and you have read mine."

He frowned. "Don't get slick with me, Miss Gautier. I'm here to investigate the murder of Ernesto Portillo. Where were you last Saturday around midnight?"

She said, "Asleep, here."

He grunted. "Anybody else in the house with you?"

She shook her head. "No, I was alone here."

"Did you and Baptiste know Portillo?"

She hesitated, uneasy about submitting to questioning by a cop she disliked on sight.

He smiled evilly. "Young lady, I want the truth from you, but you don't have to answer any questions here without the presence of a lawyer. We can take a ride to the Bellflower station."

She shrugged. "I have nothing but the truth to tell. We only saw Mr. Portillo's face on TV."

Limanski shifted his muscular frame on the sofa. "Have you ever driven Baptiste Landreau into Bellflower?"

She said "Yes, days ago... and also into Long Beach, Compton, and Carson the same day. We have done it at least twice a year to find properties for sale."

He said, "Come on girl, we know that your boss killed Portillo before he caught that train to New York. If you didn't drive him to Bellflower the other night you've got to know who did."

She stared into his eyes defiantly. "Detective, again you have read my mind wrongly. I don't believe my friend killed Portillo. So, I can't know anything about anyone driving him to Bellflower the night Portillo was killed."

Limanski stood and glared at her with hostile eyes. He looked at his watch. "I'm going to have those cars in the garage impounded for forensic examination. New York City police will be waiting to arrest your friend when his train arrives around noon, New York time… we'll sweat your role out of him. I'm gonna be thrilled to arrest you for accessory to murder. Don't try to leave California."

Helene got up and laughed in his face. "Detective, I'm sorry, but you will never get that thrill. You will not find anything in those cars to hurt me or my friend." She followed him to the front door. He opened it and stared at her for a long moment. She said, "I wish I could read your mind." He said, "I was thinking how becoming a uniform in the big joint would be on you."

He went to his car. She watched him drive away to the gate. She buzzed him through and went back to her quarters. She went into her closet of horrors to beg the loas to kill Limanski for her. She also prayed to them for Baptiste's escape from prosecution for Portillo's murder.

In her beautifully furnished four-bedroom home in Sugar Hill, Opal finished dressing in a red wool Lilli Anne suit. She went to a closet stash and got a vial of cocaine. She shook out enough for two short lines on a hand mirror. She snorted up the coke with a straw and re-stashed the vial. "I'm not a dope-fiend. I'm not hooked. I can stop using whenever I want to," she told herself for the 20th time since she had started to use. That had been six months ago when her husband had deserted her for the flashy young white barmaid.

Opal went to her pale blue Mercedes parked in the long winding driveway. She drove through Harlem toward the Grand Central Railroad terminal on 42nd Street in Manhattan. It would be easy to stop using coke now that Baptiste was coming to live with her. She wouldn't be lonely any more, she thought.

Inside Baptiste's roomette, two porters watched a passenger doctor give Baptiste an injection and then start CPR. After twenty minutes the short, stocky, & elderly white doctor sat down on the side of the bed. His shirt was wet with sweat. His face was red from the lengthy exertion. He put a stethoscope against the motionless corpse. He felt for a pulse. "He's gone... apparently he died from cardiac arrest," the doctor said as he stood up.

One of the porters said, "He was out when I answered his bell... Sure was a nice old man." The other porter said, "Sure was... and one of the best tippers I ever met."

The doctor picked up his bag and said, "You better lock this room. I'll have to talk to the police about this when we arrive in New York." The porter locked the door. Both of the porters then went to alert occupants in other roomettes that the train would pull into Grand Central within the hour.

Emilio and Frank sat in the living room of their bungalow in the rear of the big house in Baldwin Hills. Their live-in girlfriends, Pam and Grace, sat with them on a long zebra-striped sofa. They were two pretty 30ish blondes who had left the Midwest to come to Hollywood to become movie stars. Two years before, Pam had met Emilio at a pizza parlor where she worked the cash register. They hooked up quickly. Pam introduced Frank to Grace two weeks later. Grace was a receptionist for a horny old physician in downtown L.A. Both women found their 9 to 5 gigs to be unbearable. They jumped at the chance to live, eat, and get clothes for free. They had just returned two days before from a two-and-a-half-month tour of Europe and visits with their relatives in Kansas and Wisconsin. Emilio and Frank had financed everything. They had wanted to go with the women but there had been no replacements for them to guard and do Portillo's business.

Now the couples had spent most of the last 48 hours in bed renewing their strong sexual bond. Emilio and Frank kissed the women and went to a rented gray Chrysler. Frank drove them past Portillo's big deserted house. Bianca had flown with Portillo's body to Colombia for burial.

"I still can't believe he's gone," Emilio said as Frank drove into the street.

Frank glanced into his side view mirror. "You know, Emilio, I'd miss the DEA cocksuckers if they didn't follow us."

An ordinary looking dusty Ford followed them from a block away. It took Frank 40 minutes to catch an amber light at a fast, busy intersection. He went through just before the red light. The instant flow of traffic made it impossible for the agents to follow.

Frank drove to a large department store parking lot. He parked the car and Emilio and he drove away in a blue rented Lincoln sedan. Frank said, "I heard this guy Octavio Valenzuela is a hard liner, tougher than Portillo."

Emilio lit a cigarette. "He's so fuckin' small he's got a Napoleon quirk. He's a boyhood pal of Portillo's. The cartel obviously trusts him a lot... Watch your mouth Frank, and don't upset him like you sometimes did with Portillo. This runt could get irritated & blow you away."

Frank said, "Why do we have to move our stash... Glendale is so perfect. Southgate is full of creeps that draw heat."

Emilio groaned. "I hope you don't make that crack to Octavio. He's the boss now and we have to keep our thoughts to ourselves. We just take orders... that is if you want to stay alive."

Within an hour Frank drove down a quiet residential street in Glendale. It was a medium-sized town near L.A. He parked the Lincoln in front of a neat white stucco house. A large U-Haul truck was parked at the rear of the house. They walked to the front door and rang the doorbell.

The 6'6" fortyish Colombian boss of the stash house opened the door. He smiled and placed a submachine gun on a hallway table. Casper led them into the modestly furnished living room. Dwarfish Octavio Valenzuela sat on the sofa dressed to the nines in a pinstripe grey silk suit, navy blue silk shirt, and grey elk-skin ankle length boots on his neat little feet. A dove grey stingy brim hat sat on his glossy straight black-haired head. His doll face was ruined by the long-time stress of numerous murders and the constant fear of being killed. The security police in Colombia had hounded him for years. His bright black eyes studied them without wavering, with snakelike cold detachment.

Frank said nervously, "I'm sure, Mr. Valenzuela, that you will be as satisfied with us as Mr. Portillo was."

The bantam's thin cruel lips shaped a demented smile. "Portillo was a good man and my friend. But even when we were kids together, he had the flaw of infatuation with cunts of one kind or another. No man can really pursue perfection and excellence in his business and life with a cunt to distract and aggravate him. I have been celibate since I was seventeen. I was in love with a slut who fucked one of my best friends. I shot them both to death. To prove my point, remember that Ernesto was killed after he left a young tramp. So, expect to give me, a superior man, more than what Ernesto got from you. Understand that?"

Emilio said, "Yes, Mr. Valenzuela, we understand."

The pygmy gangster got to his feet. "Let's get the goods and load them into the truck."

They followed him to the basement.

Casper moved a large freezer from a trap door in the floor. Octavio hit a light switch on the floor with his foot. He watched Casper lead Emilio and Frank down a short stairway into the stash room.

Two tons of coke in plastic wrapped kilos were stacked in the underground room.

The three men started filling garbage bags with the two-and-a-half pound bundles. Within an hour-and-a-half they had emptied the room and loaded the truck.

Octavio said sternly, "Don't ever mention my name to the Wade Johnson guy that took Big Freddy's spot. I don't ever want to meet him. Understand that?"

Frank said, "We will never let him, or anyone, know you exist."

Emilio nodded. He drove Octavio in the Lincoln to his hotel suite in downtown L.A. Frank drove the truck toward South Gate. Casper held a machine gun on his lap. They would unload the truck into the new stash house. Casper would stay and Frank would take the rented truck back to the agency. He would then take a cab to the department store lot where the gray Chrysler was parked. He and Frank would return to the bungalow and party with their women.

———

At the Grand Central railroad station, two burly New York City black detectives waited on the platform for Baptiste's train, due at any moment.

Ostel Holmes, the older detective, stood near the front of the station among a group of people waiting for friends and relatives. They were waiting for the train to arrive. His partner, Johnny Burke, stood among the crowd at the middle of the platform. Opal stood near Burke.

Finally, the sleek train coasted into the station. The passengers started to leave the train to hugs, kisses, and exclamations of joyful greetings. Redcaps helped passengers with their bags.

Holmes and Burke eye-swept the passengers. A short, stout, elderly black man with white hair was one of the last to leave the train. He didn't fit Baptiste's description faxed from L.A. Burke asked a redcap with whom he was acquainted, "Melvin, did you have a tall, husky old black man with a square jaw and white hair traveling from L.A.?"

Opal moved closer to Burke. The porter said, "Sure did, Mr. Holmes... but his heart stopped after I answered his bell... that old white doctor getting off that rear car tried to save him."

Burke signaled Holmes and the redcap led him to the New York doctor, Delbert Ennis. Opal followed with an anxious face and a sick feeling in the pit of her stomach. Her legs wobbled.

The doctor held his small medical bag. "Dr. Ennis, I told Detective Burke about what happened to Mr. Landreau."

The doctor said, "I don't know the deceased's medical history, but I'm 99 percent certain that he died of cardiac arrest. Here is my card. I'll be in my office tomorrow if you want to talk to me."

Holmes took the card. "Thanks, doctor." Burke said to the porter, "Melvin, take us to the deceased."

The detectives boarded the train behind Melvin. Opal, in a fog of shock, followed.

Burke glanced over his shoulder. "Are you a relative, lady?"

Opal half-whispered, "I'm his daughter, Opal Landreau."

The porter took them to the door of the roomette and unlocked it. They entered and stood for a long moment looking at Baptiste lying on his back in his favorite peach silk pajamas. A three-carat diamond ring and diamond studded Rolex sparkled on his wrist and pinkie finger. He seemed to be sleeping peacefully.

Opal screamed. "Oh, daddy!" She threw herself on the body and wept. Burke gently helped her to her feet. Holmes pressed an ear against Baptiste's chest. "We'll have to call the coroner. Miss Landreau, you have our deepest sympathy. May we see some I.D."

She showed them her driver's license and a half-dozen credit cards. Burke put his mouth close to her ear. "Did you know your father was a suspect in the murder of a Colombian man?"

She collapsed on the side of the bed. "Why, no, that's absurd. My daddy wouldn't kill anybody. He was so kind, sweet, and gentle."

Holmes said, "Whether he was guilty or not is a moot question now… Miss Landreau, you can take his jewelry. We're going to seal this room until the coroner comes to officially declare him dead and take him to the morgue."

She took off the ring and watch. She took his wallet from a small tabletop and put the items into her shoulder bag. She took the completed manuscript off the bed beside Baptiste.

Holmes said, "Let me see that." She noticed that his breath reeked of alcohol. He riffled through the pages. She said, "It's daddy's novel, which I'm going to have published." He gave it to her.

"We'll keep his luggage for a few days or so. Give us your address and we'll send the bags to you, including the rest of his effects."

She gave him her card. She left the train in the worst depression of her life. She somehow drove herself to a Harlem funeral home to make arrangements for the retrieval of Baptiste's body, after autopsy, for burial with her mother, Deanna Stein, grandmother, and Uncle Chester.

The next day in L.A., DEA agent George Nelson had just stepped out of the shower in his downtown hotel suite. The phone rang. It was a South Central confidential informant. Nelson instantly recognized his voice.

"Hey, man, I got good news... I'm gonna almost for sure get hip to where Wade Johnson's new stash house is located. I'll jingle you. Bye."

Nelson immediately called Wiggins. "Chief, one of my C.I.'s, just called me. He's certain he'll know the location of Wade Johnson's new stash house soon."

Wiggins was ecstatic. "If we can bust Wade in that house with a large amount of coke, we can pressure him with the possibility of a life sentence... he could flip on whoever replaced Portillo & we could take him down. Excellent news, George. Thanks, and keep me informed about this matter." He hung up.

A week later in Harlem, Opal left the crowded funeral home chapel. Pallbearers closed the lid on the elegant mahogany casket where Baptiste lay dressed in a black mohair suit, black satin tie, and Irish linen white shirt. She and Helene entered a limousine behind the hearse. A long line of cars followed behind driven by her friends and acquaintances, white and black, including a number of old timers who had patronized the voodoo supply store that Baptiste had run for 20 years.

Helene returned to L.A. the next day to oversee Alonzo and business affairs for Opal.

Detective Bertram Limanski was becoming aggravated as he dug through several bags of groceries. His wife Megan had just brought in the groceries. She had rushed into the bathroom immediately after setting the groceries down.

His frantic search for the cigarettes that he had reminded her to buy were not in the bags. He needed a cigarette. It irritated him greatly that she, who had kicked her nicotine habit, had forgotten or deliberately decided not to bring his cigarettes. He stood waiting for her with a bellicose expression on his pit bull face.

Petite brunette Megan entered the kitchen. Her dark, deep set large eyes had a sad, subtle overcast of apprehension after 25 years as the wife of a policeman.

"Sweetheart, you forgot to get my goddamn cigarettes." She started to remove the frozen items to place in the freezer. "I'll go back to the market after I put these groceries away… Bert, you really ought to stop smoking. Hundreds of thousands of people are dying every year from tobacco related illnesses. Want to, just for the hell of it, do without a cigarette until tomorrow?"

He was in his shirtsleeves and the night was balmy. He went out the back door and headed for the corner liquor store. He spoke to a young couple entering their house, several houses from the liquor store. He entered the store and went toward the counter.

A short man with shoulder length blonde hair was at the counter facing Mac, the night manager. His arms were working feverishly at the cash register. Mac's body had an odd tension and his usually friendly face was tight with fear as he looked past the blonde toward Limanski.

Limanski heard the bandit say, "You son of a bitch — hurry, get it all in the sack!" The manager continued to stare at Limanski as if hypnotized. At the instant the bandit spun around, Limanski started to lunge to bear hug him and throw him to the floor. And as he looked into the barrel of the bandit's .45 automatic, he had one final thought. "You dumb motherfucker, you forgot your piece." The pistol then spewed flame that scorched Limanski's shirt front. Limanski crashed into the bandit with a slug through his heart. Mac snatched a gun from beneath the counter and shot the young bandit through the back of his head. The manager's hand shook so much he had difficulty dialing the police.

Inside Limanski's modest home, Megan finished putting away the groceries. She wondered why her husband was not back from the liquor store.

The day after Limanski's death, Helene was in the living room of the mansion when the noon TV news came on.

She watched the newscast, but she was distracted by grief and thoughts of Baptiste and Isaiah. Suddenly she was shocked, and then thrilled, that the loas had acted so quickly.

The woman newscaster reported that the night before Detective Bertram Limanski had apparently left his home without his gun. He had gone to a liquor store to buy cigarettes and had walked into a holdup. He had tried to disarm the bandit and was shot to death.

Helene went to unlock her closet of horror. The rows of shrunken heads seemed to grin at her in the red glow of the ever-burning ceiling bulb. She flung voodoo dust into the pot on a tripod. She threw a lit match into the pot. A geyser of blue flame whooshed into the air. She fell to the floor when she heard the sibilant gabbling of the loas. Her body jerked and writhed in sweet agony. "Thank you beloved loas, for the death of the hateful detective. Now I beg you wonderful spirits, send me a dear friend like Baptiste and a kind, handsome lover like Isaiah without a white witch in his head and crotch like Sabina." She lay curled on the floor in a fetal position. She was in a state of sublime serenity.

COLOPHON

NIGHT TRAIN TO SUGAR HILL

was handset in InDesign CC.

The text *&* page numbers are set in *Melior*.
The titles are set in *Novarese Ultra*.

Book design *&* typesetting: Alessandro Segalini
Cover design: Alessandro Segalini

NIGHT TRAIN TO SUGAR HILL

is published by Contra Mundum Press.
Its printer has received Chain of Custody certification from:
The Forest Stewardship Council,
The Programme for the Endorsement of Forest Certification,
& The Sustainable Forestry Initiative.

Contra Mundum Press   New York · London · Melbourne

CONTRA MUNDUM PRESS

Dedicated to the value & the indispensable importance of the individual voice, to works that test the boundaries of thought & experience.

The primary aim of Contra Mundum is to publish translations of writers who in their use of form and style are *à rebours*, or who deviate significantly from more programmatic & spurious forms of experimentation. Such writing attests to the volatile nature of modernism. Our preference is for works that have not yet been translated into English, are out of print, or are poorly translated, for writers whose thinking & æsthetics are in opposition to timely or mainstream currents of thought, value systems, or moralities. We also reprint obscure and out-of-print works we consider significant but which have been forgotten, neglected, or overshadowed.

There are many works of fundamental significance to *Weltliteratur* (& *Weltkultur*) that still remain in relative oblivion, works that alter and disrupt standard circuits of thought — these warrant being encountered by the world at large. It is our aim to render them more visible.

For the complete list of forthcoming publications, please visit our website. To be added to our mailing list, send your name and email address to: info@contramundum.net

Contra Mundum Press
P.O. Box 1326
New York, NY 10276
USA

OTHER CONTRA MUNDUM PRESS TITLES

Gilgamesh
Ghérasim Luca, *Self-Shadowing Prey*
Rainer J. Hanshe, *The Abdication*
Walter Jackson Bate, *Negative Capability*
Miklós Szentkuthy, *Marginalia on Casanova*
Fernando Pessoa, *Philosophical Essays*
Elio Petri, *Writings on Cinema & Life*
Friedrich Nietzsche, *The Greek Music Drama*
Richard Foreman, *Plays with Films*
Louis-Auguste Blanqui, *Eternity by the Stars*
Miklós Szentkuthy, *Towards the One & Only Metaphor*
Josef Winkler, *When the Time Comes*
William Wordsworth, *Fragments*
Josef Winkler, *Natura Morta*
Fernando Pessoa, *The Transformation Book*
Emilio Villa, *The Selected Poetry of Emilio Villa*
Robert Kelly, *A Voice Full of Cities*
Pier Paolo Pasolini, *The Divine Mimesis*
Miklós Szentkuthy, *Prae, Vol. 1*
Federico Fellini, *Making a Film*
Robert Musil, *Thought Flights*
Sándor Tar, *Our Street*
Lorand Gaspar, *Earth Absolute*
Josef Winkler, *The Graveyard of Bitter Oranges*
Ferit Edgü, *Noone*
Jean-Jacques Rousseau, *Narcissus*
Ahmad Shamlu, *Born Upon the Dark Spear*
Jean-Luc Godard, *Phrases*
Otto Dix, *Letters, Vol. 1*
Maura Del Serra, *Ladder of Oaths*
Pierre Senges, *The Major Refutation*
Charles Baudelaire, *My Heart Laid Bare & Other Texts*
Joseph Kessel, *Army of Shadows*
Rainer J. Hanshe & Federico Gori, *Shattering the Muses*
Gérard Depardieu, *Innocent*
Claude Mouchard, *Entangled, Papers!, Notes*
Miklós Szentkuthy, *St. Orpheus Breviary, vol. II: Black Renaissance*
Adonis, *Conversations in the Pyrenees*
Charles Baudelaire, *Belgium Stripped Bare*
Robert Musil, *Unions*

SOME FORTHCOMING TITLES

Rédoine Faid, *Bank Robber*

THE FUTURE OF KULCHUR
A PATRONAGE PROJECT

LEND CONTRA MUNDUM PRESS (CMP) YOUR SUPPORT

With bookstores and presses around the world struggling to survive, and many actually closing, we are forming this patronage project as a means for establishing a continuous & stable foundation to safeguard our longevity. Through this patronage project we would be able to remain free of having to rely upon government support &/or other official funding bodies, not to speak of their timelines & impositions. It would also free CMP from suffering the vagaries of the publishing industry, as well as the risk of submitting to commercial pressures in order to persist, thereby potentially compromising the integrity of our catalog.

CAN YOU SACRIFICE $10 A WEEK FOR KULCHUR?

For the equivalent of merely 2–3 coffees a week, you can help sustain CMP and contribute to the future of kulchur. To participate in our patronage program we are asking individuals to donate $500 per year, which amounts to $42/month, or $10/week. Larger donations are of course welcome and beneficial. All donations are tax-deductible through our fiscal sponsor Fractured Atlas. If preferred, donations can be made in two installments. We are seeking a minimum of 300 patrons per year and would like for them to commit to giving the above amount for a period of three years.

WHAT WE OFFER

Part tax-deductible donation, part exchange, for your contribution you will receive every CMP book published during the patronage period as well as 20 books from our back catalog. When possible, signed or limited editions of books will be offered as well.

WHAT WILL CMP DO WITH YOUR CONTRIBUTIONS?

Your contribution will help with basic general operating expenses, yearly production expenses (book printing, warehouse & catalog fees, etc.), advertising & outreach, and editorial, proofreading, translation, typography, design and copyright fees. Funds may also be used for participating in book fairs and staging events. Additionally, we hope to rebuild the *Hyperion* section of the website in order to modernize it.

From Pericles to Mæcenas & the Renaissance patrons, it is the magnanimity of such individuals that have helped the arts to flourish. Be a part of helping your kulchur flourish; be a part of history.

HOW

To lend your support & become a patron, please visit the subscription page of our website: contramundum.net/subscription

For any questions, write us at: info@contramundum.net

9 781940 625294